Hilary Bailey was born in 1936 and was educated at thirteen schools before attending Newnham College, Cambridge. Her first novel was published in 1975 and she has since written fifteen novels and a short biography. She lives in west London.

After the
Cabaret

Hilary Bailey

WARNER BOOKS

A *Warner* Book

First published in Great Britain in 1998
by Little, Brown and Company
This edition published by Warner Books in 1999

Copyright © Hilary Bailey 1998

A CIP catalogue record for this book
is available from the British Library.

ISBN 0 7515 2279 1

Typeset by Palimpsest Book Production Limited,
Polmont, Stirlingshire
Printed and bound in Great Britain by
Clays Ltd, St Ives plc

Warner Books
A Division of
Little, Brown and Company (UK)
Brettenham House
Lancaster Place
London WC2E 7EN

1

A grey, damp November day in London.

Gregory Addams Phillips, BA UCLA, Rhodes Scholar, Cambridge University, now assistant professor (untenured) of modern English literature at Fraser Cutts, a small but prestigious university in Virginia, walked up the cracked steps of 11, Cornwall Street and approached, nervously, the peeling front door of the Victorian terraced building. He felt a twinge in his left, quarterback's knee. The British climate, he thought. Didn't the Brits invent housemaid's knee?

He stared at the left-hand side of the entrance, bewildered by an array of doorbells, of different styles and dates, some looking out of use, some unlabelled, none offering the name he was looking for. Then he rang one marked with a printed business card, much dirtied by London smut. He waited. He had a six-month working break from Fraser Cutts and a contract with a major publisher. He had flown the Atlantic to get here, not knowing what he would find, what there was to find, whether he would be able to find it. This moment was the apotheosis of a year's work and arrangements; the ensuing moments could be the making or breaking of his career. And now as he stood on the stained concrete landing before a front door, he was too nervous to care what might happen next. He was tempted to duck down and look through the letter-box, but that would be an undignified attitude in which to be found when – if – the door was opened.

What happened next was that he heard feet coming heavily downstairs, not a young man's tread, then sounds in the hall of what his two years in Britain had taught him was an ironical exchange: 'Oh, *thank you* – thank you so *very much*.' The voice, a man's, artificial in tone, came closer to the door. 'Thank you, Mrs Bulstrode, that will be all.' It was a high, slightly unsteady voice with traces of a German accent.

Greg Phillips came to life. All his repressed anxieties leaped up like warriors from earth in which dragon's teeth had been sown. My God, he thought, it's Bruno Lowenthal. Bruno Lowenthal: the man no one had heard of, no one had thought to find, for fifty years. But I did. And in about one second he's going to open that door, and I'm going to talk to him . . .

2

Coming downstairs, Bruno thought, Yes, Mr Phillips, I suppose it is you, Mr Phillips. This is me, Bruno Lowenthal. And I'm going to tell you what I want you to know and no more. Then it will be goodbye.

The first time I set eyes on Sally Bowles it was June 1940, at Pontifex Street. I'd come in, I remember, with a string bag containing some peas and a rabbit. I'd been gone hours. I got caught in a raid. And there she was, standing in the middle of the room in a pink Chanel suit, filthy, oil stains on the skirt and an even more unpleasant smear on the jacket, her black hair all messy, as if she'd spent the night in an open boat – and, of course, she had. I noticed that the suit, though dirty, was new and that she'd hitched up the skirt, had her foot on the sofa, and was rolling on one of a brand-new pair of silk stockings.

She turned, fastening a suspender. She grinned at me and said, in her slightly husky voice, 'Bruno – darling – I bet you didn't expect to see me here, turning up like a bad penny.'

3

3

After the scuffle in the hall which involved, as Greg so dearly hoped, old Bruno Lowenthal, he was still waiting on the steps. Below him in the basement he noticed window-boxes with flowering geraniums on the sills. A fig tree was growing down there in a concrete tub, a bush he didn't recognise in another. He knew the strange way they lived over here, nothing purpose-built, houses converted into apartments then back into houses, warehouses redesigned as apartment buildings, churches, chapels, railway stations and post offices as homes, studios, offices. The dearest wish of all Britons was to live in a two-hundred-year-old hop mill called the Old Oast House.

Staring at the closed front door, Greg was surprised to find these thoughts drifting through his mind. He was confused, must be. Yesterday he had handed the keys of his office and apartment to the woman who would be taking over from him for the remainder of the semester at Fraser Cutts. Then he had driven his files, a lamp, a rug and some suitcases to his parents' house in Oakridge, California, for storage. He'd caught the plane and travelled eleven hours to London, back to a country he had not visited for nearly seven years and had left with very confused feelings. He'd taken the underground to Bayswater and booked into the small hotel he remembered from vacations all those years ago.

He had jet-lag – and more. Probably he should not have phoned Bruno Lowenthal, he thought, on the evening he arrived, at two in the morning by his body clock, and asked to come round at eleven next morning. Now he was going into a crucial – *the* crucial – interview. If he blew it, everything, or nearly everything, would be lost.

He wondered if it would be better if Lowenthal, if it *was* him in there, didn't open the door at all. He could come back and try again when he was better adjusted to the time. Had he been standing there hours or minutes? His jet-lag wouldn't tell him. Should he ring the bell again? Or turn and run? How long had he been there, like a hopeful lover, or maybe like a hunter in the bush, prey sighted, finger on the trigger? Then he heard the lock turn. Oh, God, oh, God, oh, God, said a voice in his head.

The door opened a crack. There was a chain on it. He said through the crack, 'I'm Greg Phillips. Are you Mr Lowenthal?'

And the accented voice said, 'I'll open the door.'

4

The night before, a freak bomb had dropped nearby – some lonely, lost German bomber had overshot the coast, where the battle of Britain was raging.

Now plaster dust from the ceiling lay all over the room and one of the windows was blocked by a piece of cardboard that bore the words Tate and Lyle.

Having fastened her stocking, Sally produced a compact from somewhere and began to powder her grubby face. 'Bruno – it is Bruno, isn't it? Excuse, darling. Someone told me about you and Briggs. I'm so demoralised. The time I've had. Where's Loomie?'

She meant Adrian Pym, of course. Oh, those upper-class nicknames, those Biggins, Cocos, Dumphies, Heffers, Tatas and Simsims – but at least her use of the soubriquet made it less likely that she was a full-blown German spy. She couldn't be German, at any rate. No German could have been so unselfconsciously grubby in that particularly

6

English way. Bruno was still suspicious, though. 'What's that got to do with you?' he asked.

She said desperately, 'And where's Theo? I absolutely must find Theo. It's a matter of life and death.'

He had no chance to answer for from behind Sir Peveril's dusty white sofa, which was minus one seat-cushion and not improved by the ceiling plaster, came a thin, nasty, wailing sound, like a cat at night. Sally assured him, 'Honestly, darling, it hasn't made a sound since St Malo. You haven't got a drop of milk in the house, have you? That would be lovely. And, please, darling, do tell me where Loomie is.'

Still holding the string bag, Bruno crossed the room and went to look behind the sofa, though he was pretty sure he knew what he'd find. There on the floor, lying on the missing sofa cushion, was a baby, bare-legged, barefoot and wrapped in a dirty yellow cardigan. Sally said, 'It's only a little one,' and laughed.

She was putting on lipstick now, but underneath the powder and the grime Bruno noticed that she looked quite worn out. She was about thirty, with short dark hair, a small nose, pale skin, very large brown eyes with dark shadows underneath. She would have been pretty, he thought, if she'd been a bit cleaner, a little less tired and a little more composed.

This was Bruno's first sight of Sally Bowles.

5

Greg was surprised by the figure he saw in the narrow, four-feet-wide, dark-painted hall. He knew that Bruno Lowenthal was nearly seventy-eight years old, Jewish, European-born, and had pictured a small, frail man, worn down by age – and Europe.

In the old black-and-white photographs of Bruno (in bathing trunks, at Cannes, or in a Homburg and suit, or dining in a London restaurant with friends) he had been a tall, apparently blond, muscular young man. Greg had believed – wrongly, he now saw – that Bruno would have changed over the years into a bent old fellow such as one might see walking the pavements of New York, or being helped along by a stronger wife in a retirement village in Florida. However, Bruno Lowenthal was still six feet tall, almost as tall as Greg, and his shoulders were still broad; he stooped only a little. His face was heavily wrinkled, his eyes very blue, sharp and unkind. His head was topped by a shock of unkempt white hair, yellow in front – from the effects of nicotine, Greg supposed. Indeed, he now held a cigarette in a big, wrinkled hand, smoke streaming up to the discoloured ceiling, as he stared at Greg. In the other hand he had a large bunch of keys. He wore a black roll-necked sweater and baggy grey trousers. On his feet were tartan carpet slippers. He did not, Greg reflected, look unlike some of the older professors from his Cambridge days, smart, often nasty, known, though not to him, as having had a gilded youth in the days before the war, perhaps not having reaped all the rewards due to them.

'I'm very pleased to meet you, Mr Lowenthal,' said Greg.

'Well – you'd better come in, but quickly.' He turned abruptly and led the way along the passage, which was painted dark green up to the height of about four feet, then dirty primrose yellow above. They went up linoleum-covered stairs to the first floor. It reminded Greg of some old black-and-white British movie about gritty bad times and crimes in the 1950s. And this was a high-rent area. What was going on?

As he mounted the stairs, Lowenthal kept up a good pace, wheezing as he went, the smoke from his cigarette blowing back across Greg. The house didn't smell at any rate, thought Greg, who knew the mingled odour of cooking, cats and grime that often accumulated in these old, unventilated British houses.

The landing at the top of the stairs was covered with more linoleum, in the same dark red as below. Ahead was a door of dark, cracked varnish, the original wood showing through in strips. Lowenthal bent stiffly to release a stout lock at the bottom of the door, then straightened to open another. He stuck a third key in a Yale lock, then turned the door handle. 'Please come in.'

Greg got another surprise. From the appearance of the house, the hall and the stairs, he had had the impression that Lowenthal must be eking out a poverty-stricken old age, possibly in one room with a couple of gas rings. There would be a narrow iron bed, a wardrobe, a TV, old wallpaper, some curtains sagging sadly on a bent rail at the window. Instead, he was faced with a long sitting room, furnished with modest antiques, all gleaming with polish. Long lace curtains billowed at the tall windows. At the sides were other curtains of heavy brocade, obviously old but fresh. There were some nice watercolours and a small oil painting on the walls. To the left was another door, leading, Greg assumed, to a bedroom, kitchen or bathroom.

Lowenthal waved him into a low chair, with tapestry seat and arms. 'I will make some coffee,' he declared.

'Thank you, sir, but I'd rather not,' Greg said.

'Not British coffee,' Lowenthal assured him.

Greg smiled. 'That's not the problem. I only arrived yesterday from the United States. It's six in the morning for me.'

Lowenthal shrugged. 'Very well.' He sat down opposite Greg.

'This is a beautiful room,' Greg said.

'I deal in antiques.'

'Yes. I saw from the London telephone directory you have a store in Portobello Road.'

'I have a manager but I go in several times a week. You must visit me there.'

'Thank you. I should like to.' Greg drew a breath. 'My letter will have explained clearly, I hope, what I'm trying to do. Shall I say a little more about it before I start asking you questions? I take it you don't mind questions?'

'Why else would you be here,' Lowenthal said, 'if I didn't want to answer questions?'

A little uneasy in his low Victorian chair, Greg looked directly at Bruno Lowenthal and asked, 'I'm curious about why you've never spoken out before. There's no reference to you in Charles Denham's book. Or anywhere else. Why did you decide on silence?'

Bruno's thin lips twitched. He raised grey, bushy eyebrows. 'No one asked me, dear boy. No one tried to find me. I didn't want to be found. I expect they think I'm dead. I've no wish to be thought otherwise.'

Greg paused, waiting for more. Nothing came. 'You didn't want to remember?'

'I was running a business. I still am. What good would all that gossip do to my business? None at all. Waste of time,' Bruno concluded.

'But now?' Greg asked, terrified that this determined, angry old man would, on a whim, terminate the interview. Never ask a question if you don't want to hear the answer, he reminded himself, too late.

'Now,' said Bruno Lowenthal, waving a hand, '*now*, it doesn't matter any more. Now – I will tell my own story, before somebody else gets in first – yes?' He spoke lightly, as if to involve Greg in the fun, but Greg, suddenly fearful

11

that a project similar to his own, but further advanced, was in the pipeline, asked quickly, 'Who?'

Lowenthal appreciated his anxiety. 'Don't worry,' he said, with an unsympathetic smile. 'I know of nothing else yet.'

'I'm glad to hear it,' Greg replied. But could he trust this man? He had thought to interview a man broken by the European history of war, treachery and ruin. Yet here he was, physically strong, economically viable, or so it seemed, and thinking at least on a level if not ahead of Greg himself.

'So,' he said, 'you want to tell your own story at last?' He produced the tape-recorder he'd had running in the pocket of his jacket from the moment he rang the doorbell. 'Do you mind if I use this?'

'Of course not,' replied Bruno Lowenthal.

6

'The first time I met Sally Bowles she'd arrived from Germany, if you please. She turned up at the flat in the West End I'd been sharing with three others since war was declared. She'd been living in Berlin from nineteen thirty to thirty-six, went off with a young lover to the Spanish Civil War. There the man died. Apparently she returned to Germany in 'thirty-eight. Why, I didn't know.' He told Greg of Sally's unwelcome arrival at Pontifex Street with the baby, Gisela.

'Then she went to bed,' Bruno continued, 'in Alexander Briggs's bed. I was terrified. Briggs was very fussy about anyone being in his bed – often wouldn't let *me* in it. Unluckily he arrived soon after. He was furious when he heard Sally was in the flat – he loathed her. "My God!" he said. "Look at the place!" And he stared at the plaster dust and the boarded-up window as if Sally had been responsible for the bomb that had fallen nearby the night before.

'The apartment consisted of three storeys – no distance

from Oxford Street, the BBC and Other Places, where secret work was going on. The bottom floor was a shop, selling expensive cakes. The whole building belonged to Sir Peveril Jones.

'"Where's Mrs Thing?" Briggs demanded. This was the woman Sir Peveril paid to come in and look after the flat. She lived in Croydon. Her husband, now in the Navy, had filled her up with twins before he left so what with the tots and their infant ailments, and her being, when it came down to it, in the eye of the storm where the battle of Britain was concerned, her visits were less frequent than they should have been. The other residents always called her Mrs Thing. At first I thought that was her name and once called her by it, just after we moved in, causing much offence. How was I to know that that was the British generic name for those who do such work? Even the Communists, which we were, used it. So Briggs was angry. I wasn't calm myself.

'It was I who had been faced with trading a small quantity of sugar for a baby's bottle of National Dried Milk from a woman in the street I barely knew, and put up with Sally turning the kitchen upside down when she made herself a cup of tea. There was no other milk – she helped herself from the baby's bottle.

'Briggs was upset by the disorder and the lack of lunch. He had, no doubt, been trying to analyse some coded messages from occupied countries all morning. He was even more upset when I told him Sally had had a bath and was now asleep in his bed. I said, "Briggs. She may be a spy."

'He responded, "Don't get in a state, Bruno. She's not a spy. Not if it's really Sally. And if she is, put out the flags. If she's spying for the Germans they'll have surrendered by Christmas from sheer despair."

'"She's come from St Malo, wearing a suit bought in Paris. She has a pair of silk stockings, also French. Be serious, Briggs," I urged him.

'"I am," he said. "From what you say, she thinks she can stay here. Well, she can't. Sally and her little illegitimate must take to the highroad before nightfall – better still, the moment she wakes up."

'"She asked me about somebody called Theo. She said it was urgent to find him."

'Briggs said, "Ah. So Theo's the villain of the piece. Well, I can't say I'm surprised. But there's no point in her trying to find Theo Fitzpatrick and get him to take over because, first, he can't be found and, second, even if he could be, he wouldn't."

'"Even so, you should tell the authorities about her," I said.

'Briggs laughed. "About Sally? The authorities? Sometimes you're very German, Bruno."'

7

Bruno said to Greg, 'Briggs told me, "I have a meeting at two o'clock. You must get her out by the afternoon, old chap. I can't face finding her and the infant here when I get back. Here's five pounds." Which he handed me. And departed. Leaving me to wake her up and send her off. I gave her another couple of hours' sleep. I know what it's like to have been on the run. It had happened to me five years earlier – but that is another story.'

Suddenly Bruno stopped speaking. He said, as if surprised, 'You know, I find this tiring. I have not thought of these things for many years. It seems so strange in London, now, to be looking back so far.' He paused for a moment, then went on, 'So – I knew what being a fugitive was like, as I say. Two hours later I woke her up. The baby, beside her in the bed, began to cry. I told her, "Briggs came back. He says you must go."

'She sat up in bed, naked, and all she said was, "Damn. I might have known it." Then she grinned and said, "I can imagine how glad the family will be to see me after so long, especially with Gisela." Then she got out of bed, with nothing on, went to the bathroom and came back struggling into her slip, which she had evidently rinsed out and hung up to dry. "There's nothing like it, I can tell you, the feeling of struggling into a wet petticoat," she told me. But I had seen my sisters doing the same, in Berlin. She got her suspender belt and started to pull on her stockings.

'"Your baby has wet the bed," I told her, when I looked at the sheets. It was screaming now.

'"I'm sorry, Bruno. But there it is. That's the worst of babies," she told me. "Oh, God," she groaned, then, "Oh, God." She seemed overcome with grief.

'"What?" I asked.

'"I'll have to go back to the family. Oh God – mother and father aren't going to like this at all. Maman is French. She's very correct. I used to pretend she was English, just to cheer myself up." She groaned again. Then she pulled herself together, did up her suspenders and said, "Well, there's not much choice, not with this baby." She got into her stained suit, stood in front of the mirror and began to put on makeup.

'Briggs kept his room very tidy. The furniture also belonged to Sir Peveril Jones and it was new, clean, pale-coloured, as was the carpet. I slept in the dressing room through a door, just a small bed, a wardrobe – maybe to keep up the conventions but, more because Briggs liked his privacy.

'"Who else lives here?" Sally asked, putting on lipstick.

17

I told her. "God, what a crew," she said. "Alexander Briggs, Adrian Pym, you, Julia Montrose. You'd think they'd give a girl and her baby a bed for the night." But she didn't argue. She had been on the run and when they ask you to go you go, without argument. "You're queer?" she asked, slapping a powder puff all over her face. It looked strange when she did that in that room, I can tell you.

'"Of course," I said.

'"Thought I didn't get much response from you wearing only my birthday suit," she said, with a smile. Well, she had a pretty figure, and a pretty face, also, with those big dark eyes and the full mouth. Very good teeth, also. I suppose she was accustomed to getting a reaction from men.

'And she left that day. I gave her Alexander's five-pound note, and a flannel shirt for the baby and a hand-towel for its bottom, with pins, so it wouldn't foul itself on the journey. As she left she asked, "Any news of Theo Fitzpatrick?" and I shook my head. "I'll come back and ask again," she promised and, baby under one arm, still crying, she marched off down the street, turning half-way down to fling up her arm, fist clenched, in a Communist salute.

'You can imagine – I breathed a sigh of relief and went back inside to clear up. She was very untidy, Sally. You'll want to know what I thought of her. Well, I didn't hate her. I didn't love her either. She was privileged, you see. OK, she was of the left, but when it came down to it there was the same old bourgeois background. A cold home, perhaps. But a cold home is better than no home at all. And then, look at what I was – gay, queer, a friend of Dorothy, one of *those*, whatever you call it.'

8

'It was a nightmare at Pontifex Street,' Sally told her father and stepmother some weeks later over breakfast. Through the window, the roses were out in the garden, and beyond lay the orchard, the farms, then the green swell of the Malvern hills. 'The atmosphere's gruesome, like a haunted house or something.'

Sally's father might have been listening. Sally's mother was not. Paris, her home, had fallen to the German Army. They had marched victoriously through Napoleon's Arc de Triomphe. Her heart seemed too numb for grief, her body felt like lead. She could scarcely bear to think of the defeat of France, her family and friends abandoned in that occupied country. Equally she could hardly bear to hear Sally's prattle, except to wish that she was more like her younger sister.

'I suppose it would have been difficult, with so many on the premises,' Harold Jackson-Bowles remarked, with some restraint. For several days after Sally had rung, late at night, from the station, he had shown no restraint at all. He had ranted and raved. Sally's absence – two years without a word, then out of the blue her unexpected arrival at the station, asking to be picked up, perhaps she didn't realise petrol was rationed – was of minor importance. Of more note, though, was – what she had been doing all that time. Parents, surely, had a right to know what their daughter was up to. The major issue, of course, was the baby Gisela, and who the father was.

Sally had borne almost wordlessly the attack, the questions, the appeals to common sense, smoking all the time, and in the face of her lack of response her father had wound down, finally, like a clockwork toy. Harry Jackson-Bowles was tired. Although he was long retired, a country gentleman now, he had been forced to go back to his factories, because both his managers had been called up, and he was now turning out soldiers' khaki shirts and drawers at an enormous rate. The women were doing three shifts a day in Birmingham, and Harry Jackson-Bowles four days a week. On top of that there was the anxiety. No one knew if the Nazis would invade but they had already conquered six countries in under a year. Who knew if they might not be coming up the drive at any moment? And his heart was heavy for his wife, Geneviève, and her friends and relatives who, though they had never been very nice to him, were under the iron heel.

Geneviève Jackson-Bowles, formerly Février de Roche, thought of her sister and brother-in-law in the big, high-ceilinged flat overlooking the Luxembourg Gardens, her nephews, Benoît and Charles, her other sister, Clothilde and her husband. Where were they? What was happening to them now? How many would survive? Would she ever see them again? Such thoughts must be suppressed or she would go mad, thought Geneviève.

She looked at Sally, still in a Chinese dressing-gown (where had that come from?) at the breakfast table at eight thirty in the morning. How pretty she could be, if she took care of herself – her carriage, her expression, her feet, hands, nails, skin, her hair. Why was she so badly regulated, so careless, physically and morally? She was a cross that Geneviève had to carry. It was on account of Sally that she, Geneviève, to her own family was still known as 'poor Geneviève', '*la pauvre*'.

Geneviève came of a prosperous, conservative family, in which life moved calmly and to a strict routine. On a certain date each year they all moved for the holidays from the city to the Normandy farm. On a second date, they returned to the big apartment in Paris. In autumn, they made preserves. In Lent, they fasted. In Paris the carpets were taken up for the summer, in September they were replaced. The domestic patterns were as orderly, the family finances conducted as frugally, as those of the convents in which the women of the family had received their early training. They married in the small circles in which they lived – unions that were not quite arranged but almost.

Geneviève broke the pattern when handsome Captain Jackson-Bowles of the Lancashire Fusiliers was brought home on leave from the trenches during the Great War by a relative in the French Army. Geneviève fell in love with

Harry Jackson-Bowles and married him – an Englishman, a Protestant and a self-made man, a manufacturer. That was when she had become 'poor Geneviève' to her family. But had it not been for Sally, with a successful marriage on her side, sooner or later she would have lost that name. Instead it was still 'poor Geneviève' and 'Sally – always something new with Sally', spoken in a way that, while it said little, said everything.

There had been Germany. Then the scandal when Sally went to Spain with a man – of the left! – prepared to fight on the wrong side! And now this baby, whose father she would not even name. At least, thought Geneviève, she could not undertake the painful duty of breaking this last sad piece of news to her sister Madeleine, so that she in turn could break it gently to Great-aunt Marie Claire in her convent. For there would be no news in or out of France for a long time. Geneviève did not permit herself to sigh. Instead she said, 'I think, if you have both finished your breakfast, you would like to go for a walk now, to talk.' The English often talked better to each other while walking in the open air, she knew. And Harry must find out the identity of the baby's father.

She watched father and daughter leave the house together. Perhaps it would have been better if Sally had been a boy, she thought, as she often had before. Behaviour such as Sally's was acceptable in a boy, not in a girl. That there was an excellent reason for this rule was indisputable: upstairs, in a cradle, lay the evidence.

Sally and her father were in the orchard. As they passed the lawn, half dug up now for vegetables, Harry Bowles had said, 'In six months' time there'll be no food, none at all.' Now he said, 'Sally, we're very upset. This baby – if only you'd tell us who her father is. Perhaps I could speak to him. Something must be arranged. My God, Sally,' he burst out, 'imagine a birth certificate saying "father unknown". It's too bad. It's a disgrace.'

To this Sally made no answer. Harry grew angry. 'You've been a cross to carry for your poor mother from the word go,' he said hotly. 'You're a silly girl. A very silly girl.' He turned away from his daughter and walked back to the house.

He'd always called her a silly girl, thought Sally. He was probably right. She kicked the gnarled old trunk of a Cox's Orange Pippin. Too early for that satisfying, wasteful thump of apples falling to the ground. She'd have to wait until September for that, she thought, and she wouldn't be here in September. In fact, she'd better get out as soon as she could pack her suitcase.

9

'Well, my dear, you'd have done far better to stay where you were,' Cora Blow remarked comfortably, from her deep chintz-covered armchair. She and Sally were alone in her cosy sitting room on the first floor of the Hotel Bessemer, which Cora owned. Situated in Bessemer Street behind Wigmore Street, behind Oxford Street, on the fringes of the area known as Mayfair, the hotel was on the edge of respectability, much as Cora herself had been on the edge of fashionable society for some fifty years. Her little tables, relics of an Edwardian past, were crowded with ornaments and framed photographs of a young and beautiful Cora with the notables of two generations – Cora in a big hat and a bustle with the old Prince of Wales, later Edward VII, Cora in a small hat and Chanel suit with the later Prince of Wales, who was now the Duke of Windsor, and Mrs Simpson. Other photographs showed Cora with a bouquet, Cora at the races, Cora at Cowes with a Balkan prince, Cora in Monte Carlo.

How she had come by the big, faded hotel in Bessemer Street, the width of two houses, with a portico in front, no one really knew. Someone had been grateful to her for something, and had rewarded her accordingly – unless she'd won it gambling. Those who knew the details never told.

Now she ran the hotel as a private kingdom, assisted by the head hall porter, Bates, her *alter ego*. There were twenty bedrooms but Cora was quite capable of turning away would-be guests when most were empty – because they were middle class, because they were Americans, because they were musicians. Cora liked aristocrats and loved artists but hated the middle class and musicians. In her hotel Cora's whims were law.

Now Sally gazed ingenuously at Cora, who, for this morning interview, was wearing a vast dark red peignoir, with plenty of ruffles. Her grey hair was bundled roughly on top of her head and she was smoking a thin cigar.

In turn Cora appraised Sally, thinking, Pretty, untidy dresser, nice eyes, pale. Where does she come from? Something about a Mlle Février de Roche and a bourgeois marriage with a certain Jackson-Bowles. Cora was a walking *Who's Who* and *Almanach de Gotha*, but she knew all the secrets behind their pages, too. In a hotelier this pays.

'Well, my dear,' she said, rising to pour the first gin of the day and gesturing vaguely with the cigar at Sally – who, as befitted a would-be employee, shook her head, 'well, dear, as I say, you'd do better to stay in the country, plenty of butter there, eggs, further away from the struggle, as you might put it, but in the circumstances, with all the staff

25

shortages, why not? You can have the little room in the attics, so recently vacated by Doris Strong, who decided to run off and join the Army. That's the snag, though. How long will you be here before they start putting women into war work?'

'War work?' Sally wondered.

'Yes. I've heard a whisper they may order all the women into factories or make them work on farms, planting potatoes and milking cows. I don't know how to keep this place going without staff. We'll manage, I suppose.'

'I've got a baby,' Sally announced.

'A *widow*,' Cora declared, with Edwardian firmness. 'Well, as long as you don't bring it here to disturb my guests you will be quite suitable. The Government will probably exempt mothers from forced labour. So all's for the best. Go and see Mr Bates about the details.'

'Thank you, Mrs Blow,' said Sally, standing up.

As she opened the door Cora said to her back, 'Oh – no hanky-panky with the guests, that goes without saying.' I do *not* think, she added silently to the closed door. Still, she needed someone. The girl said she was a friend of Mr Fitzpatrick's – Cora knew what *that* must mean.

As she descended the sweeping marble staircase to the hall, Sally reflected that Cora had not told her what her duties would be, or, which was important, how much she would be paid.

Frederick Bates had stood on the cold marble floor of the Bessemer behind his mahogany desk for as long as anyone could remember. Those who had faced his neutral eyes on visits to London in short trousers during their

school holidays and were now dignified grown men st
retained a healthy respect for Bates. They felt much th
same about Cora, whom they saw as the most capriciou
arbitrary school matron ever, rewarding and punishing a
she saw fit.

From behind his desk, Bates said, 'Wages? Hah. Chance
would be a fine thing. Pays you when she feels like it, which
isn't often. That's Cora Blow for you. Still, you've got a
roof over your head. That's something. And where's your
gas mask? You can be arrested for not carrying one.'

'I'll go and get one,' Sally promised. 'By the way, Mr
Bates, do you know how to register a baby?'

'As a what?' asked Bates.

Sally stared at him. 'As a baby, of course,' she responded.

'Ask a policeman,' he said promptly.

As she left he studied her pink-clad back and muttered,
'French suit! Get a gas mask? Where does she think she'll
go for it – Harrods? And registering a baby? She'd better
not bring it here.'

Two officers in the uniform of the Free French came up
to the desk. Bates said, in French, 'Good morning, officers.
How may I help you?'

10

Greg's mouth was dry. He gazed, astonished, at Bruno as the old man went on calmly, 'You know the history, of course. The Germans overran Denmark, Norway, Holland, Belgium and France in only six months. They'd already conquered their neighbours to the east. That summer Russia opportunistically attacked the Baltic states, Lithuania, Latvia, Estonia. The Germans didn't stop them. They were allies. Britain had no allies – only the help of its Empire. The RAF was defending the coasts day and night. Hitler would invade Britain, he said, when the Royal Air Force had been destroyed. In short, it was a siege.

'Until September, the desperate battles were all over the sea and coast; the cities had been fairly safe from bombing. The country was packed with troops from all over the British Empire, Australians, Canadians, West Indians. There were also men who had escaped from occupied Europe – Belgians, Dutch, French, Poles – and their leaders, monarchs, politicians and their entourages.

And we were waiting. The RAF seemed to be losing the battle of Britain. The Luftwaffe had five planes, at least, to each British one. It was a miracle they had hung on so long.

'So one summer night in Pontifex Street, we were sitting out on the flat part of the roof with a bottle of gin Adrian Pym had got from somewhere, and we had hauled some cushions and the gramophone up through the trap-door. It was dark, of course. There were no street-lamps, no lights showing from the houses, the skies were filled with the vast white shapes of barrage balloons. It was rather quiet, too – conditions kept traffic off the roads. It was like living in the country, really, but more menacing.

'We were a good-looking group, I have to say this,' Bruno told Greg. 'Briggs was a tall, slender man, very handsome in an English way – a long nose and pale brown hair, with a lock that fell forward. The most beautiful thing about him was his eyebrows, over which that lock of hair so often fell – arched, fine, covering rather narrow, long blue eyes. Pym's appearance was rather extraordinary. He was dark-haired with very blue eyes, fringed with thick black lashes. His lips were full. His body was beautiful, broad-shouldered, narrow-hipped, and his legs were superb. He was also very attractive, sexually attractive, and people, men and women alike, just fell for him. He had no inhibitions and this came out of him, like a scent. He could have seduced a bishop. Indeed,' said Bruno, 'according to him, he had.

'Julia,' Bruno went on, with a grimace, 'was an awful girl. "Terribly pretty," they used to say of her, and I suppose

29

she was, blonde, with big blue eyes and a small mouth. Oh, those "terribly pretty" cold English blondes.' Bruno smiled an old, cynical smile at Greg. 'You will be thinking that Lowenthal, the nasty old queen, can see only the attractions of men, eh? Perhaps – but I don't think so. So there we were, none of us yet thirty, like you, beautiful and afraid. I myself,' he said, with some vanity, 'was tall, blond and pretty, Aryan to the fingertips, to one who did not know the truth. I was twenty-one. Hard to believe, isn't it? Bruno Lowenthal – tall, handsome, only twenty-one years old.

'So there we sat, with the music playing, and I remember Briggs looking up, saying, "You can see the stars. It's such a good opportunity to learn astronomy." He was sitting on a cushion, and his hair was very neat even after the scramble up the ladder and through the trap-door to the roof. His shirt, open at the neck, was clean, his trousers still had a crease.

'"I'd rather you took up astrology, Briggs," said Pym. "Then you could put on a fringed shawl and earrings and tell us all our fortunes." The doorbell rang downstairs. We ignored it.

'"Good idea," said Julia Montrose. Well, we all knew what she wanted an astrologer to tell her. Sir Peveril was running a branch of the intelligence services at the time. She was his secretary, and his lover. She hoped he would abandon his wife and children, who were living in the country, and marry her. But at that time Sir Peveril was not thinking of making any changes in his private life. His work was making too many demands on him. Or so he said.

'Julia was sitting, tidily, on her cushion, blonde hair in a roll at the back. Pym was lying down, a bit drunk, looking as ever like an Italian angel, with his perfect golden skin, smooth dark hair, large eyes with the long lashes – oh, everybody fell in love with Adrian Pym, though he never fell in love with anyone.

'And he said, in a Romanian-gypsy accent, "I see you, my dear, wife of a handsome man in his fifties, with a brood of tall sons about you, ruling over wide, rolling acres in the West." When I say he sounded like a Romanian gypsy, he did. He had an uncanny ear for accents, a gift for languages, a nasty tongue, also. Julia winced, for he was telling her what she most wanted – and that meant he knew.

'At this point the doorbell rang again, for a long time. The caller had stuck their thumb on it. "Hell," said Briggs and, "Loomie, you're a cad," said Julia to Pym.

'"Worse than that, dear, much worse," he said.

'Then the bell stopped ringing and a voice came yelling up through the darkness from the silent street. "Pym – Briggs – Julia – somebody! Let me in!" It was a woman's voice.

'"Who's that?" Briggs remarked, without much interest.

'I knew. "It's Sally Bowles," I said.

'"Shit!" exclaimed Pym. "Keep down, everyone. Pretend to be out."

'The voice came again. "I know you're in. I can hear the music. Let me in. Don't be rotten. Loomie – let me in."

'"She'll wake up the whole street," Briggs said. He stood up.

31

'"No," Pym protested.

'"Sally! Shut up! I'm coming down," Briggs said, over the parapet. "My God! What have you got on?"

'"It's my uniform," she shouted back. "Open the door."

'"Just stop yelling," he called. "She's wearing a maid's uniform," he told us, as he went to the trap-door.

'As I followed Briggs down the ladder I heard Pym suggest, "Perhaps she thinks we're having a fancy-dress party." And there at the door Sally was indeed dressed as a maid in a black dress, black stockings and a white frilled apron. In her hand she carried what had evidently been a maid's starched white cap. She came in and Briggs shut the door quickly so the light could not escape.

'When we got upstairs, Briggs said, "Hello, Sally. Nice to see you. Sorry about having to ask you to leave. We're overcrowded here as it is. Tell me one thing, why are you dressed like that?"

'"I'm a maid," Sally explained. "I've just slipped out to see you." Then she came to the point: "I wondered if there was any news of Theo."

'"Well, Sally," he said, "quite honestly, even if I knew, I'm not supposed to say."

'"I love him. He's the only man I've ever really loved," said Sally, emotionally.

'"Oh, crikey," Briggs said. "Well, since you ask me, I actually don't know where he is."

'This was not enough for Sally. Soon she was on the roof, her uniform, especially the apron, much the worse for having climbed the ladder. She began to ramble on about Theo, the days in Berlin when they'd shared a room in a working-class house in a slummy area, the romance of it, the full moon over the Unter den Linden, the simple goodness of the honest working folk with whom they'd lodged. And who had been glad of the money, I thought. I knew that life.

'She was talking about the mid thirties when she had been singing in tatty little cabarets and Theo had been collecting material for the *Witness*, a weekly magazine he ran at the time. And working for *The Times*. And reporting back to . . . somebody. The German authorities suspected him of spying, not wrongly, I think. To many he was a hero – young, handsome, brave, a man with a cause. Well, it was dangerous enough there, at that time, God knows, but nothing was ever going to happen to Theo. He was too quick on his feet, and always had enough connections to get him out of trouble. As always, at any time, there were Theo and his kind and there were the rest of us, the natives, with cardboard in our shoes and no ticket out. He may have been a hero, Theo, but the rest of us were martyrs, and I know which I'd rather be. I said nothing like this at the time, though. Briggs, to his credit, knew how I felt. He was tough, a martinet, a disciplinarian, of himself and everyone else. Something so harsh, so cruel in his past had made him see through everything.

'Pym was different. He didn't care what I or anyone else felt. I've never understood what Pym did care about. I suppose his actions were dictated by rage. He was upper class, but had no money. He was homosexual, so a criminal under the law. With care, by hard work and concealment, he could have risen high, but when he looked about him he didn't want to rise high in this country where wealth came by accident of birth and where the law would put him in prison.

'Of the three of us, I suppose Julia was the most sympathetic to Sally's account of her Berlin romance with Theo Fitzpatrick. You only had to show these well-brought-up young women a good-looking young man, with a day's stubble, a worker's cap on his head, giving the clenched-fist salute, and common sense deserted them. Even today – I see the pop stars on TV sometimes – there's still the same old glamour. The allure of rough trade. It's not so exciting if you grew up in that milieu, in a cap, ill-fitting shoes, not so clean.

'But I lose the point. It was Pym who interrupted this romantic tale and got down to brass tacks. "Sally," he said, "it's rumoured you have a baby. Would it be tactless to ask if Theo's the father?"

'Sally was a bit drunk – she'd confessed to some Free French cognac taken earlier in a hotel bedroom at the Bessemer while she was doing whatever she was supposed to do, turning down the bed, dusting the dressing-table. On the roof she'd had the best part of a tumbler of gin. She put on a dignified voice and told Pym, "I don't think that's any of your business."

'"Come off it, Sally," he said.

'"Well, it isn't."

'"If you want us to find Theo, don't you think you owe us some information in return?"

'"You're a spy, of course, Loomie. That's why you want to swap secret for secret."

'"I only asked—"

'"And you got a dusty answer, Pym, so shut up," Julia said. "If Sally doesn't want to tell you who the baby's father is, it's up to her. Actually, Sally," she said, "all I know about Theo is that he's been at a sort of secret code-cracking place in the country, but he's been agitating to go abroad to do liaison with the patriots in Norway and the last news indicated he'd succeeded."

'"Does he speak any Norwegian?" Briggs asked.

'"His theory is he can get by with German and Anglo-Saxon," Julia explained.

'"Thank God those in charge have worked out a master-plan. Theo will quote *Beowulf* at the Germans until they surrender. This is an amateur's war," said Pym.

'"Brilliant improvisation, that's the term," Briggs said.

'There was the beginning of a gloomy silence. Briggs then asked Sally, "After you and Theo parted . . . ?"

'But Pym interrupted, "I think I've been invited to a party in Tite Street. Do you want to come along with me, Sally? I'm after a golden Norwegian, but I think he'll like you better. Will you be my decoy?" He added, with transparent cunning, "He may know something about Theo."

'"Count me in," said Sally promptly.

'The last we saw was the pair of them going off up the dark and silent street, arm in arm, singing, "It's a long way to Tipperary, it's a long way to go—"

'We heard before we saw a convoy of trucks coming towards the crossing at the top of Pontifex Street. It came slowly across the road as Pym and Sally approached the corner. There were whistles and shouts from the soldiers in the lorries and a responding chorus, "But my heart's right there."

'"Well, Sally's out for a good time," said Julia, a bit sadly. Then she mentioned she was getting cold, so we went inside and to bed.'

'I'm a little tired myself now,' Bruno Lowenthal said to Greg Phillips, in the sunny room at Cornwall Street. 'Do you mind if we finish for today?'

'No, no, of course not, sir,' Greg said, startled, coming back suddenly to the present, into the antique-filled room. He looked at the old man opposite. 'Thank you. It's been most interesting. I'm impressed by your memory.'

Bruno said, slowly, 'I seldom think of those days. The last time I really remembered it all was when the participants were exposed, disgraced, fled to Moscow. Now it all comes flooding back. But it is very tiring.'

There was a silence. Greg was not sure how to respond and was fearful that, if he got it wrong, Bruno would escape him. He said, tentatively, 'Should we perhaps leave intervals between sessions, sir?'

'Call me Bruno. No, no. Come tomorrow, to the shop, at one o'clock.' He got up and took a card from a bowl on the mantelpiece. 'Here is the address.'

The audience was over. Greg, who had been listening in silence for two hours, his head reeling, took his leave. He could not believe, as he found his way back to his cheap hotel, that this was happening to him.

11

'Katherine?'

'Yes,' said the woman's voice, at the other end of the line, uncertainly. 'Yes? Who are – my God! Oh, my God,' she said, half amused, half horrified. 'It's you, isn't it, Greg?'

'Yes, it's me, Katherine. How are you?'

'I'm fine,' she said. 'Are you here?'

'Yes. Katherine, can we meet? I realise you may not want to see me. You got my letter?'

'Yes. Of course I want to see you. Greg, it's been six, nearly seven years. I often think of you.'

'I often think of you. You're still Miss Ledbetter, I assume.'

'Dr Ledbetter,' she told him.

'I'm imagining you in a study overlooking Newnham's immemorial elms, fire burning, surrounded by books—'

'Grey hair piled on top of my head, held up by hairpins, fashionably dressed in a baggy tweed skirt and lisle stockings. No, I'm in my jeans looking out over the immemorial bus-stop in Histon Road. How are you getting on?'

'That's the point. Did you ever hear of Bruno Lowenthal?'

'Bruno Lowenthal? I think so. But it's just a name. I know almost nothing about him. Do you want sources?'

'Not sources, Katherine. Background. Can you help me – please? I'll pay for the dinner.'

'Where?'

'Cambridge.'

'I don't know if I can help. Now I think about it, I can't even remember when he died.'

'That's because he's not dead. I've just been talking to him.'

'What! He's alive. You found him. How? Where is he?'

'London. He runs some kind of antique shop.'

'How the hell did you find him? Who put you on to him?'

'Unlike in Britain, life in the United States sometimes happens without us having to contact our own or someone else's cousins. What I did was get a British telephone directory, look up Lowenthal under L, then I called him. Neat trick?'

'Phew!'

'So, dinner tomorrow night? Give me the address and I'll collect you.'

'Not tomorrow.'

'Tomorrow you're having a working dinner with Professor Thomas Thomson-Thomson, who's married to your godmother. The affair's a secret, but everybody knows.'

'Greg, you're psychic. Or maybe just psychotic. I've sometimes wondered why we ever parted. Now I've remembered.'

'Because, like Dracula, you couldn't live in daylight.'

'Cancel the dinner.'

'No. I'm coming the day after.'

'No – the day after that.'

Later Katherine Ledbetter, who was indeed sitting at a book-laden desk in a room overlooking the gardens of Newnham College, Cambridge, including its immemorial elms, put the phone down and whispered, 'Oh, Christ.'

While Greg, in his Bayswater Hotel, measured his length on the dismal raspberry-coloured bed-cover and groaned, 'Oh, God – Katherine, Katherine.'

It had been many years since they had had their mad affair in Cambridge, followed by a terrible parting. Like Dracula again, it wouldn't die, never had for Greg, anyhow, and now that he had spoken to her, he knew it had not died for Katherine either. She couldn't disguise it. He knew her voice too well.

In Cambridge, Katherine planned rapidly to cancel their meeting on some spurious grounds. Then she made a phone call to a relative.

Meanwhile Greg, in London, had decided that she was deciding to do this and resolved to take effective counter-measures next day. He would leave for Cambridge as soon as his second meeting with Bruno Lowenthal had taken place. He would arrive twenty-four hours before they had agreed to meet and cut her off at the pass as she tried to escape him.

12

The day after Sally's visit to Pontifex Street she arrived in the foyer at the Bessemer at six in the morning, somewhat drunk, her maid's uniform dusty and torn. From the desk, Bates's eye was gloomy but unsurprised.

He reported her, of course, and Cora Blow sacked her. 'You've been a chambermaid here for two days – two days too many,' Cora remarked unemotionally.

'Mrs Blow, I left the hotel at ten last night and returned at six this morning. Surely you can't expect me to be on duty all day and all night as well.'

'Can't I? In the good old days there was no such thing as time off. Your off-duty time is when I say it is,' Cora replied implacably. 'Moreover, there's the damage to your uniform and a complaint from Colonel le Brun.'

'*He* complained about *me*?' protested Sally.

'Be that as it may,' Cora said. 'It's your job to stay away from the guests.'

'He said he knew my mother.'

'Perhaps. Perhaps it was even true. I fail to see what difference that makes, especially to a Frenchman.'

'So I'm sacked.'

'Up to a point,' Cora conceded. 'It's plain you haven't even the vestiges of the making of a chambermaid. But I have another position to offer you.'

Sally, who was feeling dizzy, looked at the astonishing old woman with apprehension. What was she about to suggest? It might be anything.

But Cora's plan was music to Sally's ears. The deep basement was part kitchen – if the guests had only known what it was like they would have paid not to dine at the hotel – part repository for old furniture and part cellar. Cora's idea was to clear out part of this area, put in a bar and paint the place pink: La Vie en Rose would be created, bomb shelter and club in one. With a band or, at any rate, a pianist, so that people could dance – and a cabaret.

'You'll do,' said Cora. 'Don't worry, I won't let in anyone I don't like. Hand your uniform to Mr Bates. It'll be ten shillings for cleaning and repairs. I'll have the money now.'

Sally handed it over. Cora put it in her pocket. She said, 'There's another artist, a singer who plays the piano. She'll double as manageress so you'll have to take your orders from her. I'm sorry about that but quite honestly, Miss Bowles, I couldn't put you in charge of a rice pudding, and Vi Simcox, who sings under the name of Lola Laine, is a thoroughly competent young woman. She's not exactly out of the top drawer but you'll have to make the best of that.'

Sally went upstairs to her narrow bedroom under the eaves, penniless now and homeless. She stripped off the uniform and, no longer a maid but an artiste again, lay down for a long, daytime sleep.

13

She was woken by a voice saying, 'Whoops! Sorry.' She opened her eyes. The door was closing. 'It's all right,' she called. 'I'm getting up.' The door reopened promptly. A small woman in her twenties with very blonde hair, very red lipstick and very high heels stood there. She wore a smart little burgundy hat on one side of her head. 'I didn't mean to wake you up,' she said. 'Bates told me you were here so I came up to introduce myself – Lola Laine, chanteuse, otherwise Vi Simcox. Pleased to meet you.' She advanced, holding out her hand. Sally sat up and shook it. Then she got out of bed, picked up the skirt of the pink suit and put it on. Vi looked at it. 'That's a damn good skirt,' she observed. 'But it could do with a good sponge and a press.'

'It's all I've got for the moment.'

Vi looked at her impassively. 'Let's go down and have lunch,' she suggested.

'Will that be all right?' Sally asked. She was terrified of Cora Blow.

'I'll square it with Bates,' Vi assured her.

Sally put on her pink jacket and followed her down the linoleum-covered stairs, which led from the staff bedrooms in the attics to the red-carpeted sweep of stairs that went down three further flights to the hotel foyer.

'Many in for lunch, Bates?' asked Vi.

'An air vice-marshal, two counts and the exiled King of somewhere. I regret I can't allow you to lunch in the dining room.' And he looked calmly at Sally's stained suit.

It was at this point that Adrian Pym entered with a man carrying a bowler hat and a younger one in work-stained corduroys, who gazed uneasily around him at the faded grandeur of the Bessemer.

'Well, Sally,' said Pym.

'Loomie, darling, lend me a pound,' she responded.

'What will you do for me?'

'Anything you want.'

He produced a large bundle of notes from his pocket and peeled one off. This he gave to Sally. As he turned to go into the dining room, she said, 'Any news of Theo?'

He sighed, 'Really, Sally . . .'

Sally and Vi got a bus to the Lyon's Corner House. It was full of women with shopping bags and parcels and men in uniform.

Vi said, 'I'm gasping for a cup of tea. Cora said you'd had a baby girl and lost your husband. I'm ever so sorry. Was he in the forces?'

'I'm not married,' said Sally, bluntly.

'Oh – like that,' Vi said sympathetically.

'It's a long story. I won't bore you with it.'

44

'Up to you,' Vi responded, a little huffily.

'You married, or anything?' asked Sally.

'I look after my brothers. Ted's a docker, so he hasn't been called up. Jack's nine. After my dad died three years ago my mum went off. She met a feller who didn't want to take Jack on so off she went. Left a note saying she was sorry.' Vi looked down at her egg on toast. 'It looks hard. I don't fancy it somehow. I'm fussy about my eggs.'

'Have something else,' Sally suggested.

'This took long enough to get here. I haven't got time to start all over again,' and she attacked it vigorously.

'It must be hard to manage the house and your own career,' Sally said.

'My gran helps out,' said Vi. 'She used to be in the profession herself. She had quite a name on the music halls. Violet Lavengro. Bit too fond of the gin now. Well, she always was. So what kind of stuff do you do?'

'I've worked mostly in cabaret,' Sally told her. 'In Germany.'

Vi looked at her. 'I've heard about those cabarets.'

Sally shrugged.

'Did you take all your clothes off? Fellers in dresses, that kind of thing?'

'Sometimes.'

'We can't go in for anything like that, not in London. Nor you singing in German – not with a war on. Can you manage some of those little French songs, "La Vie en Rose", that kind of thing?'

Sally nodded.

'That'll do,' Vi said briskly. 'It all hangs on the band

and God knows what they'll be like, with everybody in the forces. Cora's getting them in herself, which I *don't* like.' She leaned back and gazed at Sally from big blue black-fringed eyes. 'What have you done since you left Germany? Had the baby, I suppose.'

'We only got here ten days ago,' Sally said.

'Ten days!' exclaimed Vi. The war had begun in September 1939 and now it was June 1940. A massive rescue force, including a flotilla of private boats, had just sailed out to rescue the British Expeditionary Force, trapped on the beaches of Dunkirk under heavy bombardment. Army doctors had drawn lots to decide who would remain in France to take care of the wounded.

Sally told her, 'At first I was ahead of the Germans getting into France and then somehow I was behind. I came over in a fishing boat from Brittany. There were lots of men on board who were going to join up with the Free French over here.'

Vi was puzzled, veering towards suspicion. After all, Sally had confessed to nine months in Germany after the declaration of war. 'The baby came with you?'

'I was let down by a man,' Sally said.

Vi continued to scrutinise her.

Sally went on, 'It sounds funny, I suppose. All that happened was that I got stuck in Germany with no money – and the baby. And suddenly we were at war. I ended up singing on the stage for the wives of German soldiers. They're all blacked out and rationed, you see – frightfully depressing – so they have a policy of trying to persuade the women to bear more children for the

Fatherland. They put girls in scanty costumes on the stage to encourage what they call "healthy eroticism" so they'll want to have more children, which people sometimes don't want to do, if there's a war on, they say. I couldn't get enough money to escape – and by that time I was an enemy alien. The winter was grim,' she recalled. 'Very cold, dark, and I had someone else's papers, someone who's left Germany, and I was getting scared I'd be captured.'

'So how did you get out?' asked Vi.

'His wife paid,' Sally said.

'If she wanted to get rid of you, why didn't she turn you in?'

'She didn't want to go that far.'

'My dad was in the last lot. He used to say the only good German's a dead German.'

'People are people, wherever you go.'

This was when the Spaniard spat on Sally. He was coming past their table with another man, stopped, looked back at her, turned and took a pace back to where they were sitting, said two words to Sally in a vicious tone and spat in her face.

Then he rejoined the other man and they walked on and out of the restaurant.

'Filthy pig!' exclaimed Vi. She opened her handbag and handed Sally a small bottle of cologne. 'Use this,' she told Sally. 'It'll freshen you up. Why did he do that? Do you know him?'

'Oh, God – oh, God,' Sally said. 'Is my makeup all over the place?'

'You're looking a bit the worse for wear,' Vi said, and handed her a small mirror.

'I'd better go to the ladies' and make running repairs.' She got up and left, with rapid steps. Apparently no one else had noticed the incident. When she returned she was freshly made-up. She sat down.

'What did he say to you?' Vi asked.

'Communist whore,' she replied. 'He was Spanish. He must have recognised me from there. I don't know what his sort are doing here, now we're fighting Hitler who helped them so much.'

'Everybody's here,' Vi said. 'French, Norwegians, German spies, Czechs and Poles, Jewish refugees from all over. We'll sink, at this rate. So, you were in Spain. We're Catholics – not good ones, but that's what we are. But quite a lot of the blokes at the docks where Ted works went out there for the civil war to fight for the Reds. Well, I suppose at least that means you're not a German spy. You had me worried.'

'I know, darling,' said Sally, with a laugh.

'Politics, eh?' said Vi, dismissively.

Sally put a pound note on the plate with the bill on it.

'Let me pay,' said Vi, 'if that's all you've got.'

'No, I insist, darling,' Sally said.

'Split it,' said Vi, fishing out her purse. 'The point is, Cora won't open up till September. It'll take all that time to get the place fixed up, what with the manpower shortage. She's begging and bribing all over the place, the carpenter's so old he must have worked on Noah's Ark and the bricklayer's an invalid from the Great War

48

and he's being helped by his son, and if that boy's eleven, that's all he is. And then there's the band – we'll end up with a one-armed pianist, that's my opinion. There'll be no pay, during this summer. But we ought to work out some numbers. Where can I get hold of you?'

'I don't know where I'll be. Cora kicked me out of the Bessemer. I'll go and bang on some doors.'

'Blimey – you *are* in trouble.'

Sally sighed. 'I know. I can get a job, I suppose. There's plenty now they've called up all the men.'

Vi rummaged in her bag. 'Here's my agent's card. Go and see if he can fix you up with something. Say I sent you and I'll leave messages for you there.'

'What will you do for money?' asked Sally.

'I used to do a summer season in Bournemouth but I don't know if that's still on, because of the war. At a pinch we'll all have to live on my brother's wages. Well,' she said, dabbing powder on her nose and scrutinising her face sceptically in a small mirror, 'I'll love you and leave you.' She stood up, ''Bye, Sally, don't do anything I wouldn't do,' and she was off, her high heels clattering over the marble floor.

In Shaftesbury Avenue, Sally went to Victor Kane's office below which was a small shop selling umbrellas and walking sticks. She went into the tall building, climbed a flight of stairs and went through a door with a frosted-glass window on which was painted *Victor Kane, Theatrical Representative*.

A well made-up woman with dyed blonde hair in corrugated waves sat behind a desk knitting a jersey in a complicated Fair Isle pattern.

She glanced up at Sally, then the phone rang. She placed her knitting carefully on the desk and answered it. 'No, sorry, Bobby. Nothing today. It's the war. Will you ring tomorrow, darling? Good, that's good. Toodle-oo.'

She looked at Sally again. Once more the phone rang. She picked it up. 'Hello, Mrs Kane. Yes, Mrs Kane. I'm putting you through, Mrs Kane.'

Immediately there was a burst of speech from behind the door leading off from the office. The woman picked up her knitting.

'Can you help me, darling—' Sally began.

The male voice beyond the office door grew louder and wilder. 'Mrs Kane's got herself in a shocking state about the war,' the woman confided. 'That's what it's about. Well, don't just stand there. Advance and state your case.'

'I'm looking for a job,' said Sally. 'Cabaret, revue, that sort of thing – Lola Laine sent me. We're opening in a club in September.'

'I know,' said the woman. The man's voice went on and on. Then came an impatient shout and the door was flung open to reveal a portly figure in a green waistcoat, with an unlit cigar in his hand. Victor Kane looked shaken. 'I'm volunteering! I'm joining up,' he declared. 'You'll hold the fort for me while I'm gone, won't you, Yvonne?'

'You don't want to do that, Victor,' she told him. 'You'd make a rotten soldier.'

'Well, I can't stand any more of this,' he said. 'Will you do it – keep the business running?'

'You'll have to draw up a document,' she told him. 'I can't have Mrs Kane interfering all the time.'

'What about pleading with me? "Don't go, Victor, don't go and get killed."'

'You'll survive,' she said, unsympathetically.

He went out.

'Will he do it?' asked Sally.

'I shouldn't think so. He'll stop off at the Café Royal on the way to join up and that'll be that for the day. Mind you, he's very wrought up. Mrs Kane's got relatives in Poland and she's saying they'll all be killed. Jewish,' Yvonne mouthed at Sally. 'She's driving him mad.' She flipped open a card index, then copied something on to a piece of paper, which she handed to Sally. 'You're in luck. *Pull Up Your Socks* has just lost a soubrette to the Army. If you get the job come back here and sign on with the agency. That okey-doke with you?' The phone was ringing again. She picked it up. 'He just went out. I'm not sure where he's gone, Mrs Kane. No, I haven't seen the paper today.' She covered the receiver with her hand and said to Sally, 'For God's sake, clean yourself up a bit before you go. You look as if you've just got out of bed.'

Sally did an audition on a dusty stage, to a piano accompaniment played by the theatre manager, who happened to be in the building at the time. She sang a song popularised by Gertrude Lawrence, 'The Physician', lightening, as far as possible, a voice too low and husky for the music. 'See your legs, dear?' came the weary request from the producer's nephew, who had been the only other person there, apart from the manager, when Sally arrived. She raised her skirt to reveal her last pair of silk stockings.

He called her down into the stalls. 'Can you start tonight?

The conductor's got the music. You'll have to go over to Camden Town to get it from him. And don't expect the show to last, the way things are.'

'I won't,' she promised him.

In Camden Town she stood on a doorstep looking down a dusty passageway, which contained an old pram. The conductor's wife, a harassed woman in a floral pinafore, gave her the music. Then she took another bus and headed across the river for Kennington, where her friends, Spanish exiles Ricardo and Antonia, agreed to put her up on the couch in their flat.

From then until July Sally, in an electric blue evening dress borrowed from Vi in exchange for Vi's use, when required, of the pink suit, did six shows a week, and a Wednesday matinée, in *Pull Up Your Socks* – 'witty, farouche, gossamer-light', read the notice outside the theatre. She sang two numbers, one bitter-sweet, '*It was forever, you told me on Monday, but eternity ended that day*' and one madly gay, '*Dance the tango through the night, Tango, fandango, till early light.*' Then she got the last bus back to Kennington.

She spent her afternoons in the cramped South London flat on correspondence for the local Communist Party. On Saturdays she sold the *Daily Worker* outside Piccadilly Circus underground station.

When the show closed Sally borrowed ten shillings here and there in order to eat and help out with Ricardo and Antonia's rent until September.

There had never been any doubt in Cora's mind that, war or no war, La Vie en Rose – or the Pink Urinal as

it was cruelly christened by the Pontifex Street crowd –
must open in September, and only in September, when
the better sort of people returned to town. The date of
the opening was fixed for the seventh.

14

Greg was impressed by his first sight of Bruno's shop on the bottom floor of a low house at the smarter end of Portobello Road. It stood on a corner, beside a cobbled mews at the end of which were two garages that must once have been stables. The shop had large windows on two sides, overlooking the street and the mews. The windows gleamed; the paint was trim; above the shop the name 'Lowenthal' was painted in gold letters.

Inside stood small items of furniture, an early Victorian upholstered chair, a rosewood table. Old china and silver had been placed on various surfaces.

As Greg approached, a thick-set man and a tall, pale girl in jeans were unloading a kneehole desk from a van in the mews. Bruno stood nearby, watching. When he saw Greg he said, 'Good. I've booked a table at a restaurant in Hyde Park, but first I must see this done.' The man and the girl carried the desk past them, into the shop. 'Hurry up, Fiona,' Bruno said. 'I want the van moved so I can get my car out.' He and Greg watched as the pair, having disposed of the desk, returned to the van and started to unload a large tall-boy. They began to move it towards the shop. 'No!' cried Bruno. 'In the workshop! What did I tell you before?' They turned and carried the tall-boy to the end of the mews. 'No one remembers what you say,' Bruno grumbled. Finally, they were finished, but before the van moved off Bruno said to the young woman, 'I'm going to have lunch, Fiona. Be careful. No accidents, not like last time.'

'Yes, Bruno,' she said meekly.

They walked to the garages at the back of the mews. One was obviously used as a workshop and storage area. Bruno opened the door to the other and revealed an antique more impressive to Greg than all the rest, a gleaming black Wolseley, all fresh paint and chrome, dating from some time in the 1950s.

'Mr Lowenthal,' he said respectfully. 'What a car!'

'I used to dream of such a car,' Bruno said. He opened the door and got in. Greg followed suit on the passenger side. The interior was immaculate: the seats were polished leather; the walnut dashboard shone. As Bruno twisted the ignition key Greg heard the sound of a perfectly tuned and maintained engine. 'Ah,' said Bruno, happily.

Greg thought that this must have been the car you wanted when few Europeans had cars. It spoke of wealth and authority. It was like the cars out of which men leaped in darkened streets to hammer on doors, drag people out—

The air was damp, grey clouds hung low. They sat by

the restaurant's window, looking over the misty composed vista of trees, grass, water.

'I like your shop,' Greg said. 'How do you acquire the things you sell?'

'Sales, buying trips. Other dealers come to me, I go to them. There's a grapevine. I'm training the girl, Fiona, to go to sales for me. But she's not good. As you may have seen, I specialise in Regency and early Victorian objects. I like them very much – they are cosier than eighteenth-century things but not so ornate as furniture became later in the nineteenth century. In the nineteen fifties there was quite a lot about in houses and attics. It was not so much valued – you might find a card table in a greenhouse, with flower-pots on it, a chair, original upholstery, in a spare bedroom. It's not so easy now, but that was when I began to deal in it, and learn.

'You see, Greg, once the war was over I became a junk-dealer in an area of junk-dealers, men with horses and carts going round buying old gas-cookers, baths, broken chairs. When I got a van I became an aristocrat. All London was dilapidated at that time. What was not broken was old and this neighbourhood was as bad as anywhere. One of my distinguished professional rivals – he had a shop not three hundred yards from where I am today – was a famous mass murderer. He had the bodies of six or seven women buried in his flat and his back yard. So, I dealt in old pots and pans, chipped plates, second-hand electric fires, cookers – not very nice. Then slowly I began to collect better things, quietly, and sell them. I haven't done so badly, eh?' he asked. 'Not for a poor immigrant boy, a refugee. You're an American. You understand such things.'

'You left Pontifex Street?' Greg said.

Bruno shrugged. 'After the war, Briggs dumped me. He found someone more attractive and that was it, goodbye, Bruno. I wasn't sad. I was fed up with him. Out of decency – and because I knew too much – they fixed me up with papers and Briggs gave me a little money to get started. Not much but, to be fair, all he had. He was not a wealthy man. What I minded, though, was that I never saw him again. I phoned once, then I wrote. Nothing. He was cold, Briggs.' He paused then told Greg, 'They were all cold – Pym, Briggs, Julia Montrose – cold in a way I don't suppose you could imagine.'

They had ordered and the waiters brought their food. Bruno tucked into his veal with appetite. Then he looked up at Greg and asked, 'Tell me about your book. How long have you to write it?'

'There's no set deadline. But I hope to begin writing some time next year. I can't tell you how much it means to me to have you talk to me, sir.'

'I told you to call me Bruno. These days I am too much "Sir" or Mr Lowenthal. That happens when you get old. Well, you want more information, you ambitious young man, in a hurry. Where were we?'

'Sally had gone off to a party with Adrian Pym. But first, Bruno, can you tell me what happened to Sally? I can't find any record of her. Of course, women marry and change their names. Do you know how she finished up?'

'She's dead, I suppose, like so many of us,' Bruno told

him. The thought appeared to give him no pain. 'But here she is again,' he said briskly, 'in spirit. That's enough. Turn on your little recorder and let's go on. You have your career to consider.'

Greg placed the recorder on the table and shot Bruno a quick, intense look, as if by catching the old man unawares he could work out who he was, and what approach he was taking. He knew – just knew – that there was more to Bruno Lowenthal than met his eye. His glance did not escape Bruno, who smiled knowingly, as if he had guessed what Greg was thinking. Sitting in the restaurant, with its view of the park, Bruno's cracked, precise voice went on: 'This park used to be full of barrage balloons. The ropes securing them were all over the place – you'd fall over them in the dark. Sometimes the balloons were on the ground, huge and white. It was completely dark at night, of course, because of the blackout. The whole city was dark. We lived by looking up, I suppose, at the moon and the stars, the searchlights – and the aircraft overhead. Often, you would see the swastikas painted on their sides. People made love in the park, on the grass with the bombers going overhead.'

Greg smiled. 'Did you?'

'Sometimes,' the old man said. 'When I thought Briggs wouldn't find out. You could meet anybody in the dark.' The old blue eyes took on a gleam. 'Yes, well,' said Bruno, in a more practical tone, 'it was a long time ago. Now, where were we? Ah, when the Blitz began . . .'

15

'The battle of Britain was over then – all those dull little places with dull names, Ramsgate, Hastings, Bromley,
Orpington, had been bombed. The people would look up
and see the planes fighting just above the trees, lower
sometimes. They called it hedgehopping. And the average
life of a Spitfire pilot in those days was, they said, three
weeks. The attack on the cities was still to come. But
before that, and before La Vie en Rose was due to open,
Sally arrived suddenly at Pontifex Street one evening with
her luggage, an officer of the Free French Army and a
mattress. There was an attic upstairs, just a room about
twelve yards square with a sloping roof and a skylight and
two very small windows, high up. You had to climb a ladder
to get up to this room. And Sir Peveril Jones, who, you will
remember, was our landlord, had told Sally she could have
it. She was moving in.

'When she arrived Briggs and Pym were there having
a drink. I was cooking supper. Briggs fought back. "You

can't possibly stay. There's only one bathroom," he said, and instantly phoned Sir Peveril at his secret War Office number. He was on the phone to Sir Peveril when Julia came in, making a fuss also. She didn't know Sally well, but I don't think she wanted to be associated with Sally in people's minds. It was a matter of her reputation. After all, Julia was having an affair with Sir Peveril, who had a wife and several young children tucked away in an old manor house on the Welsh borders. Sally, though, was open in what she did – she never had an ulterior motive. Julia believed that if Sally was about, people would connect them, call them both tarts – and Julia was being very careful for she wanted to marry Sir Peveril and be Lady Jones of the Elizabethan manor house.

'But it was Briggs who made the most fuss. He raised his voice to Sir Peveril, which showed how angry he was because Sir Peveril was much senior to him at his office – *and* his landlord.

'I only heard Briggs's end of the conversation, naturally, but it sounded as if Sir Peveril was determined. He told Briggs that Sally would be singing at La Vie en Rose and would need a base nearby, and that, as you could say, was that. I thought at the time that Sir Peveril must have some old connection with Cora Blow and that that was why he gave Sally permission to stay in the attic at Pontifex Street. Briggs went on arguing but then he had to stop. He was achieving nothing, except to annoy his landlord – a generous landlord, I might say. He charged little rent, paid readily for repairs and breakages and probably Mrs Thing's wages. He was not a man to upset.

'While this was going on Sally and the French officer were humping her mattress upstairs and Pym was lying there in a chair with his shirt off and a glass in his hands, looking quite detached. He'd brought home some tough in the uniform of the Foreign Legion, a brute with no neck and frightening eyes who was sitting on the sofa drinking and looking round him like a murderer. Then Briggs had to end his call, because Sally came in with her Frenchman. The Legionnaire started telling the story of an incident in North Africa where the Legion had gone to punish a village for some act of defiance. It ended with torture and massacre. He was a dreadful man. Briggs listened with horror, Pym as if the man were telling a story about going to buy a newspaper. Then I seem to think we all drank some whisky and many people arrived – Charles Denham, who was a novelist, and a young Air Force officer, Ralph Hodd. And there was a man from SOE who had been at Eton with Briggs, and a cousin of Julia's and her friend, who were both WAAFs in uniform, and Geoffrey Forbes, whose name you may remember. He also became famous later, not in a good way. I had prepared dinner but I could see how the evening would end. I went upstairs and began to move things out of the attic, a broken chair and so forth, and sweep the floor.

'When I came down the ladder Sally was coming out of the bathroom, wearing an evening dress I knew belonged to Julia. Well, that meant trouble. By the time she got back into the room Pym had said something to make one of the other girls cry – he could be very cruel. Julia, of course, began to complain about her dress. "But I'm going dancing," Sally was saying, "and you said you were staying in." Julia was telling her that that was not the point, but I don't think Sally could see it that way. As this went on the French officer sat down at the piano, which was an impressive Steinway, and started to play Chopin. The Legionnaire got up, grabbed at the WAAF who wasn't crying and started to swing her round the room, holding her very close and bending over her as if they were in some working-class cabaret. I don't think she liked it. And so the evening went on, with people coming and going – a vase was broken when Charles Denham tried to rescue the WAAF from the Legionnaire without success, so Sally broke in between them and went on dancing with him while the young woman fled upstairs.

'I can't tell you what that atmosphere was like, always, at Pontifex Street,' Bruno told Greg. 'You would have had to have been there. We were young, young as you are, Greg, we were facing a war, we didn't know what would happen – we thought we would probably die. Our fathers had died in millions in the Great War, why should we do any better? And everybody, nearly everybody, was doing secret work.' Bruno shrugged. 'You can't describe it. I've forgotten it myself. Just sometimes, when I pass a building, perhaps, or hear a certain piece of music, do I remember. Anyway . . . anyway . . .' His voice trailed off.

Then he said, 'I went to sit in the kitchen. I was fed up. I was supposed to look after the household. This was my contribution. But it was a nightmare. No one helped. No one thanked me. My relationship with Briggs, who had saved me, got me into Britain, describing me as a servant, was terrible. I had no status in the country, no friends, no relatives, no certainty. And I had lived in Germany until nineteen thirty-five. I knew very clearly what would happen if the war was lost. I was sitting at the kitchen table, ignoring the noise – they had the gramophone playing now – and people were coming in and out. I felt very low, very depressed. Then Briggs came in. He said only, "I'm going upstairs. I've work to do."

'There was a crash, and laughter and the doorbell rang again. There were feet on the stairs and cries of welcome. A very handsome young man put his head round the door, "Alexander!" he cried. "Where's Loomie?"

'"I really don't know, Casimir," said Briggs.

'Then in came Charles Denham and sat down at the table with a sigh. Briggs said to him, "Charles, I'm heading upstairs. I've work to do," but Charles replied, "Gerda's staying in Gloucester with her aunt."

'Gerda was his lover, but she was married to an American diplomat and would not leave her husband and children for him.

'"Rotten for you," said Briggs, but without much concern in his voice. He turned to leave the room.

'Charles halted him. "No," he said. "Listen, Briggs, do you know a man called Jonty Till?"

'"No, I don't think so."

'"I've got a suspicion he's Gerda's latest."

'"That's no good, if it's true."

'"You couldn't find out for me, could you?"

'"Me? Why?" asked Briggs, astonished.

'"Well, you're supposed to be a spy."

'"My dear Charles, first, I'm not a spy, and second, even if I were, what makes you think I'd spend the Government's money hanging about outside Gerda's house to see what she's doing? I suppose you'd want me to wear a false beard."

'"Oh, God, I'm so unhappy. It's the uncertainty. If only I *knew*. I'd rather have the truth, whatever it was."

'"I shouldn't think you would," Briggs said. "If you knew for certain this Till character had supplanted you, you'd feel even more unhappy. Look, Charles, what with there being a war on I really *must* go away and look at my papers." He added, "Have you asked her about Till?"

'"Yes. She said there was nothing between them."

'"I suppose she might anyway."

'"Quite. I think I'll go and see if there's anything to drink." Denham got up and swayed out of the room.

'Briggs said, "Oh, my God. Doesn't he realise? I think it's escaped him we're fighting a war against Hitler and his fascists."

'Sally, bright-eyed and red-cheeked, was in the doorway. "But how nice it would be if someone helped – the Soviet Union, for example," she said. Because, of course, Stalin and Hitler had signed a pact which meant that Russia wouldn't fight.

'"You know the party line," Briggs said sternly. "But what *I'd* like to know is how you persuaded Sir Peveril to let you have the attic."

'"I didn't persuade him at all, darling,' Sally said. "I just rang up and asked him and he was an absolute sweetie and said yes, of course I must move in if I wanted to. He's a darling, but honestly, Briggs, I do hope we're all going to be great friends here and get along like a house on fire, with never a cross word between us."

'"I hope so, too," said Briggs, "but I'm not optimistic. Still, while we're chatting, Sally, do tell me, what did you do with your baby? Leave it on a bench at King's Cross?"

'"Don't be so utterly foul, Briggs. The baby's in the country with my family. My old nanny's gone back to help."

'"If anyone asked me for my advice," Briggs said deliberately, "I wouldn't recommend them to hand over another child for her to bring up. Not after you."

'"Aren't you a bastard, Briggs?" Sally said. "Nanny Trot's absolutely wonderful. I think it's horrible to say things about a person's nanny." She turned to the young officer with whom she had arrived. "Pierre, sweetie, I'm desperate to get out of here. Shall we go to the French, darling?' And they disappeared.

'"She's going to be such a nuisance," Briggs said, and went straight upstairs to do his work.

'Not long after that I saw Pym and the Legionnaire staggering up the stairs together. Pym had his hand in the back of the Legionnaire's trousers. I wondered how much work Briggs would get done. Briggs and I slept in the larger bedroom upstairs and Pym's bedroom was at the end of the passageway. Julia had the room further along, between Pym's and ours, opposite the bathroom, but that was all right. It was Pym and Pym's boyfriends – pick-ups, really – who were the problem.

'I think that before war was declared the flat had been

rented to a young couple who kept it as a base for when they wanted to come to parties and other things in London, and it was consequently well decorated and furnished. As time went by, of course, standards declined.

'I went and sat down in a chair by the window. The WAAF who had cried had fallen asleep on the sofa. The other was searching in a cupboard for gramophone records. Then she started dancing with Hodd, the RAF officer. Sally and her French officer were still there – they had not gone out. The music stopped and I heard her saying to Charles Denham, who was standing by the fireplace, "No, Charles. It's not Jonty Till. It's his brother, Vernon. He and Gerda spent a weekend together in Scarborough – everybody knows." She never had any tact.

'Meanwhile Pym had rolled downstairs, in a pair of jodhpurs, and was rummaging in a cupboard for a bottle. He straightened up, holding it. "Scarborough – funny place to go," he remarked. "And, Charles, I hope we're not going to hear of any more of those tired old suicide attempts of yours."

'Charles crossed the room and tried to punch him on the nose, but only hit his cheek because Pym turned his head aside at the last moment. Charles tried again. A girl in a beret who had just come in screamed. Someone pulled Charles away. It wasn't hard. Pym staggered off upstairs. Then everyone who was left woke up the WAAF and we all went off to the French pub.

'We rolled through the dark streets singing, "You stepped out of a drain. You looked quite insane. That's why I loved you—"

Bruno sat quiet for a moment. He cleared his throat and went on. 'Then La Vie en Rose tried to open. There were more cellars behind it and these became useful later on during air-raids – we'd sit on the old empty casks Cora had kept there since Edward VII's time, or on a carpet on the floor or in a set of dining chairs she had cleared out of the hotel in the twenties. It was quite luxurious compared with the tube stations or the cramped air-raid shelters in people's gardens.

'You entered La Vie by going down the steps from the street into the basement. The main entrance of the hotel was next door. Once down there you banged on an unpleasant purple door with whatever you had in your hand, the women used to take off a shoe sometimes to hammer with. Then at some point someone would open up, Cora, perhaps, or Vi – or one of the band or a guest, even. One night young Hodd, a bit the worse for wear, was beating on the door crying out in an Irish accent, "Will you open up in there, for the love of God? What does a man have to do to get a drink round here?" Then the door opened and he was looking straight into the face of an air vice-marshal, who just said, "Thank God you're not in uniform, Squadron Leader," and let him in. Of course, Hodd *was* in uniform.

'The legend went that one day two girls in evening dress, looking for their boyfriends, had the door opened to them by Winston Churchill, who said gallantly that if they couldn't find who they were looking for they'd be welcome at his table – where his private secretary, a cabinet member and a general were sitting.

'The rules for membership of La Vie en Rose were the same as the rules for staying at the Bessemer. If Cora liked you, you got in. If she didn't, you stayed out. The room was very small, rectangular, only about twenty-one feet by fifteen, with a bar at the back, next to the stairs, a tiny platform at the other end, hardly big enough to take the band, which usually consisted of a piano, saxophone and a couple of drums. There was just enough room on this dais for Vi or Sally, who worked in shifts. Apart from that there were ten small tables, crammed together and in front of the platform a tiny space where you could dance – almost. People were jammed together on busy nights but in places like that they like to be crowded together.

'The whole place was painted strawberry pink, which looked horrible in daylight, but was somehow comforting at night, when the lights, also pink-shaded, were low.

'The beer was terrible – Cora didn't care. Where she got the other drinks from it was better not to ask. I don't know how she did it but throughout the war when the pubs, even, would have to put up signs saying NO BEER, Cora managed something. There was almost always gin, whisky and brandy and sometimes there would be a miraculous arrival of wine, or plum brandy, or Calvados.

'How Cora found the drink was one mystery. Where she got the band from was another. They started with an old pianist, Vincent Tubman, who had been an accompanist in his younger days for many famous singers, including, by his account, Dame Nellie Melba. He claimed to have stood in when her own accompanist was taken ill. However, the drink had got to Vincent. He wasn't bad when he was sober but he often wasn't. Sometimes I saw him carried unconscious from his piano stool. At first, too, there was a furtive saxophonist, who seldom spoke. He came and went guiltily each evening. Briggs thought he was a deserter who thought he'd be safest from detection in a place full of senior servicemen, what they called the "brass". Pym's theory was that he was a bigamist, hiding from several wives. The drummer was a tired young man who worked as a postman during the day – they couldn't call him up because he had bad lungs. And, of course, there were Vi and Sally.

'Pontifex Street had decided to turn out in force to celebrate the opening on the seventh of September. But at five o'clock the sirens went and the big raid began. The West End of London where we were was much less affected, but it was a shock. The bombers just came straight in through southern England, crossed the Thames and bombarded the docks, railway lines and homes of the East End.

'People had never experienced this before and they were terrified. The fire services and ambulances weren't properly prepared, the ack-ack batteries weren't in place. There weren't enough air-raid shelters. The bombers flew off and returned two hours later, when it was getting dark. The raids went on for twelve hours, until dawn next day.

'It must have been about seven, getting dark, when I stood with Pym on the roof at Pontifex Street, and saw what we were to see often again – the sun setting in the west but appearing to set also in the east, where a glow of fire four miles away stretched along the whole horizon.

'Then we heard the bombers coming back and the sound

of the second attack. The sirens started up again. Puffs of smoke began to appear on the burning horizon. We heard some planes coming towards us. Pym said, "Bloody hell," and we scrambled through the skylight into the attic, through Sally's cluttered room and down the ladder to the upper floor of the flat. Then we fled into the shop below.

'There was a cellar door set into the wall beside the back door and Pym hammered on this as the bombers droned overhead. There was an explosion that seemed near us, though it was perhaps a quarter of a mile away. Later we were to think of such a hit as distant.

'"Louisa! Anne!" Pym was shouting. "Let us in!" These were the names of the two gentlewomen who ran the cake shop downstairs. But they had bolted themselves in and it was some time before they opened up, as if they thought the Gestapo was already there. When Louisa pulled back the bolts Anne was sitting on a crate, wearing her gas mask, just in case.

'I was surprised to see Briggs already there, sitting on the dirt floor, leaning against the wall at the back, smoking a cigarette. "I strolled back to get a clean shirt," he told Pym. "Otherwise I'd be safe and sound in our secret bunker miles below the earth." This was the coal cellar of their offices in Baker Street. "It's opening night at La Vie," he added gloomily. "I was rather looking forward to it. You didn't think to bring anything to drink, did you? The sirens went off just as I was opening the front door."

'"Is that all you can think of?" cried Louisa. "We've nothing – no food, no water – we could be here for days. We could all be killed."

'"Better to be drunk, then," observed Pym.

'A bomb whistled down outside. There was a great thump, some dust rose from the floor, some plaster came off the walls, the overhead bulb flickered but did not go out.

'To me it sounded very close, but I couldn't place where it was. Later we would learn how near, and where a bomb had landed and say, "There goes the post office." But at that moment my fear of the unaccustomed bombardment was less than the fear of a German victory, invasion, my own capture and death. These seemed suddenly much closer. My freedom in Britain had always been conditional. I saw the prison gates, the grave.

'"If this is going to happen very often," Briggs said looking round, "we'll have to do something about this place." Pym looked a little tense, but Briggs showed no fear. Anne began to cry and had to take off her gas mask to wipe her eyes. Louisa tried to comfort her. The noise went on. The worst was not knowing what was happening outside. We sat there for about fifteen minutes until in a lull Pym said, "Sod it. I'm going out to see what's happening."

'"Don't do it," Anne cried.

'But Pym ducked out of the low door, straightened up outside in the dark and said, "Christ!"

'"What's the matter?" one of the women said in alarm.

'Briggs stood up quickly and went out. I followed him. And there was Sally, standing in the yard in a tin hat, with a raincoat over her filthy evening dress, a blue number, but now dirty and torn. Her face was streaked black. Something was struggling in a grey blanket in her arms.

71

'"Where *have* you been?" Briggs asked her.

'It seemed she'd been in Kennington with her friends when the raid began. They were right under the path the planes were taking to the Thames. Bombs were already dropping.

'All three had been bombed in Madrid, you see,' Bruno said, signalling for the bill. 'So apparently they dashed out of the house, got on their bikes – Sally borrowed one – and rode under the bombers down into the East End. There, they helped the rescuers. Someone said later they'd seen Sally, illuminated by the flames of a warehouse, digging frantically in the steaming rubble of a house.

'She said, "It's awful there. And my dress is ruined. But I don't suppose Cora will want to open up. So depressing – my big night!" She dropped the bundle, and what appeared to be a cat streaked out and away somewhere.

'I hope someone frightfully nice will adopt it,' Sally said.

'The rest of us were listening to the sound of a solitary bomber approaching.

Sally went on. '"Quite frankly, in Madrid the bombardment just made people angry and obstinate, like apes being furious when another lot of apes starts throwing coconuts on their heads out of the trees." The noise of the bomber grew louder.

'"Actually," Pym said, "I'm so frightened all I want to do is fuck and fuck and fuck." Then there was a massive explosion two streets away. The sky flared up, the ground shook. We all, except Sally, flung ourselves on the ground.'

Here Bruno paused to call for the bill, and now he and

Greg went into the battle of the wallets. Greg knew early on in the struggle that Bruno, determined, would win.

Once the bill was paid and Bruno was tucking away his wallet, he told Greg, 'Briggs said later, "You must admit it's frightfully irritating, us hiding in a cellar while Sally digs people out of the rubble. And being so superior about having been bombed before – it's almost intolerable." Then Pym remarked that Sally was rather brave and there was an odd look on his face as he spoke, but I didn't understand it at the time.

'Well,' Bruno said, standing up. 'Thank you so much for your company. Where can I drop you?'

They walked out into the still gloomy afternoon. As they strolled towards the car Bruno said, 'The raids went on, night after night, but La Vie opened a week later.

'Vi was a nice singer – she had a clear soprano but with a few true deep notes. Sally's voice was small and husky, but she had the knack of putting a song over which made up for some of her deficiencies. When she sang "The Last Time I Saw Paris" I must say there were a few damp eyes and a bit of swallowing. She'd often end up singing "Please Don't Talk About Me When I'm Gone".

'Oh, my goodness,' Bruno said suddenly, as they approached his vehicle, 'I can suddenly see her again, singing under the pink light, and all the time you could hear the crashes in the distance and the sounds of the fire engines coming and going.' He smiled at Greg and walked towards the car, singing in his harsh, unmusical voice, '"Makes no difference how I carry on, Please don't talk about me when I'm gone."'

16

Katherine Ledbetter and Greg leaned, side by side, over the bridge crossing the Cam near King's College. Before them the college stood white, soaring, like Gothic Lego, in its acres of green turf. Rooks cawed and hopped on the grass.

A man in corduroys was propped at the other parapet, reading. Two ducks eddied, unresisting, under the bridge.

'You shouldn't have done this, Greg,' said Katherine, in her clear voice.

'I figured you planned to leave town before I came,' he answered. 'That's sneaky too. Whatever else I am, I'm an old friend, aren't I? Who's the guy?'

'What guy?'

'The guy you're having an affair with.'

'Greg,' she said, 'it's been six years. And it's no business of yours.'

'Just a friendly question. You haven't changed a bit. Still evasive.' Then he added, 'Still beautiful.'

She was a tall, slender woman, with a long, pale face, very big brown eyes and a mass of shiny dark brown hair piled at the back of her head and secured by a tortoiseshell comb. She had a large, curving mouth. She wore moccasins on her feet and a long black linen dress with a brown coat over it.

'Still beautiful,' he repeated. 'Still the same old snappy dresser.' He put his arm round her. 'Why don't I buy you lunch? We'll have some wine then go back to your book-strewn studio apartment for a cup of instant coffee in a chipped mug. I'll say I need to pick your brains about the war-time cabinet but in fact I'll be after your body.' He put his arm round her.

'No, Greg,' she said.

He squeezed. 'That's not what you used to say.'

She pushed him away, saying more loudly, 'No, Greg.'

The man at the other parapet slowly moved his book aside and turned. 'Katherine,' he said, 'I didn't notice you. Will you be at the Williamses tomorrow?'

'I think so,' she said. She introduced the two men. 'Ken Jerome, Greg Phillips.'

Jerome nodded at Greg then said, 'I'll probably see you at the Williamses then.' He put the book in his pocket and strolled off.

Greg glowered at his retreating back then bent over the parapet again. 'Smug English bastard. Why didn't he say "hi" when we came up?' he complained.

'He was reading. His attention was attracted by your trying to kiss me and my resistance. It's the kind of thing people notice.'

'He certainly gave me the evil eye,' Greg said. He straightened up to face her. 'Well, maybe it was a friendly, welcoming look. Perhaps I've been away too long to tell the difference.'

'Fuck you, too,' said Katherine. 'You've been away six years, Greg. We broke up before you went, mainly because you wanted to go back to the States and I'd been offered a lectureship here – do you remember that? It was by mutual consent, but it cost me a lot to do it. It did, Greg,' she said. 'So now here you are again – "Look, I'm here." You're right, I was going to dodge you. But what did you expect me to do? What do you want?'

'All right, I'm sorry,' he said. 'I've got the opportunity of a lifetime here, to write this book, make some kind of a name for myself. I'm jumpy – OK? But I am glad to see you, very glad. Parting wasn't easy for me, either, but what choice did I have? I didn't have much of a future here. Shall we go get some lunch? Please?'

She softened. 'Never refuse a meal,' she said. 'OK, let's go.'

They walked arm in arm along King's Parade, then turned off down a narrow street with colleges on either side. Huge gateways showed grassy squares inside the old walls.

'How's it going, the book?' enquired Katherine.

'So well I'm scared,' he told her. 'Everything's right, nothing's wrong and still I'm paranoid.'

'Well, you know what they say about that,' she said.

'It doesn't mean someone isn't out to get me.'

A bird in a tree overhanging a wall cawed. 'Lunch,' he said, leading her across the street.

*　　*　　*

They were in bed in Katherine's room in college. Student voices came up from the lawn below.

Greg, lying with his arms behind his head, said, 'This is a lot better than the old days. Two whole rooms, big ones, all to yourself. Who does the furniture belong to?'

In her sitting room were a sideboard, some small tables and a picture or two, which did not look like standard college issue. Though who knew what these dignified foundations thought suitable for their staff?

'They're borrowed from a relative,' she told him.

'Who's that?' he asked.

She yawned.

'Tired?' he asked.

'I'm trying to complete a paper about government regulations covering employment between nineteen forty and nineteen forty-one. It'll be part of a bigger project, the effects on people of the civil measures taken in Britain during the Second World War. Oh, Greg,' she said, turning to him, 'I shouldn't be doing this.'

'Once more won't make any difference.'

On the train back to London he was happy. The winter landscape streamed past him. Crows flew across dark, ploughed fields. There were grazing sheep, orchards, bare trees and hedgerows. There was something to be said for Britain, he thought contentedly. Quite a lot.

17

Greg woke next morning under the pink coverlet from which his feet poked out. His gaze fell on the shaky, brown-stained wardrobe. He didn't feel as cheerful as he had the day before, and was not sure why.

It was raining outside but, conscientiously, he took the underground to the British Library periodicals department and looked at the reports for the aftermath of the first big raid on London, hundreds killed, thousands injured, many more rendered homeless. The raids grew worse daily. By the end of September 1940 7,000 people had been killed and 9,000 injured. No panic, just stoicism, they said. Oh, yeah, thought Greg. He still felt gloomy and oppressed when he got up and went off to meet Bruno for lunch. This time it was to be his treat. They went to a pub and sat in a corner.

'No panic?' questioned Greg. 'Britain can take it?'

'Under constant bombardment? With tube stations, one of the safest places, barred and guarded by the police?

People attacked the gates at Liverpool Street to get in during a raid. No panic? What do you think? People left the city and went and slept in the fields.'

'What was happening at Pontifex Street?' Greg asked.

'Well, on the night of the first raid we got to sleep in the end. Briggs set his alarm as usual but when he got up he found the keys to his little car were gone from his dressing table. He ran out and found it had been taken. He set off to work on foot and found the car parked in a square not far away. The back seat was covered in clothing, including a fox fur. There were blankets and a lamp. Then Sally came down the steps of a nearby house, carrying an eiderdown. On top of it were lodged some pots and pans.

'He walked up to her and held out his hand for the car keys. "I didn't give you permission to take my car," he said.

'And Sally said, "I'm collecting for the East End."

'Briggs told her he didn't care and made her unload the car. She had to heap everything up on the pavement and give him the keys, whereupon he stepped into the street and hailed a taxi. The driver looked at Sally and the heap of clothes and bedding, and said, "I'm not a removal van. Get Pickford's."

'Briggs,' said Bruno, sipping his beer, 'started threatening the man with the Hackney Carriage Office but Sally called that she was taking the stuff to the East End and the cabbie agreed to take her. She was loading the items she had collected into the taxi, the driver helping, when Briggs drove off. Sally yelled, "Property is theft," after him but he didn't hear – or didn't want to.

'Briggs couldn't stand having his things used by others,' Bruno told Greg. 'It was pathological, almost. He returned to Pontifex Street and phoned Sir Peveril again, demanding that Sally leave the flat. It was strange that Briggs, who was so handsome and clever and privileged – I think his father was a senior clergyman at Salisbury Cathedral – reacted as violently as he did to Sally. I didn't want her at Pontifex Street, either, but at such a time what could one do?'

'You stuck by him, though,' suggested Greg.

'I had no choice,' Bruno replied. 'I was a refugee. Briggs was a British official of the class that can always pull strings. I thought he could have got me interned – anything. He was my protector. I was young. I suppose I loved him.

'So,' he sighed, 'the raids went on, almost every night, for three months. We became experts at knowing the weather conditions that would keep them off and studying the phases of the moon – they couldn't come when it was too cloudy and dark. The RAF recovered from the devastation of the battle of Britain, guns were mounted to fire on enemy aircraft – they were as good as useless, but it helped morale. Sally spent a lot of time in the East End. The Communists down there were very noisy, probably because they knew the rule "Organise", so she spent a lot of time agitating about the tube stations which were now being used as shelters where conditions were horrible. Also about the rest centres where people went when they were first bombed out, and about housing the homeless people. They laughed at her at Pontifex Street. She went on working at Cora's, though. It was the only money she had coming in and it wasn't much – Cora was not a generous employer. And there was never any question of Sally's family helping her. She never stopped talking about Theo Fitzpatrick, though, "the only man I ever loved".

'I can still see her,' he said, 'one evening, with her face covered in powder, big tired eyes, standing there singing, "Alexander's Ragtime Band", and old Vincent Tubman played his piano louder when a bomb went off nearby. The place was crammed with young men and women in uniform, girls in evening dress. There was a hammering on the door and three soldiers with girls were revealed when Cora cautiously opened the door. "This is a private club," she told them.

'"Come on, Mother, let us in," said one. "There's an air-raid on."

'"You should take shelter in the tube, then," Cora told him.

'"We're fighting for you," he told her. She let them in, and Sally went on singing. Then we heard a bomb whistling through the air. Everyone threw themselves under the tables, Vincent and Sally were under the piano together. There was a deafening explosion. The walls – even the floor – shook. Dust came down all over them. Then came the sound of fire engines as they all got up and shook themselves off. Vincent Tubman started to play again vigorously. Everyone sat down and Cora went out with Pym and Sally and me to examine the damage. What a sight,' Bruno said. 'Searchlights lanced the sky and in and out of them you could see the black shapes of fighting planes. The firemen, tiny against the blaze, were spraying water on the house next door. A man in a tin hat marked

ARP told Cora, "You should be inside, dear." He said to Sally, standing there in evening dress, "What do you mean, bringing your mother out into all this?"

'"I'm the owner of the hotel there," Cora said coldly, pointing. "Is it damaged?"

'"Probably not too bad. If they can get this fire out. Anybody in there, do you know?"

'"Only the housekeeper, Mrs Harding, over there with her dog. The owners are in the country."

'"Very nice for them," he observed.

'Cora called, "I'll put you up, Mrs Harding, till you're settled." She turned to Sally. "I think you owe me another couple of numbers," she said. "Sing something cheerful, for God's sake."'

Bruno looked round the busy pub. He greeted a woman in a shawl and dangling earrings with a nod. He turned back to Greg. 'A different world,' he said. 'But I must get back to my shop, now. On Sunday,' he said, 'we shall meet again, but this time at Covent Garden. I haven't been there for some time and it will be a chance to see what they have. I may buy something, who knows?'

Greg would have preferred to go to Bruno's flat where he could be sure of the quality of his recordings, but noted that since their first meeting Bruno had never suggested this. His own room was, he felt, too dismal for this proud man, this man of good taste, to visit.

Outside the pub Bruno said to Greg, 'Next time I'll tell you about Sally's engagement.'

18

Wandering among the stalls at Covent Garden Bruno muttered, 'Well, there's nothing here. Everything – even the area – fake. It's attractive, though, but of course it's a film set. Do you like it?' he asked.

'Well, I do,' said Greg. 'But I'm an American. It looks real to me.' He gazed at the arcades and across the piazza to an old building.

'It's thinking back, I suppose, to London as it was then, black, covered in soot and, of course, in nineteen forty full of bomb-sites covered in rubble and people walking to work through broken water mains and piles of bricks, carrying gas masks. Well, they took out the gas masks and used the boxes for carrying sandwiches and makeup most of the time. This area was no pretty sight then,' he said, reminiscently. 'Too close to the river, I think. And there was something a little raffish about it, perhaps.'

'Strange at night, in the darkness,' Greg said.

'Yes,' Bruno said, obviously remembering.

'Sally's marriage?' prompted Greg.

They found a bench and sat down. 'It wasn't a marriage,' Bruno said, 'just an engagement that should not have happened, I suppose. Sally was rather lonely, in some ways. Theo Fitzpatrick having played his part, allegedly, in Norway was now said to be being a hero elsewhere – there were stories about that later, but never mind. So Sally began a whirlwind affair with the brave flier Ralph Hodd. He was brave, there was no doubt of that. He flew in Spitfires throughout the battle of Britain. He'd survived, but he'd seen two-thirds of his squadron killed. When Sally came into his life it was like a blessing – he fell head over heels in love.

'It took three weeks in all, and then Sally and he left for Hodd Hall, the family home, in Northumberland. Cold as a tomb, Briggs said. He'd been there. But he was delighted to see her go. He gave a huge party the night she left.

'It wasn't to be, of course,' Bruno said with a sardonic grin. 'Could you imagine Sally as the lady of Hodd, presiding over a gloomy mansion in the far north – no, it was impossible.

'I was sorry for Ralph Hodd during the time he spent with Sally at Pontifex Street. Although he was a well-born landowner they treated him as badly as me – because he was straightforward and the Pontifex Street residents were tricky. He was no more than intelligent – perhaps less – and they, in their way, were brilliant. He was a flier, they were desk-bound. He was open, they were like icebergs, nine-tenths below the surface.

'Ralph Hodd was only twenty-four. When he finished

university he took over at Hodd from his father, who had been a sick man since he had been gassed in the Great War. Then the second war started and Ralph joined the RAF as a pilot. Then came a year of constant demands on nerve and stamina. It didn't show on the surface, except sometimes in his eyes. He was quite conventional and would say things like, "These working classes are the salt of the earth," meaning his ground crew.

'One evening he came downstairs into La Vie with Sally to find two young soldiers having an argument. Suddenly one picked up a bottle and hit the other over the head with it. He stood there with blood running down his face. Hodd said, "Crikey!" What sort of word is that? It goes with buns and ginger beer. I don't know – and I don't know what Sally saw in him. Of course, after that he dashed in and helped with the injuries, tried to sort out the quarrel.'

'Perhaps that was what she liked,' Greg suggested.

'Well, he'd never have let her down,' Bruno said. 'How they mocked him. He'd come round to Pontifex Street in the early evening in a nice suit, well shaven, to pick her up and perhaps find Pym playing the piano and Briggs having a quiet drink after work. He and Sally would go off and when they returned the place would be like hell, the air thick with smoke, gramophone playing loud jazz, Pym on the sofa with his arm round a sailor, some kind of a row in a corner, a girl in tears, a political argument in the kitchen. When Ralph proposed to Sally he said, in the nicest politest possible way, that he'd take her away from all that, it was not the manner in which she should be living.

'In the morning Sally said to me, waving a cigarette about in the kitchen, "Darling, what *shall* I do? It means leaving London, my career – and think of Theo, poor Theo." I noticed she didn't mention the baby.

'After she'd accepted him Briggs wondered if she'd told Hodd, the *Boy's Own* hero, of Gisela's existence. "If she hasn't," he said, "I certainly won't. All I yearn for is Sally's marriage to good old true-as-steel Ralph Hodd. I wouldn't do anything to prevent that."

'One morning at eight the doorbell rang and I let in a couple, a burly man in tweeds and a very soignée lady. Sally's parents! We weren't prepared for them – Pym was in the sitting room in an Arab robe, reading *The Times*, and there was a Dutch captain, still drunk, on the couch with bottles and glasses all over the place.

'Briggs saved the day. He arrived downstairs, looking impeccable, and actually bowed over Geneviève Jackson-Bowles's hand. He almost clicked his heels. She was charmed. All this gave me time to warn Sally, who was upstairs in bed with Hodd. They got up and started to blunder about giggling.

'Ralph came downstairs, Pym made introductions – Geneviève was frosty towards Pym. I made us all tea, of course.

'Geneviève sat, straight-backed, in a chair and Harry looked about, trying to get the measure of the situation and his son-in-law-to-be. "It's very sudden," he said to Ralph Hodd. "It's typical of war-time, I know. How do you see your future when this lot is over?"

'"I suppose I'll go back and take care of things at

home," Ralph Hodd told him. "Things" meant about half of Northumberland.

'"Yes, well, jolly good," replied Harold Jackson-Bowles. Then he seemed to remember what Ralph's present life must be like. '"I expect you're too concerned with the present – you're hard-pressed, doing a wonderful job, you chaps. We all owe you a debt." He coughed.

'Geneviève said to her daughter, "When's the wedding? What must we do? It's so difficult, with all these shortages." She smiled at Ralph.

'"I'm going up to Hodd for a bit," Sally told her. "There's no hurry."

'"Oh, well," Geneviève said. "I suppose in war-time everything's different. At least you'll be away from this terrible bombing."

'"You shouldn't have come, Mummy," Sally said. "There could be an enormous raid at any moment. It's frightfully dangerous."

'Neither Geneviève nor Harold looked disconcerted when she said this. Harold Jackson-Bowles said, "We planned to catch an afternoon train. I've booked a table at Rules."

'"I'm most terribly sorry, sir," said Ralph Hodd. "I'm due back on duty soon. I can make it in a couple of hours on my motorbike, but I ought to start more or less now in case of delays."

'"What a great pity," Geneviève said.

'Not long after, Ralph left and Pym and I were persuaded by Sally, who could not face Harold and Geneviève on her own, to make up the party at Rules. Here, in a gloomy and smoke-laden atmosphere, aged, rude waiters staggered about under huge plates of pheasant and hare, seemingly unaffected by war-time shortages. Pym turned on the charm and Geneviève, though she did not like him, softened. Harold was polite but plainly did not trust him. Geneviève set about Sally. "Darling, you really should do something about your hair. Sally's always been so very independent-minded, hasn't she, Mr Pym? Too much, do you think?"

'Well,' said Bruno, 'my enemy's enemy is my friend, that's how the saying goes, doesn't it? Geneviève Jackson-Bowles couldn't stand her daughter, nor could Pym. It was enough. I began to see why Sally rarely went home.

'"Betty's so very different, of course," said Geneviève. "Quieter and less ambitious, somehow. And her little boys are so charming. Tell me," she asked Pym, "what's become of that delightful man, Theo Fitzpatrick? We all thought Sally was going to marry him – well, I think you did too, Sally, yes? And now look what's happened."

'"Theo's a slippery fish, Mrs Jackson-Bowles," Pym said.

'It was terrible, like when the picadors go in after the bull. I could do nothing. I was a stranger with doubtful credentials. Sally's father either did not observe what was happening or thought nothing about it.' Bruno gazed with a jaundiced air at a juggler in motley out on the piazza and remarked, 'I'm an old queen and we're supposed to understand women, but the reasons for women hating their daughters have always eluded me. What do you think?'

Greg shrugged, 'I think it was more common years ago.'

'It was almost a relief when the siren blew and we all had to go down into the cellars. There we sat amid the barrels and racks of wine – the waiters had carried in the chairs from the restaurant – and conversation became more general among the clientele. Geneviève was remarkably courageous, considering this was an experience she had not met before. Harry, who had been at the front during the Great War, sat there dourly and said to another man of his own age, "I wonder what we'd have thought, going through the last lot, if we'd known this was going to happen twenty odd years later?" The other just shook his head.

'The All Clear sounded not long after. Geneviève stood up, dusted herself down and said to Sally, sincerely, "Thank goodness you're going up to Northumberland, darling."

'I think it was expected that Sally would marry and spend the rest of the war there, but in the end there was no wedding and Sally was back three months later, just after Christmas.'

Greg and Bruno stood up to go. Bruno offered Greg a lift back to Bayswater. They found his car parked off the Strand on the large area in front of Somerset House. 'I have friends,' Bruno said mysteriously, when Greg exclaimed over his access to this exclusive parking space. On the drive Greg said, 'If you've no idea where Sally Bowles is – or even if she's alive – do you have any clue about her parents? Or where I could find her sister? I'd like to talk to her.'

'The Jackson-Bowleses are dead,' Bruno said. 'And I know the sister and her husband emigrated to South Africa after the war.'

'Do you know where?'

Bruno, driving slowly up the Mall, shook his head. 'How could I know? As I've told you, the Pontifex group threw me out in 'forty-six. I rented the shop and Pym, Briggs, all the rest of them, were leading their lives in embassies, or in Whitehall ministries, wearing good suits and going off for weekends in country houses. Julia Montrose managed to marry Sir Peveril. Still,' he added, 'without Briggs I would probably have died in the camps. He gave me the language, also,' said Bruno, 'and, of course, he trained my taste so that when I could afford to venture into the antiques trade I was able to do so. That's not so bad, is it?'

'Perhaps it isn't.'

They pulled up outside Greg's building. 'I won't ask you in,' he said. 'It's pretty depressing. But will you tell me what went wrong at Hodd?'

'Soon,' Bruno said. 'I'm going away next week to attend some sales. What will you do?'

Greg concealed his disappointment. 'Research,' he said stoutly. 'Go to libraries, read old magazines and newspapers.'

'Good,' Bruno said. 'That's good. Then we will go on with our story.'

19

For two months Sally had been at Hodd Hall near Jedburgh, some twenty miles from the Scottish border. The house, not far from the east coast, was cold and getting colder. One morning she was standing in the drawing room, which was long and heavily panelled, full of rather gloomy pictures and mounted antlers, staring glumly at the rain beating against the window-panes, when her future mother-in-law opened the door. Sally froze.

'*Dear* Sally,' said Lady Hodd, in an affectionate tone. 'Now – what shall we do with you today?' She wore a very good tweed suit. Sally was in brown corduroy slacks and a thick blue jersey.

'I think I'll go to the dairy. I promised Jessie I'd help her move the cheeses into the store,' Sally said.

Lady Hodd could shift Sally from the house and towards some form of useful work as if by magic. 'Oh, yes, of course. What a good idea,' she said.

In the icy yard a tall girl in clogs was sweeping manure into a pile.

'Time for a cuppa,' Sally called.

'All right,' she agreed.

Soon they were ensconced in the warm kitchen, drinking tea with the estate manager, Tim Ferris, who had been invalided out of the Army after Dunkirk. Sally asked, 'Have you ever wondered why the Hodds have all this and you haven't?'

His answer was cautious, since he knew that Sally would one day become the next Lady Hodd. 'It's because of the way things are,' he told her, a humorous glint in his eye.

'Do you think it's fair?'

'Fair? What's fair got to do with it? It's like the weather, isn't it? You can't alter it.'

The cook, who was stirring a large pot of soup on the stove, pursed her lips, and Sally squeezed Tim's knee under the table. That was the moment at which Lady Hodd came in, observed the under-the-table movement and decided not to believe her own eyes. 'Another tea break! Heavens! No one would ever believe there was a war on.'

When they were out in the yard again, in the wind, moving cheeses the size of bicycle wheels from the shelves in the dairy down to the cellar, through a trap-door in a wall, Jessie asked, 'Is there any news from Mr Ralph, Sally?'

'Very bad,' said Sally. 'The squadron's been in the air twenty nights out of the last thirty.'

'That's awful,' Jessie said.

'I'm going to London to meet him this weekend,' Sally said. 'He only has a weekend pass, so it's too far to come here. Oh, God!' she wailed, looking down. 'My hands! My nails!'

'Dip 'em in whey – that's what we do round here,' Jessie advised her.

They went into the dairy and hauled another cheese from a shelf. They contemplated each other from either end of it. 'Whey?' said Sally. 'I'll try it.' As they trudged to the trap-door Sally asked, 'You don't think I'll last here, do you?'

Jessie did not reply.

Lady Hodd was screaming, 'My God! With Ralph's father ill in bed again with his wound and Ralph fighting for his country, you – you – disgrace!'

The dining room at Hodd was even gloomier than the drawing room. More stags' heads lowered down on them through the misty light of a December afternoon.

Sally, who was wearing dungarees and wellington boots, said, 'I don't know what you expected. I know I've been working hard here for two months in the national interest, or so you say, but I think it's in yours, really. I think you're hoarding food.'

'What the hell—' exclaimed Lady Hodd, almost speechless. 'What the hell has that got to do with what we're talking about? You've been sleeping with my bailiff – my *bailiff* – my son's fiancée and Tim Ferris from the village. What decent girl could do that, with her fiancé at war? How could you? And now I'll have to discharge him.'

'You'd better discharge me,' said Sally. 'You need me less. I'll go.'

'I think that would be best,' said Lady Hodd.

Sally turned in the doorway and asked, 'I suppose there's no chance of any wages?'

Lady Hodd seized a complicated china fruit-stand, made of twisted, coloured porcelain, from the table and hurled it at her son's fiancée, but by that time Sally was outside the door. She heard it thud against the wood and smash to pieces, then Lady Hodd's anguished cry as she appreciated what she had done.

Tim drove her to the station. 'I'm sorry she sacked you,' Sally said, lighting him a cigarette.

'It doesn't matter,' he said. 'I'm going to try to join up again. There must be something I can do . . .'

'Come and see me in London.'

'If I can.' He stopped outside the little station. 'Hurry, or you'll miss your train.'

20

'Of course,' Bruno remarked, 'everyone at Pontifex Street laughed. Laughed, as they used to say, like a drain. "I laughed like a drain,"' he quoted.

They were sitting in a café in Bruno's neighbourhood. Bruno had bought his lunch, a solid plate of sausages, fried egg, baked beans and chips. Greg had a greasy omelette and left half of it. The door opened occasionally and a workman, or a man in a suit with a briefcase, or a local tradesman entered in a blast of cold air. His tape-recorder was on the table in front of him, concealed from the rest of the customers by a sticky sugar dispenser.

During the week in which Bruno had been off on his buying trip Greg had checked that there had indeed been a squadron leader named Ralph Hodd at Farnborough during the Second World War. He found out, too, that Hodd Hall existed and was still occupied by a member of the family. He had also talked his way into the house in Pontifex Street once occupied by Sally and her friends.

The present occupant, an American woman, was initially suspicious of him, but let him in, made him a cup of coffee, and said, 'Yes, I heard we were living in the apartment that had once housed those British spies. I asked the landlord's agents about it but they didn't know much.' And the landlord, she told Greg, was still Sir Peveril Jones.

Greg had even gone into the loft, no longer reached by a ladder but up some stairs, for it had been converted, and looked from the same windows, he thought, through which Sally Bowles and the others must have seen the searchlights and barrage balloons of war-time London's darkened skies.

By the time he and Bruno met again, he was convinced that Bruno Lowenthal was telling the truth – or most of it. There was no way in which the old man could have conveyed, so off-handedly, so much random yet detailed information. Bruno was giving him the real stuff of Sally Bowles's life. Sometimes, though, he had the idea that he was on an archaeological site which had been excavated by a madman so that all the layers had been tumbled into each other. And he worried, too, that Bruno might have an agenda he didn't understand. But, all in all, he thought, if Bruno wanted him to listen to his tale sitting in a puddle in the middle of a field he would do it without complaint. Hell – he'd do it naked in Trafalgar Square, if that was what Bruno wanted.

However, at least he now had a hope of being able to meet Bruno somewhere out of the cold and damp of wintry London: Katherine had phoned to say a cousin of hers was going off on an archaeological dig for a few months. His flat in Bloomsbury would be empty and she was trying to persuade him to rent it to Greg. If that worked out, thought Greg, it would give him a base where he and Bruno could meet, away from the public places which for some reason the old man preferred.

Now he sat back in the steamy atmosphere to listen.

'Sally,' Bruno said, 'was not very forthcoming about what had gone wrong at Hodd. She said, "It was ghastly – so cold – and an absolute nest of traitors. They were all Nazis. Lady Hodd said it would be a good idea to put the Duke of Windsor on the throne when Hitler won the war. While I was there she put a Christmas card from Wallis Simpson, the Duchess of Windsor now, on the mantelpiece. It was the last straw."

'Everyone laughed – and the engagement came to a natural end when Ralph was shot down in France. He survived – that time – and was taken prisoner. Sally spent Christmas with her parents in Worcestershire and Ralph Hodd was in a prisoner-of-war camp in Germany. In those days things happened quickly. He wrote releasing her from the engagement and she went on sending pots of jam and woolly jumpers until he escaped. As he did because, of course, he was a hero, poor man.' Bruno looked round. His eye lit on a young man sitting by the window, reading. 'So young,' he said, 'and so many of the clichés are true. Those pilots saved the country and many, many died.' He looked at Greg. 'Ralph died too, later. So did the others, the Hermann Schmidts and the Carl Brauns. But that's war,' said Bruno. 'There was a terrible raid at the end of December. And Theo Fitzpatrick turned up.'

21

'You'd have done a lot better to have stayed up north, Sally,' said Vi, as she swept broken glass and plaster through her back door into her small garden. The wall at the end had been hit and where it had stood was a vast heap of crumbly bricks and splintered wood. Beyond that were the two walls left standing after the house opposite Vi's had been struck in a previous raid.

'Can you lift while I fix this?' asked Sally. She was trying to put the back door, which had been blown into the garden, on its hinges.

'Christ! My nails!' exclaimed Vi. 'This is men's work. Let's leave it for Ted.'

'You said yourself he was working round the clock. If we wait for him you'll freeze.'

They wrestled with the door for another five minutes, and got it roughly into place.

'That'll have to do,' said Vi. 'I can wedge a chair against it to keep it closed. The warden says not to try to use the gas. I'll light the fire and boil up the kettle on it. I've got plenty of wood from up the street – the poor buggers it belonged to won't need it any more.'

The narrow street where Vi lived was a shocking sight. On either side of her home two big craters represented two houses. Rubble was piled along the pavements. Workmen were repairing a broken water main. A smell of burning still hung in the air.

As soon as they had closed the back door there was a knock at the front. A woman in an old coat, her face drawn, was standing there. She said, 'Potter sent me round from the Rose and Crown. Your Jack's at King's Cross – he phoned the pub. He wants you to go and collect him. He hasn't got any money. Potter said to stay where he was.'

'Oh, my God,' said Vi. 'What's he doing there? He's meant to be in the country.'

'He told Potter he didn't like it so he ran away.'

'The little—' exclaimed Vi. 'I'll go and collect him, I suppose.'

She and Sally set off for King's Cross. Some months before Jack Simcox had been evacuated to Lancaster with a small suitcase and a label bearing his name and address strung round his neck. Large numbers of London children had been sent away to be safe from the air-raids. However, it was not unusual for their parents to bring them back. Few, though, took the law into their own hands, as Jack apparently had, and returned alone.

On the bus, Vi exclaimed, 'Silly little fool. What's he think he's coming back to? A house with all the windows boarded up. No gas. Spending all night in a tube station –

well, these days Ted and me go into the Phillpots' air-raid shelter up the road, but it's horrible. You sit up all night because there's no room to lie down. You have to run down the garden to the outside lav through the middle of a raid if you need to go. The baby cries. Jack was all right up north. He was living with a vicar, in a vicarage, for God's sake. He had fresh milk, eggs, meat. My God, what wouldn't I do for a good breakfast, with bacon and eggs and a bit of sausage? Now how am I going to manage? Even my gran's disappeared – gone up to Scotland to plonk herself on an old admirer. Jack'll have to go back, if they'll still have him.'

'The vicar's probably a bastard,' observed Sally, lighting a cigarette.

They found nine-year-old Jack on a seat in the busy station. He was talking to a soldier with a kit-bag at his feet. Jack had his gas mask with him and nothing else. His first words were 'I didn't like it there. Don't send me back.'

The soldier said to Vi, 'It doesn't sound any good there, miss, if you'll pardon me putting my oar in.'

'Oh, I don't know,' said Vi. 'Let's get you home first, what's left of it.'

'Did we get bombed?' Jack asked keenly.

'Yes – weren't we lucky?'

'Part of it was that he was worrying about you, see,' the soldier explained helpfully. 'He kept on thinking you and his brother were dead and no one was telling him.'

'All right, Jack,' said Vi. 'Stay here and live on grey bread and marge and spend all night in a shelter with the rest of us – I don't care.'

'Thanks, Vi,' Jack said, in heartfelt tones.

Over tea and a bun in the station café he told her, 'Mrs Rathbone, the vicar's wife, kept shaking me. I thought my head would drop off.'

'What had you done?' Vi asked suspiciously.

'Chased a few hens,' he told her. 'They weren't hurt. She had no call to slam me up against a wall. I think she's potty.'

'I'll write a nasty letter to the billeting officer,' Vi promised. 'But what am I going to do with you? Your gran's gone. You'll have to go round to the Phillpots while I'm at the club. I can't leave you alone in the middle of air-raids. I can't even trust you not to disappear now you've apparently got the knack of taking long train journeys by yourself. Lancaster to London! You know our mum never left the East End in all her life – never even went up West once. Never went further than Aldgate.' Vi made this sound like proof of virtue and respectability.

'I'll take your turn tonight,' Sally volunteered.

22

'That evening Theo turned up at La Vie,' Bruno reported in the steamy café. He mimicked a rather husky, upper-class voice, '"The only man I've ever loved, darling."' Reverting to his own voice he added cruelly, 'I don't think. Vincent Tubman, a cigarette dangling from his mouth, was playing the opening bars of 'Plaisir D'Amour'. Sally began to sing, standing in the spotlight in a blue and green chiffon dress, heavily made-up and holding her hands slightly behind her back to conceal the damage caused by her activities with Vi's door. She had been unable to repair the nail polish, as stocks had run out at her local chemist's.

'There were twenty people in the club, some in uniform and some officials, their womenfolk in scrupulously cleaned and repaired evening dresses. They seemed to sigh, collectively but inaudibly, as Sally sang – the words of the song recalled pre-war France, travel, dancing, food, sunshine, the luxury of private life, but in imagination they were dancing on summer lawns in England to the strains of a gramophone, they were lounging in a boat under willows. Perhaps some were in Provence, walking hand in hand over dry, herb-scented grass, drinking coffee at pavement cafés.

'Then, Theo was standing by the stairs and Cora was embracing him. Over her head, his eyes met Sally's. She faltered for a beat, then went on singing. He was a tall man, very thin but broad-shouldered,' Bruno told Greg. 'He had a lean face, tanned and intelligent, brown eyes, and long, narrow lips. A lock of his hair, which was black, persistently fell forward, so that he would have to brush it back with one well-shaped hand. You know the type,' Bruno appealed to Greg.

'Yes, I know the type,' said Greg.

'He was wearing corduroys, an open-necked blue shirt and a huge tweed jacket, probably someone else's, with bulging pockets. He was carrying a bottle of something foreign, which he presented to Cora with a bow. He had that kind of attractive English style,' Bruno said, 'great aplomb, nice manners, but still rather boyish and endearing.'

'When they tell you something, believe the opposite and then start looking for the third thing,' Greg said.

'Yes, well, they made very good double agents,' said Bruno. 'Though I was never sure whether Theo was involved or not. He was never found out, but his career staggered when the others were exposed. But that was later. That night Theo moved forward – he had physical grace, too, what a lucky boy he was – and got Sally down from the little stage just as she finished the song, and they began to dance. Vincent was sober that night, by a miracle, and played 'Plaisir D'Amour' again. It was very romantic.

'I don't know when they'd last seen each other. Sally'd been in love with Theo since she'd been at school but there was Berlin in those strange days before the war, all heightened senses and danger and sex and – oh, you couldn't describe it. You can imagine them as the linden trees greened and the sun came out, walking hand in hand past cafés with open doors and the smell of coffee coming out – and all the time, the terror continuing. Ah well,' said Bruno, 'we all grew up under the Chinese curse, I suppose, "May you live in interesting times." After Germany they'd met in Madrid, where Theo was reporting for *The Times*.

'So – it was years since they'd been in Spain, but Sally had kept him in her heart, even though there had been plenty of others in her arms. I couldn't tell you how real this love of Theo was – what does real mean? Who can tell about another person? She believed it anyway, at that time.

'She told me they walked through St James's Park. It was very quiet and, as usual, searchlights cut the air. The grass gleamed with frost. They kissed under a tree. She said, "I love you."

'He said, "Oh, God, Sally, you know how it is – the war and everything. You know – I could not love thee, dear, so much, loved I not honour more."'

'It was an old joke between them. Later, when she was feeling bitter, she told me it was always an old joke between false lovers and their women. This time, though, she said she gave the correct response. She said, "Lucky Honor Moore."

'"Let's go home," he said, and they walked over the

grass, she leaning against him, past two soldiers supporting a third, an air-raid warden on a bike taking a short-cut, figures pressed against trees.

"'Oh, Theo, I'm so happy. I'm dancing on air.'"

23

'He was a devil for women.' Bruno glanced at his watch. 'I must go soon. I have a difficult tenant in my basement. There are complaints about the plumbing.' So the old man owned the house he lived in, Greg thought, without surprise. He wondered vaguely why the meticulous Bruno hadn't fixed the place up better. Standing up, he said, 'OK, thank you.'

'No – I have to talk to the plumber, but not just yet,' Bruno told him. 'The photographs you may see of Theo do him less than justice. They could not show his lightness, intelligence, his speed of movement. Or his charm and glamour. There was an exciting touch of haggardness in his features. He was an adventurer. He was a radical, sacrificing himself for a cause – a hero, a young girl's dream, if that young girl was in rebellion from a bourgeois family. As Sally was – as so many girls were, at that time.

'Perhaps they were a little spoilt, those young men of that generation. So many of their fathers, uncles, older brothers had died in the Great War. These, the survivors, were precious and it was believed much rested on them.'

'I guess it might have been thought they would have to go to war themselves,' Greg said. 'As they did.'

'All Europeans expect to have to go to war,' Bruno told him dismissively. 'With you, war may be a disturbance in the natural order. Here, even when you think it's all forgotten, it's just in hiding, waiting to come out.'

'I hope not,' Greg said doubtfully.

'Ah – I'm an old pessimist,' Bruno said. 'However, Sally's honeymoon with Theo lasted less than a week. In the attic – and New Year's Eve at the Savoy, with everybody in uniform and wondering what the next year would bring – how gay they were. Then, suddenly, one morning Theo was gone. He left a brief note on the dining-room table, pinched a kit-bag that one of Pym's pick-ups had left in the sitting room, put his few things in it – the pipe, his father's VC and a volume of Xenophon – and went off to whatever secret thing he was doing next. Pym's poor soldier boy was punished for losing his kit-bag. Briggs said Theo had stolen away like a thief in the night and recalled some ugly incidents from their Cambridge days. Sally was distraught but stood up for him, saying he'd only left so early not to disturb anyone.

'Pym was furious. If you drew a chart like a family tree of that group but showed only who had been to school or university with whom, who had grown up with whom, who had been in love with, slept with, desired but not had whom, well, it would be a big, big map with many, many names on it, some surprising. At that time I thought Pym's rage was because he, like Briggs, had been in love with Theo. Imagine that adolescent greenhouse of a school they had all been to. Imagine all those boys trapped there, like a prison. Then imagine Sally and Theo coming downstairs arms draped around each other – think of baby Gisela, positive proof of their love. I saw Pym's face one morning when they came into the kitchen. It was glowing, frightening almost – he went very pale and his eyes burned. He had to turn away to conceal his feelings.'

Bruno paused for effect, then said casually, 'I thought that was why Pym blackmailed Sally into dropping into occupied France.'

'What?' exclaimed Greg. 'Sally dropped into France?'

'Oh, yes,' said Bruno. 'I'm surprised you didn't know.' He glanced at his watch again. 'I must go. I shall be busy until the weekend. Will you be available then?'

'Will I!' said Greg, and sat on after the old man had left, thinking, Sally? France? When? Where? Why? Was it true? Was Bruno leading him astray? Above all, what kind of a book would he end up writing?

24

Greg spent the next few days on research concerning the men and women parachuted into or landing secretly in occupied France in 1941.

Since his last meeting with Bruno, he had been increasingly worried that the old man was misleading him. Before he had embarked on his attempt to write Sally's biography, his chief source of information about her had been the novelist Charles Denham's *Autobiography of War* in which there had been no mention of her having been dropped into France. However, finally he discovered her name in a volume of reminiscences by a former SOE operative. The reference was ambiguous: 'Among the others who played their part during the early years of the Second World War were Captain N. M. Armstrong and Miss Sally Bowles.' Not much, but when Greg read these words in a dusty book at the British Museum his heart soared and his confidence was restored in Bruno Lowenthal. He clapped the book shut and bounded out of the library.

That day he rang Katherine and told her. He called his editor in New York and told him. The editor was not very excited – but Katherine was. 'Greg, darling,' she said, 'I'm trying to arrange a few days in London. But ring me as soon as you hear what Bruno says. God, I'm looking forward to seeing you.'

'Me too,' said Greg, with feeling.

He was also delighted to hear from Katherine that her cousin had now agreed to rent him 13D Everton Gardens, a flat on the second floor of a forbidding red-brick Edwardian block near the British Museum, overlooking a small street and a sad square of unhappy-looking trees surrounded by iron railings.

The apartment consisted of a sitting room ten feet by ten feet and an even smaller bedroom. It was approached by a narrow stone staircase or a minute lift with tricky folding grilled doors. In America, Greg thought, this tiny hovel, with its hissing gas fires and ancient kitchen, which resembled the sort of apartment featured in a forties public-information film, would have seemed fit only for a prisoner out on parole or an unsupported mother. However, he had come to understand that it represented a peculiar kind of British luxury, the kind, somehow, that the Katherine Ledbetters and their kin seemed able to command.

In return for the favour, Greg saved Katherine's cousin's life by disconnecting the gas fire, pulling it out and clearing from behind it eighteen inches of accumulated rubble. He cleaned the fire itself and replaced it, feeling fairly certain now that neither he nor the cousin would die of carbon-monoxide poisoning due to trapped fumes escaping into the room. He decided not to tell Katherine about this, for she and others like her believed that only paid strangers were capable of doing such jobs properly. He also cleaned the kitchen and bathroom and that, with his reading, kept him occupied until the long-awaited visit by Bruno.

On the day Bruno was due to arrive Greg stood at the window of the flat, staring down into the rainswept trees of the square. He brooded. Would Bruno lie to him? And if so, why? If the old man was, as Greg had originally supposed him to be, lonely and fairly embittered then Greg and his questions might be just an entertainment for Bruno, a way of alleviating boredom. But he doubted this, while recognising how little of Bruno's life he knew. Bruno had shown him his flat, his shop and his car which had told Greg only that he was prosperous. He had revealed nothing of other parts of his life, such as his present friends and acquaintances or how he spent his spare time. Bruno had put Greg in a sealed box, apart from the rest of his life.

Greg had seen from the outset that Bruno did not much like him, but he had not taken this personally for he suspected that Bruno did not much like anybody. The old man's attitude had been civil but distant, masking, but not very carefully, a kind of contempt for Greg based on Bruno's greater age and experience, and on what Greg had come to know as the deadly European contempt for the American, which said, silently, 'You may be perfectly nice, but that's easy for you. You're soft and sentimental. You've been privileged. You've never had to find out what life is all about. We Europeans know all that.'

Greg was also beginning to suspect that sometimes he

bored Bruno. But if Bruno didn't want to talk to him, why was he doing so? The advantage seemed to be all on Greg's side. Could this be some terrible game he was playing, Greg thought in depression – misleading foreigners for fun?

Suddenly, unexpectedly, homesickness swept over him. He wanted to be back in America. He wondered if he might not have been better off lecturing at Fraser Cutts and putting together a paper on some small subject requiring minutely detailed knowledge and concerning something that had happened so long ago there were no living sources, just books and bits of wood and broken pottery, not awkward and possibly untrustworthy human beings.

Greg was the son of liberal parents, his father a lawyer, his mother a former social worker. Both had been civil-rights activists in their youth. They had been freedom marchers in the South; they had worked for Bobby Kennedy. Greg had no quarrel with their attitudes, was merely slightly embarrassed and depressed by them. He felt he could go for a long time without hearing about redneck attacks, police charges on Vietnam demonstrators, tear-gas, the Scottsboro Boys or the three assassinations that had ended their era. Some of the most mortifying occasions of his boyhood had been at the annual reunion barbecue his parents held. He recalled the stoned, greybearded man who had tried to pull him on to his knee when he was ten and had said into his face, 'Keep the faith, boy. All we ask is that you keep the faith.' As soon as they could, he and his sister had found reasons not to be there on what his sister called Old Revolutionary Day.

However, his background meant that Greg was no stranger to the idea of conspiracy, government chicanery and the abuse of power. Those who looked at him and chose to think him a well set-up, prosperous young American, innocent, unsuspecting and *naïf*, were, as far as he was concerned, welcome to do so. In fact, Greg Phillips had a *naïveté* deficit. Where hope, trust and belief in authority should have been, there was a big, black hole.

He knew this. He thought Bruno was beginning to know it too. But he couldn't rid himself of the nagging feeling that Bruno, like a skilled chess player, was leading him towards some disastrous end. Yet he knew, too, that he and Bruno were beginning to understand each other.

Finally, Bruno came. Greg went down to meet him and took him up in the lift. Jammed together, they creaked up slowly.

'One of my friends from Cambridge found me this flat. It belongs to a cousin.'

'A lady-friend?' hazarded Bruno.

'A lecturer at Cambridge. I knew her when I studied here.'

'Ah – so,' Bruno said. The lift stopped. They got out and entered the flat. Bruno looked about him and went to the window. 'Yes,' he said. 'I recognise the style.'

Greg had bought provisions. Now, hoping to please his unyielding guest, he offered coffee and cake. Bruno accepted and Greg set about producing the snack.

When this was done he placed it on a low table by the gas fire, set up his tape-recorder and said to Bruno, 'I saw from the memoirs of a Captain Clegg that Sally was dropped over France, but he didn't say why.'

'He probably didn't know,' said Bruno, biting into a cake. 'It was all secret. Pym's doing. He must have threatened her otherwise she wouldn't have gone – she was brave but not that brave, and you must remember, too, that Sally was a Communist and Hitler and Stalin were still allies. Whether they liked it or not, the British Communists had to go along with it. Stupid, of course. When were politics not stupid? But she had to go to France. I think it was in the early summer of nineteen forty-one.'

25

Sally's ears were full of the drone of the ancient Whitley bomber pushing across the Channel by night. She was sitting on an ammunition crate in her pink suit, which had been meticulously cleaned and restored at the expense of the British Government, which had also supplied her with makeup, stockings and the evening dress lying in a small but expensive suitcase at her feet. They had set out just after midnight from the secret airfield at Tamworth, Bedfordshire. Sally was trembling. Her escorts in the aircraft wore fleecy jackets and big boots. All she had was a jacket draped over her shoulders and a parachute strapped to her back. The blasts of cold air from the floor of the aircraft had frozen her legs and her feet. Occasionally the Whitley gave a convulsive shake, accompanied by a rattle. The first time this occurred her two companions laughed, and the mechanic said, 'The old girl's been on the gin again.'

'Did you work on this one after she crashed?' the other enquired.

'Yes.' He turned to Sally, holding out a silver flask. 'Don't worry, Miss Bowles. We'll get you there.'

She knew it didn't need two of them to get her to France. They'd done it to be friendly.

Sally took the flask and drank. 'Quite frankly, sweetie, I'm not so worried about getting there as getting back.'

'Not to worry,' the officer said. 'Your return ticket's valid for six months.' He sported a huge moustache, as many pilots did. It was intended to stick out at right angles from the face, but his drooped, giving him the look of an apprentice Viking.

Sally handed back the flask but he pushed it back to her. 'Take another nip,' he said. 'We're over France now.'

'How long?' she asked. She continued to shake with cold, fear and anger. She was furious with Pym for making her do this. Hadn't there been anything she could have done to stop him? No, she thought, there hadn't. He had threatened, as they said in plays, to tell all and she hadn't the slightest doubt that he would have done so, the bastard.

The mechanic tapped her knee. 'Feeling all right about the jump?' he asked. Sally nodded.

'Jolly good show,' said the officer.

The exit from the plane was a hole in the floor, a yard square. She had practised jumping through such a hole many times, at Templeford. You sat on the edge, legs dangling. Then, to put it crudely, they pushed you out to land on the mattress beneath. But this was different. She hoped, as she was falling, that the parachute would open. If it did, she'd have to start hoping they'd dropped her over the right spot, a clearing, not on top of trees or into a lake – or straight into German hands.

And, of course, they all hoped they wouldn't be attacked in the air before she could even jump.

Now she sat, her legs dangling into space, buffeted by air, her bottom on the edge of the hole, as the young officer said to her, 'We'll be back to pick you up in a week or two, then. Good luck.'

'Thanks,' Sally said, through stiff lips. 'Safe trip back.'

The other said, 'I think you ought to be going now.'

He took hold of Sally's shoulders and she went out and down into a rush of air. She pulled the cord of her parachute. By now she knew it wouldn't open – some Nazi sympathiser had probably packed it at the factory – she was going to die and that was that. Her skirt blew right up – and the parachute opened. She swung down and down over the darkened landscape of northern France. Up in the sky she heard the plane turn and head away, back to England.

'Plucky girl,' the fair young man said to his companion. 'Pretty, too.'

'Hope she makes it,' said the other.

They had both been awake for sixteen hours and were asleep before they landed.

'Whoops!' Sally landed in a field, remembering to throw herself sideways on landing so that she didn't hit the ground on her feet. She lay, winded, on grass, with her eyes tight shut. She just knew that when she opened them she would be surrounded by German soldiers with rifles. She had sailed down with her suitcase and now it was lost. Oh, God. Oh, God. She opened her eyes slowly. Yes, she was lying in a field, alone. A cow ambled up to look at her.

'Oh, God,' said a voice, her own. She was all tangled up in her parachute, which lay behind her, billowing up whitely. She groaned.

'Shh,' a man's voice hissed. Strong arms were pulling her to her feet. In the darkness she made out a tall figure in a dark jacket. He held her against him as he cut away the harness.

'My suitcase,' Sally said, in French.

'Shit,' he said. They searched the field, Sally falling over tussocks. Her feet went into a cow-pat. It was very quiet.

'Got it,' he called across the field, softly. She stood up, with a sigh of relief. He rejoined her. 'What about the password?' she said faintly.

'Bugger the password.' From somewhere, he had produced a spade and went over to the parachute. He picked it up, dragged it towards a hedge, dug a hole and buried it.

In the narrow road he looked at her critically. 'I like the suit. It's very smart. But God knows why you're wearing it.'

A lorry was parked nearby. Once inside it, Sally opened her case and struggled into a mac. She put on a head-scarf.

'Well, that's better,' he said, and started up the engine.

A few minutes later, as they bumped along the road, he said, 'You're going to Paris with my brother. He's taking a consignment of beef there for the Germans. They'll fill his lorry with sacks of concrete for the return trip. Got that?'

'Thank you.'

'If we're stopped, you're a widow. We've sneaked off for fear of the neighbours. Why that suit, in God's name? Is it Chanel?'

'You have an eye.'

'I used to sell dresses.'

They arrived at a gate, turned in, entered a farmyard. Inside the dark kitchen, lit only by one candle on a table, sat a second man, in a cap. He stood up as they entered, and said, 'Bravo! We're loaded up. *Bonsoir*, Madame. Would you like to eat before we start?'

'I'd rather go now.'

'Good.'

After hasty farewells, Sally and Pierre Legrand were on their way to Paris. This time, though, the lights of the lorry were on.

'How are things here?' Sally asked.

'Bad – but they'll get worse. What about Britain? We see their bombers visiting you.'

'The raids on London were worse last year. I think if they'd kept it up it would have been over.'

'We listened to the BBC and wondered. What a mess.'

'It's useful, being an island.'

He did not ask her anything about herself. And, in spite of the fear, as they got closer and closer to Paris Sally's spirits rose and she began to feel excited.

As dawn came they picnicked under a hedge in a field outside Paris. It would be safer to enter the city, which was under curfew, when it was busier. The air was full of birdsong. Pierre raised a glass of red wine. There was a slice of bread in his hand.

'*À vous*, Madame.'

'*À vous, aussi.*'

He did not wish her luck.

26

In the Bloomsbury apartment Greg Phillips looked at the big flat face and the sturdy old body opposite him. He had a dizzy feeling, as if he had gone through the looking-glass. He pulled himself together.

'So, how did Pym blackmail Sally into going to France?' he asked doggedly.

'I didn't know anything definite,' said Bruno. 'But after she came back – what an arrival that was! – she told me something. I put two and two together. It was in May,' he said, 'and there'd been terrible raids on Liverpool, Belfast, Clydebank, Southampton, Plymouth, Portsmouth. In London alone twenty thousand people had been killed. The damage was appalling. I saw people weeping in the streets.

'Poor Vi – her house was already half ruined and then more bombs came down and finished the job. They were all in the shelter down the road, and when the All Clear sounded they came out – she and her two brothers – and walked up the street in all the smoke, at dawn, and there was no house, just a pile of rubble. After they'd been three nights in a rest centre Vi found a flat through her agent's secretary. It belonged to a chorus girl who'd joined the ATS and she said they could have it as long as they left a corner for her in case she needed it when she was on leave. It was two big rooms upstairs in a Victorian terrace house in Pimlico. The kitchen was a curtained-off area in the front room, the bathroom was along a passageway. After living in the rest centre, which was full of bombed-out people sleeping on cots in a converted school hall, babies crying, Vi thought it was the Ritz.

'Anyway, Sally persuaded me to help her and the Simcoxes to take whatever they'd saved from the ruins, which wasn't much, from the rest centre to their new place. Think of me, twenty-one, all skin and bones in one of Briggs's old suits, carrying a sack full of pots and pans from Westminster Pier, where we got off the bus, to Pimlico. Vi had an old pram, piled high, Sally had two suitcases. Vi's small brother was carrying a canary in a cage. My God, what a spectacle! I felt humiliated, as only a working-class boy from Berlin could. The streets were full of gaps. You could look up at the sky through the windows of the houses. Or there'd be a wall gone, and half the floor, with a sofa, or a bath hanging over into the void. It was a brilliant day but everyone was pale. The rationing was beginning to hit – we were always hungry. And you didn't get much sleep because of the raids.

'So, we had taken our walk, with the Simcoxes and all their remaining worldly goods, and seen them in, and then we got a bus back in the direction of Pontifex Street. I was looking down into Trafalgar Square. It was a sea of uniforms – French sailors with pom-poms on their berets, nurses in scarlet-lined cloaks, soldiers in turbans, in bush hats, in kepis. The sight of the world in arms to defend this island should have been encouraging, but constant bombardment and lack of sleep had got us all down. And I said to her, in a low voice, "I don't think this can go on."

'All she said was "Hang on – it may be all right," in that cheerful voice she had. She was wearing trousers and an old shirt and plenty of lipstick, as usual. She'd brought a year's supply back from France. And other stuff, too. My God, we could have killed her at Pontifex Street, as she wafted about in a cloud of Je Reviens. We kept thinking of cognac and sausage and all the other things she could have brought instead. As I say, we were hungry. Instead, she'd got cosmetics, scent, underwear, a pair of shoes. She'd probably risked her life to get them.

'Anyway, she sounded hopeful, even confident, as she spoke. We were on a bus – and I had a German accent – so this was not the moment to ask questions.

'But she told me something that night. The sirens started at about nine. She was just about to set out for La Vie but it was impossible to go. The others were all elsewhere and the two cake-shop ladies had left London months earlier – they couldn't take any more. We went together to the cellar, which we'd made quite comfortable by then with a mattress, and a table and chairs. We'd hung up some hurricane lamps and we had a little spirit stove on a table and shelves made of planks held up by bricks. So we sat there, drinking tea and condensed milk out of enamel mugs, just like most of the rest of London, and hearing aircraft going over and explosions – by then you only worried when they were close.

'I was in the armchair and Sally was lying full length on the mattress. "It's surreal, our little house," she said sleepily.

'Now at this time there was a buzz about Sally, all over the place. No one – except Pym and a few others, I assumed – knew where she'd gone or why or what had happened. But everybody knew there'd been something – her numbers at La Vie were greeted with extra applause. Winston Churchill came down and asked her to sit at his table with General de Gaulle and a pretty woman. He laughed at what she said.

'Even at Pontifex Street she got more consideration. She could spend hours in the bathroom without someone coming up and banging on the door and swearing at her. Julia stopped bothering about her borrowings, especially after Sally gave her some makeup and a hat with a feather in it she'd brought back from Paris. People treated her differently.

'There was a loud crash. I said, "That sounds like Oxford Street."

'She murmured, "It's quieter in Paris at night."

'"Nice for Paris," I said.

'And she said, "It's an awful silence."

'I asked her, "Sally, are you going to tell me?"

'"What?"

'"Why were you in Paris? What happened? How did Pym get you to do it?"

'She laughed. "I looked up an old boyfriend."'

'Jesus,' Greg said. 'Who was that?'

'Have you any brandy?' inquired Bruno. Greg went to get it. Bruno took a few sips then went on, adopting cadences and using words Greg thought might have come direct from the lips of Sally Bowles, so long ago. Sometimes Bruno's memory did this, he had noted – produced near total recall.

It was like listening to a ghost now as the old man said, '"You see, darling, there's a very important officer in Paris called Christian von Torgau. He's terribly handsome, blond and blue-eyed, just like those posters they have in Germany showing big strong Aryan men. And he's amazingly clever and totally cultured. He'd been brought up in that terribly strict way they have – eat your soup, *eins*, *zwei*, *drei*, sleep flat in your bed, arms outside the covers, beatings for your own good, no slouching, walk like this, sit like that. He'd been in the Army, but when I met him before the war he'd resigned. While he was still a soldier he'd made a suitable marriage to an icy bitch from a family even older than his, which went back to Genghis Khan or something. What an iceberg. One glance from Julia von Torgau and the fire would go out, literally, darling.

'"I knew Christian very well – you know what I mean, sweetie? He wasn't a Nazi then and neither was his wife, of course. They thought Hitler was rather horrible – and common, you know, like those families do. They believe he's a ridiculous, vulgar little man, that they're just using him. They'll find out soon, if they haven't already.

'"Oh, God." She groaned. "I'd forgotten – it's just come

125

back. How frightful. Years ago Julia caught us once in a bedroom in a sort of castle he had. She had been away but she came back early. It was a big stone room and you could see for miles from the window, huge fields with little figures bent over here and there, all toiling away for the von Torgaus. We had big logs burning in the vast fireplace and there was a bearskin on the floor in front of it. Well, there we were in front of the fire, up to our monkey tricks, when in came Julia. She took one look, icicles started dropping from the ceiling, the air froze. She stood there, then turned on her heel and walked straight out and Christian didn't see her for a year. Dreadful, wasn't it?" Sally said. Then she giggled.

'She went on, "We went to France and Italy – oh, it was lovely, Bruno. Christian was so handsome – of course, he spoke all known languages, even Hungarian. It was wonderful."

'And,' said Bruno, 'in the middle of an air-raid with the building quivering round us, Sally looked up at me from her mattress with big eyes, remembering this Nazi and trying to seduce me with her memories.' He gave a harsh laugh. 'You can imagine how successful she was with me. Then she frowned. "Well, Bruno darling, you had to hand it to Christian. He'd gone from ramrod-backed officer of the old school to Bohemian sensualist – sometimes he went a little too far, darling, even for me, if you know what I mean – and then suddenly, Nazism. I think he was one of those people who can go from one thing to another with total belief – like St Paul, or something – so up to then, he'd seen Hitler and his boys like all the other aristocrats did,

126

useful for the country, appealing to the working classes and the petit bourgeoisie, nothing whatever to do with them, a silly little man with a silly little moustache. Then he began to convert, just like someone taking up religion. He started going on about racial purity and Germany's destiny and all that awful stuff – oh, Bruno, it was horrible. We started to have the most fearful rows. I left and went to Spain to get the taste of Germany out of my mouth. Not that it went away because Hitler sent the bombers to Spain to kill us."

'Then she paused,' Bruno said. 'She had a lot to remember. She said, "I went back to Germany after Spain and got trapped. Christian was a Nazi and, of course, in the Army again. The war came. I left, with difficulty as you know, then Pym told me Christian was on the staff of the commandant for Greater Paris, von Studlitz. Pym made me go over there to see what I could find out. He had the goods on me."

'The All Clear went then and she got up and dashed out of the cellar, to get to La Vie and do her turn. Cora didn't pay her if she didn't show up, regardless of what had prevented her.

'After she'd gone, I remembered I'd met the von Torgaus just once, in Berlin, just after I'd come together with Briggs. One evening he dragged me to the large house the von Torgaus had there – I remember it well. Who wouldn't? There was I, a big youth in patched boots, clutching my cap in my sweaty hands as if someone were going to steal it, standing in the massive hall, all tiles and marble and old furniture being greeted by the svelte blonde wife of von

Torgau. She wore pearls and had piled-up blonde hair. She was immaculate. I was grubby. My God, it was so embarrassing. A musical evening at the von Torgaus! Me?

'We went into the music room. It was elegant beyond words. I'd never seen anything like it in my life, the chandeliers, the old paintings. At the end of the room there was a concert piano and music stands. I sat on a gilt chair, gripping a small drink, an elephant at a ball, while the musicians, there were three of them, played the kind of music I had seldom heard – Bach, Scarlatti, I don't remember now, just the sounds.

'Von Torgau was sitting beside me, very handsome, very correct, and completely absorbed in the music. His wife played the piano. A dark man was playing the violin – his appearance gave the idea that he was probably a Jew but a man of good class, that too I could see. Bent over the cello, with a lot of brown hair falling over her face, was a woman. Briefly, afterwards, we met the violinist and the cellist. The woman was called Claudia. She had an intelligent, kind face – I remember nothing else. I was so uneasy. Briggs had to take me home.

'Anyway, Greg,' Bruno said, holding out his glass for more brandy, 'that was how I met, just once, the von Torgaus and their friends, Simon Stein and Claudia, whom Simon was to marry. Sally had rushed off – I never bothered to tell her later. Nor did I ask her what she'd meant by Pym having the goods on her. I was so shocked, Greg, that Pym, even Pym, could be so ruthless. He sent her into the heart of the German Army in occupied France! Can you imagine what would have happened to her if Christian von Torgau had chosen to turn her in?'

'She was very brave,' Greg remarked.

'Oh, yes,' Bruno said. 'Sally was brave. She couldn't clean a bath. She was careless with money and property, her own and other people's. She was very irritating in a thousand ways – but she was brave.'

27

Sally was forced to spend the morning in a small room at the back of a warehouse, where the carcasses of six pigs hung from hooks. She was allowed to make one call from the office while the men were on a break.

'*Bonjour*, Rover,' she said, to her cousin Benoît, using her childhood nickname for him so that he would know it was her. '*C'est moi*, Singette.'

The conversation went on in French.

'Where are you?'

'Paris. Can you give me a hand?'

'I'll try, but my leg's broken,' he replied. 'Come here at twelve. I'll send Célestine out.'

'Thanks. I'll be there.'

'Will it be fun?' he asked.

'A little – not much,' she told him.

She spent more hours with the pigs. She had known her twin cousins, Benoît and Charles, would help, knew that Benoît had rapidly guessed the nature of what she was doing.

At eleven thirty Sally, smartly dressed in her pink suit and carrying papers that identified her as an assistant at a big Paris department store, left her cellar. They had told her in London that one person in the store would back her story if she was challenged. They had also said that unluckily there was a second person who might not be so helpful.

On the bus her pink suit was coolly examined by the other passengers as they rattled through the streets, which were almost empty of civilian vehicles. Three grey-uniformed soldiers got on. The pavements were full of troops and there was, to Sally, the shocking sight of swastikas hanging outside public buildings.

Surrounded by the soldiers of the Reich, Sally walked, back straight, in her fashionable suit and shoes to the big nineteenth-century block of flats in which Madeleine and Bertrand du Tour, Geneviève's sister and brother-in-law, lived.

She opened the gilded door, with its metal fretwork, into the foyer, and took the small lift upstairs.

She rang a brass doorbell beside a highly polished wooden door. No one answered. Heart racing she rang again. Then the door opened. Benoît, short, stocky and dark-haired, grinning broadly, was there, balanced on crutches. He nodded her into the vast hall, where statues stood in niches. All was as it had always been, even the fragrance of the furniture polish, which was made at a convent somewhere in the country and sent annually to Paris.

Benoît swung himself into the salon and sat down heavily on an upholstered sofa, with a gilded wooden back and legs.

He waved at a long table on which bottles and glasses stood. There was also a loaf and some cheese. 'Help yourself,' he said. 'I've sent Célestine off to visit her family. Charles is at his philosophy lecture at the Sorbonne. I brought in what I could from the kitchen. I thought you might be hungry.'

'Thanks,' Sally said. She poured some wine and helped herself to bread and cheese.

'You can take more than that,' he told her. 'Old Jean bikes up once a week from the farm. It's not so good for others.'

'I can imagine.'

'The news says you're being bombed into dust.'

'It would. What happened to your leg?'

'A long story.'

'And Uncle and Aunt?'

'They're in Normandy at the farm. In general, they're saying it's best to co-operate with the authorities. But Charles and I know it will get worse. They're softening us up. Soon the Gestapo will be sent here.' He smiled. 'Some of us are in a gang which goes out killing Germans. The patrol got to us one night and I had to jump out of a window. That was how I broke my leg. Mother and Father think I fell off my bike.'

'That's very dangerous, Benoît,' Sally said.

'Thank you for telling me, as you're such an expert on personal safety. Why are you here?'

'I have to get in touch with a German major at the Hôtel Crillon. I knew him in Berlin.'

'My God.' He gazed at her in dismay. 'What are you – a negotiator?' Then he looked at her disbelievingly. 'You can't be a collaborator?'

'Don't be stupid, Benoît. I'm a spy.'

'Oh, my God.' He put his head in his hands.

'Don't worry, I won't stay here long,' she told him. 'One phone call, a bath, and I'll go. I have another address—'

'You must stay, but only till Célestine gets back the day after tomorrow. It wouldn't be safe after that. I don't trust her. What on earth persuaded you to be a heroine, Sally?'

'A very nasty man,' she said bitterly. 'Adrian Pym. If I'm killed, remember his name. Ask Bruno Lowenthal.'

'Bruno Lowenthal,' Benoît repeated.

Minutes later she was saying into the telephone, 'Christian – you know who it is. I wish to see you. Darling, I'm in Paris. Don't push me away.'

Her voice rolled over Benoît, husky and blandishing. She closed her eye. Winked at him.

That evening Sally Bowles, in evening dress, walked into the glittering restaurant. All the white-covered tables were occupied, chiefly by high-ranking German officers, many accompanied by good-looking women. As she was approached by the head waiter, Albert, in his immaculate coat, Christian von Torgau hurried up to her

He was still tall, blond and very handsome. His clear-cut face was pale and firm. He put out a hand. 'Sally, speak French, if you please.'

Albert led them to a table at the side of the room and seated them politely.

'Why here?' Christian asked, in an undertone, just before the waiter arrived at their table.

'Anywhere more private and you might have bumped me

off,' Sally told him, then smiled graciously at the waiter, who impassively handed her the menu.

'Why are you here? What do you want?'

'Darling – such questions!' Sally said, as Albert came to the table to make his recommendations. The choice was negotiated, wine poured. 'You look so handsome in your uniform.'

'You must surely see that this is very embarrassing for me,' he said. 'Where have you been all this time, anyway?'

Sally, relieved that he was unaware she had reached England, said promptly, 'Spain. But it got on my nerves, so I came back to France.'

'You know quite well it's my duty to have you arrested.'

'You say the sweetest things. How could a girl resist?'

'I'll arrange for you to go back to Spain,' he told her.

That night in this occupied city, over these well-ordered tables, in an atmosphere of good scent, good food and good wine, many a plan was being laid, many a deal struck. Sally, for the time being, agreed. 'Well,' she said, 'you look most important, and where is Julia?'

Here the waiter brought their food. They were silent while he placed the plates before them and removed the covers with a pre-war flourish.

'At home, in Germany,' Christian said, when the man had gone.

'Guarding the castle while her crusader is away?'

'Exactly so.'

'Have you been in a battle yet? What was it like?'

'Unhappily there has been no battle for me. I have hopes, though, for the future. Where are you staying?'

Sally looked at him. 'I don't quite trust you, Christian. I love you, of course, but I'd rather not give you my address, not just yet.'

'Sally,' he said, 'if you think there can any longer be anything between us, I must tell you, there cannot.'

'Oh, Christian – Berlin, the Riviera, Rome, don't you remember?'

'That was the past. The future, Sally, will be different.'

There was silence between them, as quiet talk continued all around. A roar of laughter came from a group of officers in the middle of the room.

'Well, I'm disappointed,' Sally said.

'I'm sorry. But you must see it's impossible.'

He dug his knife into a small game bird.

'This is a nice posting for you, anyway, Christian. Paris – *ville lumière* – all the theatres and cabarets. Do you remember the cabarets in the old days? Joséphine Baker?'

'Paris is a soft posting, too soft,' he declared.

'You're only doing your duty.'

'Well, Sally,' he said briskly, putting down his knife and fork, 'I confess I do not want to prolong this meeting. Shall we eat? And then we'll go back to my office and I'll arrange your documents for your return to Spain.' He picked up his knife and fork again.

'What a pity. I was enjoying this,' she said. 'Oh, Christian, this awful war. How dull it makes everything. But I know you must put duty first.'

Christian, tight-lipped, attacked his bird. Sally, dry-mouthed, ate as heartily as she could.

Later, as they walked through dark, quiet streets, many

averted their eyes from the spectacle of well-dressed Sally with her high-ranking German. An old man, with one leg, spat in the gutter. The city seemed dark, though street-lamps burned. Sally was terrified as she stepped through the grisly portals of the Hôtel Crillon, guarded by soldiers. What was she doing here? How would she get out? Only the knowledge that turning back would be even more dangerous – fatal – kept her moving.

They ascended a massive staircase. At the top, where once some large picture of a battle or a French dignitary would have hung, was a portrait of the Führer, in uniform, resolution emanating from his undistinguished face. Christian took her arm. They went into his office, where lamps burned. The room was shadowy, huge and alarming. A dark painting of a seventeenth-century nobleman hung over the ornate fireplace. The heavy desk was bare.

Quickly von Torgau closed the door behind them. Sally went up to him straight away and twined her powdered arms around him, flinching at the touch of his Army tunic. 'It's not very intimate,' she murmured. He pulled away from her.

'Sally,' he said, erect and stern, 'intimacy is not what I want. I am a German officer. You are English. You must see that your presence here compromises me greatly. All I desire now is to be sent to fight for the Fatherland. Any taint, any suggestion that I am not wholly loyal, can prevent that. Or worse.'

Sally moved close to him again and gazed, wide-eyed, into his face. 'Oh, Christian, you wouldn't turn me down? Don't you remember?'

136

'No, Sally. I don't remember. I don't want to remember. You – you were an aberration, a corrupt part of my life I wish to forget. My one wish is to get you out of here and on your way back to Spain.'

'Oh, Christian,' she said, in a low, desolate voice. Standing on her toes she put her arms around his neck again and kissed him on the mouth.

He pulled free and held her by the shoulders. 'Stop that! Stop that – or I shall become very angry with you! I'm going into my secretary's room to find the official stamps for the document I'm going to give you. Sit down. Stay where you are. Don't make a sound. Don't move until I return.'

But as he spoke Sally was unbuttoning the metal buttons of his tunic. 'Oh, Christian, just one more time . . .'

He pulled his arms from the tunic, leaving it in her hands, and crossed the floor rapidly to his secretary's office. 'Do as I say!' he shouted. 'Sit down!'

Inside, Sally heard him opening and shutting drawers. While he did so, Sally, who had sat down as instructed, went rapidly through his tunic. In the breast pocket she found the letter, which was later to be named, in official circles, the German Letter. As she read it she heard Christian banging yet another drawer shut. He swore.

The letter, dated three days earlier, came from Adolf Hitler's office. It was a personal letter, amiably informing Major Graf von Torgau that at last the writer was able to comply with his most urgent requests to be sent on active duty for the Reich. He would be attached shortly to the command of General von Runstedt for the launching of the attack to the east. The letter concluded by hoping that

Gräfin Julia remained in good health and ended cheerfully, '*Auf Moscou*'. It was signed by Hitler himself.

Sally stood up, holding the letter, and ran across the room. She let herself out as quietly as she could and found herself at the top of the big staircase with no choice but to go down and pass the guards at the entrance to the building. Everything inside her screamed for a less dangerous course, but there was none, so she went down calmly, always expecting to hear Christian behind her. However, he must have remained in the smaller office for longer than she had thought. She knew, though, that as soon as he entered the room in which they had been he would immediately discover the loss of the letter. She passed the guards, saying in German, 'Major Graf von Torgau asked me to meet him outside,' and went through the gates unmolested.

Once she was out of sight of the Crillon she began to run. She hoped there would be a gap between the time Christian found she was gone and his discovery that the letter from Hitler was missing – and that Christian would hesitate about making public Sally's embarrassing – to him – departure.

Mercifully it was thirty minutes before curfew and people were still in the streets. She slowed down: a running figure is always conspicuous. She found a tram, and began to make her way back to the warehouse.

There was still no hue and cry, no Army cars speeding about, no soldiers launched into the streets. Perhaps the letter was a hoax. But how likely was it that Christian von Torgau would be carrying anything but a genuine letter from Adolf Hitler? In his tunic pocket, next to his breast?

Perhaps, she thought, as the tram rumbled on through the dark streets, that he had not yet discovered it was missing. More likely he had, but was making every effort to get it back quickly without exposing himself as the officer who had permitted a woman to obtain an important letter from the Führer.

At the warehouse a man was throwing sacks furiously into the back of a van while the driver sat in front, engine running. He shouted something at the other from the window. They were trying to leave Paris before curfew. From the corner of the yard, where she was hiding, Sally saw the loader start back into the warehouse just as the driver bent over to light a cigarette. She raced across the yard and dived into the open back of the van, crawled in and was pulling some sacks over her just as the man returned with another heap and threw them in. He closed the door with a slam and the van started. In the darkness Sally finished covering herself, breathing heavily. So far, about half an hour after her theft of the letter, she had been lucky. However, by now they might have declared an emergency and closed the checkpoints. But when the van stopped the enquiries she could hear from the interior of the van were brief and sounded routine. Then they were on their way again.

She was safely out of Paris, but she had no idea where they were going. She could bang on the back of the vehicle behind the driver's seat, attract his attention and cause him to stop. But would he turn her in? They seemed to be going north, the right direction for the Channel coast so she decided to risk staying there quietly. She might be able to get out when eventually the driver opened the van door. That part of her adventure was almost the worst of all, being bumped along in darkness to who knew where – a German Army base, perhaps?

The van turned into a farmyard. Dogs barked. The back was flung open, the driver reached in for some bales of empty sacks and pulled them out. A man's voice, close to the van, said, 'You've got the money?' Sally stayed quite still.

It seemed to her that she was on the supply line, bringing food from the farms to Paris. But she could not be sure that those who owed their living to the German authorities would be prepared to help her. She'd better get out unseen. But the activity around the van did not stop, money was handed over, news about crops and families was exchanged, the van doors were slammed and they were on their way again.

There was another stop, almost the same, and then, an hour later, four hours after they had left Paris, they pulled up. Sally thought the driver must be taking a nap.

She, too, tried to sleep, but could only doze. Then for no reason, she started, so violently that her leg hit the side of the van. Fully awake she lay still, hoping that the driver had not heard. She had just relaxed when she heard the van doors open and she was blinded by the light of a torch.

Her story was ready. As her papers showed, she was a shop assistant. She was being pursued by an ugly German major and, to avoid trouble, she thought she would disappear secretly to Dinard where her father had a chemist's shop. This she told the driver, who listened without sympathy.

'You understand, Monsieur?' she said. 'I have money. I can pay you for my journey.'

'How much?' he said. 'And what else can you give me?'

Finding herself on a dark road late at night with a burly man asking about money and other potential benefits, Sally was afraid. 'I think I'll walk,' she said, and turned away. He came after her and she crippled him as they had taught her while she was doing parachute training. She got back into the van and drove four miles to the next village where she dumped it, knowing that when her would-be attacker recovered he would report the loss to a countryside that must by then have been thoroughly alerted. She found a stone wall beside the road and hid behind it. But at dawn on these country roads, in her pink suit and city shoes, she would be as noticeable as an elephant, so she was forced to get back into the van and drive north through the night. At dawn she abandoned it and walked the last mile to the farm where she had been received on landing. Her host drove the van ten miles and rolled it into a ditch.

Some days later the same antique aeroplane came in through dark and heavy cloud to rescue her. Though fired on by enemy bombers, the cloud protected them. They landed safe; Sally's mission was over.

28

'Anyway,' said Bruno, 'the letter Sally brought back was strong confirmation of what other reports were indicating – that Hitler planned to attack Russia. It was very useful. She went to the Cabinet Office to tell her story. Some suspected the letter was a trick, intended to decoy the Allies into believing that Germany intended to invade Russia and altering their strategy accordingly. But in the end the story was accepted, chiefly because Churchill himself believed it and acted accordingly. When the attack on Russia by Germany actually came, Pym was in clover. He began to take the credit for organising Sally's mission. He became famous in the intelligence services as the man who had brought off this great coup. It has been said that the matter so enhanced his reputation that it kept him safe from suspicion for years after he should have been detected. There was always someone around, when doubts arose about Pym, who would mention the famous German Letter. Briggs couldn't prevent himself from saying that he'd always thought French letters more Sally's style.

'Some of the glory rubbed off on Pontifex Street. Sir Peveril filled the flat with flowers and Pym was promoted. I don't know for certain why Sally didn't get a decoration.'

Bruno stood up to go: 'It's late for an old man,' he said, and left Greg wondering about this strange episode in Sally Bowles's increasingly mystifying life. He decided suddenly to put into operation an idea that had been crystallising in his mind. '*Auf Moscou*, Greg,' he advised himself.

29

'We're lucky – the snow's not bad there yet,' Alistair Bradshaw remarked comfortably, stretching out with his whisky in his club-class seat. 'But, in case it gets worse, my wife's packed my skiing gear.'

Alistair was the businessman brother of Greg's friend Hugh, with whom he, Katherine and two others had shared a house in Cambridge during their student days. 'I heard this Pym guy was trying to come home years ago,' he added. 'There was an outcry. He must be, what?, eighty plus now?'

'Eighty-three,' Greg agreed.

'You wouldn't want to be that age in Moscow today,' said Alistair.

Club class of the BA flight to Moscow was full of businessmen, British, American, Canadian, Russian and others whose origins were harder to decide. Documents were read, laptops were used, some low conversations broke the silence.

With unwanted candour, Alistair told Greg about his girlfriend, whom he wished to make his third wife, though his second wife was not yet aware of this. 'It'll cost a bomb,' he told Greg. 'But luckily since number one, Deborah, remarried I'm not paying alimony to her any more. I could have kissed the bloke she married, poor sod.'

Greg gave a noncommittal answer and began to wonder if it was such a good idea to have hooked on to Alistair as a travelling companion. Hugh had said his brother knew the ropes, having made several business trips there already, that what a traveller needed in Russia, these days, was expert guidance. And since Alistair, opportunely, had been leaving in a few days' time, and there turned out to be room on the plane, Greg had tagged along. However, the club-class fare was higher than the economy one he would have paid if travelling alone. And he wasn't sure why Alistair was going to Russia or how he planned to spend his time there. He had spoken vaguely of investigating the prospects of his merchant bank's setting up an office there. But what did that mean?

To Greg's eyes, the plane's cabin looked like a combination of the eight-fifteen commuter train to London from some prosperous suburb and a dining-car full of gangsters heading for Cicero in the 1920s. There were Russian faces, seamed and battered, ones you wouldn't want to meet alone in an alley on a dark night. There were American and European predators, too, looking less like men out on parole after serving a term for manslaughter, but probably, Greg suspected, just as dangerous in their way as the others.

He cheered up, ordered a drink and grinned. He said to Alistair, 'It's great to be moving.'

'Do you think you're going to find Pym?' asked Alistair, his face indicating his suspicion that Greg was mad. Adrian Pym had been in exile in the Soviet Union since 1951 when, exposed as a double agent, he had fled to Moscow with Geoffrey Forbes of the Foreign Office. Greg had obtained Pym's current address in Moscow from Hugh, who had contacts on a newspaper. Hugh had only handed it over on condition that Greg told him what he found out when he talked to Pym.

'You tell me everything,' Hugh had told him. 'I want the tapes. It may be a story. Either Pym's going to die or he'll get repatriated on compassionate grounds. The last time he tried the Cold War was still on and there was no way. The Yanks would have hated it. But now it just might come up again. But remember to stick with Alistair.'

Meanwhile, Greg himself was not sure if Pym would talk to him, or even be fit enough to do so. To Greg he seemed a fantastic, legendary figure, like a dragon, a man left behind by Khrushchev, then Gorbachev and the ending of the Cold War.

Alistair said now, 'Be careful, Greg. Russia's not a safe place unless you know what you're doing. Any doubts, check with me.'

Greg regarded him dubiously. Since the end of Empire men like Alistair had reverted to the old buccaneering habits of their ancestors, travelling the world looting like privateers. How could he tell that Alistair wouldn't shaft him – sell him – lie to him? He'd do it to anybody else.

Meanwhile, Alistair had moved on from his sexual war wounds to the grim obsession of his class. Greg wasn't sure which monologue he liked least. 'The heap . . . needs a new roof – water coming in everywhere – Heritage . . . entail . . .' No point in asking why not get rid of the ancestral home. Hard-up Hall, there to be passed on to young Rupert, Hereward, Joe or Nick, was as close to a religion as Alistair would get, and was probably the basic reason for this trip, this bit of business, and so many before and to come. His roof would be repaired if it took blood – other people's – to do it.

They got off the plane into the grey of Moscow's October and repaired to a hotel, marbled, gilded, luxurious. There was a bowl of fruit in Greg's room, peaches, apples, grapes, plums. Outside the hotel were tired grey Russians, groups of youngsters in Levi's, girls in heavy makeup.

Greg made a phone call. To his astonishment there, suddenly, at the end of the phone, was the legendary spy, Adrian Pym. 'Do come round, dear boy. Any time will do. I'm not going anywhere.' In Pym's light, rather sardonic voice he heard the tone and accent he sometimes caught in Bruno's speech. Like the clothes in an old photograph, those voices had the style of their times.

If he had expected to find Adrian Pym in a two-room flat in a tower block miles from the centre of Moscow, up four flights of concrete stairs, he had been mistaken. Somehow Pym had made a deal. He lived a short walk from Greg's hotel. Greg took wide and windy streets under a grey, swirling sky, past the American Express office, with its crowd of hopeful crooks and traders outside, to find himself opposite a park and outside a big pre-Revolution house in the expensive Patriarch's Ponds area.

He entered the hall, where a man in uniform dozed on a gilt chair, and walked up a handsome staircase to the first floor of the silent building.

He was let in by a thin young man with cropped blond hair, wearing a faded Russian Army uniform and trainers. 'I've come to see Mr Pym,' Greg said, trying to glance into a rather gloomy interior, from which came the smell of soup. The young soldier nodded, and Greg stepped into a large twilit hall then into a high-ceilinged room where, in near-darkness, Adrian Pym sat. From his window, Greg guessed, he had a pleasant view of the pond, the yellow and white pavilion, trees and bushes.

'Mr Phillips, welcome,' said Pym. 'Forgive me for not standing up.' Greg advanced, holding out his hand. The face turned up to him was thin and lined. The hand he shook was limp, wrinkled and cold. Pym was a sick man. He smiled up at Greg from the huge, ornately carved wooden chair in which he sat. A brightly coloured rug was tucked over his knees and a big enamelled stove blasted out heat.

He gestured to the chair opposite him, an upholstered armchair of the kind you might find in any house in Britain or the USA. The hieratic chair in which Pym sat gave him the air of some old, cunning medieval Pope and was, perhaps, for show, Greg reflected. He noted that from where he himself sat he could see a small television set peeping out from under the carved legs of a wooden table. The light from the window was on his own face; Pym was sitting in shadows. Now Pym clapped his hands and the soldier reappeared. Pym spoke to him in Russian.

'This is Ivan,' he said. 'He speaks very little English. He's in the Army but he helps me for pay. The Russian Army's starving, as you'll know. We'll have a drink.' During this speech Ivan left the room and Pym said, 'As for speaking next to no English, how can one tell? If you have anything confidential to say, wait until he's out of the room.'

It was very quiet. The dark walls, on which paintings hung and two icons, seemed scarcely visible in the gloom. It was as if Pym and Greg were on an island of heat, thrown out by the stove into the vast room.

Ivan returned noiselessly on his trainers with an elaborate metal tray on which stood a bottle of vodka, one of Scotch and a carafe of water. He bent over the low table, which stood in front of the red-hot stove, and placed the tray on it. 'Hop off, Ivan,' Pym said dismissively, and this Ivan seemed to understand, for he left the room.

'Good-looking, isn't he? So are you,' Pym said.

Greg, who had previously suspected, uncomfortably, that a factor in Bruno's co-operation with him had been his own youth and good looks, was now embarrassed by the same sensation. Worse, he wondered if Pym wanted anything from him, like some form of sex, in exchange for information.

'I'm very grateful that you've agreed to talk to me about Sally Bowles, sir,' he began. 'I'm sure anything you have to say would be enormously useful. I wonder – why have you decided to speak to me?'

'Well, first,' Pym said, 'there's no question of recording what I say. I hope you understand that. Do you agree?'

'I'd have preferred to tape it,' responded Greg. 'But, of course, if you don't wish me to . . .'

'I'm afraid I have to ask you to be searched by Ivan on your way out.'

'I assure you I'd never tape anything secretly,' Greg said sharply.

'I don't believe you would. But I must be careful.'

'I suppose so. I agree,' Greg said. The idea of Ivan searching him was not one he relished, but having got as far as Pym's apartment in Moscow he saw no point in refusing to jump the last fence.

'Good,' said Pym. 'Now, will you pour me a Scotch, with just a little water? Make it a large one. And one for yourself, of course.'

As Greg did so, he continued, 'You ask me why I'm ready to co-operate with you, give you information for your book.' As Greg bent to give the old man his drink Pym gave him a sharp look from his dimming eyes. 'I want you to do something for me.'

Greg took a step back. 'What's that, Mr Pym?'

'I want to come back to England. It's terrible here. Everything's falling apart. My pension is sometimes unpaid. The hospitals are collapsing. Sometimes the doctor doesn't come. I need to go back to Britain.'

'You tried some years ago, I heard,' said Greg. 'Perhaps the British administration would be more sympathetic now Communism has gone from Eastern Europe. Have you made a request to them?'

'It's a bit more complicated than that,' Pym told him. 'I want you to take a message to a certain person.'

Greg's eyes widened: this man was a fugitive traitor in exile from Britain, officially still subject to trial and even execution there.

Greg turned over the problem in his mind. He knew that he was dealing with a notoriously cunning brain, that Pym was blackmailing him crudely. He was to act as Pym's mouthpiece in return for Pym's co-operation over his book. Greg was not surprised, and on the face of it there was no great harm in it from his point of view. On the other hand he had to recognise that Pym was almost certainly cleverer and more subtle than he was. Was he being led into more trouble than he could imagine? He played for time. 'I'll do as you ask, Mr Pym,' he said. 'But couldn't you do it just as well, maybe better, yourself from here?'

'They won't talk to me, dear boy,' Pym said. 'I've become a subject they don't want to think about. There are those who got away with it, you see, informing on me, pushing a lot of paper into the kitchen boiler, calling in a network of favours carefully built up over the years. These people want me here and quiet, far, far away.'

'Aren't you afraid that I'll agree to do what you ask and that after you've talked to me about Sally I'll go back and forget about it?'

'You won't,' Pym said, giving him a knowing, complicitous look, as if he knew more about Greg than he did himself. 'No, that'll be all right. I trust you.'

That's great, Greg thought, Adrian Pym, one of the most notorious spies of his generation, the man who had been the conduit for atomic secrets to the Soviet Union, who had been responsible for sending hundreds, thousands to their deaths, trusted him. Yet, he thought, having given his word, he would probably keep it, as Pym believed. Let's face it, that was the type of person he was, even though he suspected the deal he was keeping would not be the deal he'd thought it was when he bought in. How could it be, when it had been made with this old, experienced spy, a byword for treachery, a name to be mentioned in the same breath along with Benedict Arnold and Judas Iscariot?

He said, 'So, Mr Pym, let's say I know what you want me to do and that I'll do it. Will you tell me something about Sally Bowles?' He stood up and refilled Pym's glass.

'Sally? God knows why anyone would be interested in that ghastly slut. Still, I gather things have changed in the West, with women's rights and all that. Hard to live with, I'd imagine. Well, Sally,' he continued, recalling himself, 'I remember her from Cambridge, in the early thirties when she was always hanging about. How she came to join us is a mystery. I believe her father had met Briggs's father, in the First World War. Briggs's father was the padre, of course, and the two men wouldn't have known each other well. Of course, the minute Miss Bowles found Briggs, Pym and all the rest of us, Charles Denham, Francis Keene, Geoffrey Forbes and so forth up at Cambridge, she wouldn't go away. We were too fascinating, the *jeunesse dorée*, we were going to do everything, change everything. Handsome, gifted, intelligent – strange, isn't it, how it came out?' He paused, then said, 'First, she ran away from school to Cambridge. She was sixteen and had no money. Briggs had to rescue her and return her. She did it again. He found it a nightmare. She latched on to Theo, who was her first lover. After that, there was no stopping her. Theo encouraged her, of course. We kept telling him to get rid of her but he wouldn't. Next thing, he took off for Germany, to work for *The Times*. I don't know if he took her with him or she followed him. She began her career, so-called, as a singer. Even I, though, was never sure whether it was all as innocent as it seemed. Theo was a Communist. I don't know if Sally was ever a Party member.'

This was a statement Greg found hard to believe.

'Still, who wasn't, duckie, in those days?' Pym said. Then he leaned over the side of his chair and, his hand unsteady, pushed the arm of an old-fashioned record-player. Loud, energetic music filled the room. 'Prokofiev,' declared Pym. Ivan stole into the room – to listen, perhaps. 'Sit down!' Pym said autocratically, and Ivan slid down the wall and sat on the floor, his legs in the faded military trousers extended in front of him.

'We spend many hours together, listening to music,' Pym remarked wearily.

'Are you tired? Would you like me to go and return tomorrow, perhaps?' Greg offered.

'No, no, dear boy. Better out than in,' he said. 'I remember Henley. We all turned out for Theo – whites, boaters, what tarts we were, all for the Party, of course. Ladies in hats and floaty frocks, champagne, champagne, champagne. Green, green grass and tight-bummed oarsmen. I remember Sally there, in a little straw hat, all legs, looking as if she should still have been at school. Perhaps she was.

153

She was on Theo's arm, the handsome devil. He must have seduced her by then. God – I was in love with him. Funny – I was never in love with anyone else except, perhaps, myself, and in any case I was always drunk, but Theo . . .' He paused.

Greg remembered Bruno Lowenthal's perception that some of Pym's animosity towards Sally came from his thwarted love for Theo Fitzpatrick. 'What a day. We were all young, we all believed we were working for a better world – you have to remember that all this sunshine and glamour was set against the background of the depression. There were millions out of work. Still,' he said, 'what a day! We wouldn't have turned out to queen around like that if Theo hadn't dictated we must improve our social standing, make our mark in circles that mattered. I suppose he'd had instructions.'

'From the Russians?' asked Greg.

'Well, it wasn't from the Portuguese,' Pym stated, holding out his glass for more. 'Hand me one of those cigarettes,' he requested, and Greg, having replenished his glass, took a Marlboro from a packet on the table. He lit it for Pym, who started to cough.

'I've not long to go,' Pym gasped, when he had finished coughing. 'Stress that when you talk to them in Britain.'

Greg nodded. 'Bruno Lowenthal remembers that day at Henley,' he told Pym.

Pym started to speak then began to cough again. Finally he got the words out, 'That old bugger. Is he still alive? You've been talking to Lowenthal? How astonishing. I first met him in Berlin, after Briggs picked him up. That was when Theo and Sally were there, him reporting for *The Times*, her singing and dancing in louche cabarets, all working for the Party, so in love. "Bliss was it in that dawn to be alive But to be young was very heaven," as the poet remarked about the French Revolution, which was a considerably more successful effort. Christ – Lowenthal. Where is he?'

'He runs a rather successful antique shop in Portobello Road.'

'Bloody hell. That was where he elected to go when Briggs turned him out, wasn't it? The last I heard was that he was selling rags and any old iron. I wouldn't believe all he tells you – in fact, if I were you I'd believe very little of it. I'd hate to write a book based on Lowenthal's distorted memories.'

'He seems very acute,' Greg said. 'But, of course, I can't assume that what he tells me is accurate.' He decided to take a step forward. 'He mentioned something about Sally's going to France on a secret mission.'

'To see von Torgau,' Pym said absently. The music ceased. 'Turn the record over and pour me another drink,' Pym called over to Ivan, who, apparently understanding, did so. 'Why the hell write a book about Sally?' Pym asked. 'She was nobody, you know, nothing and nobody.'

Pym was not going to discuss Sally's French venture, Greg suspected. He observed that his host was getting drunk. The music started up again, bold and dramatic.

'It's a method of approach,' Greg told Pym. 'A story that hasn't been told and perhaps never will be, fully and completely, but I plan to add piece after piece to it, using Sally as my centre.'

'You'll never get away with it,' Pym said blurrily. 'And if you did you'd get it all wrong.' There was a pause. Then he declared, suddenly, 'You'd better go. But before you do just you remember this, Mr Innocent American, that – that . . .' he groped for his thought '. . . that, silly tart as she was, Sally Bowles was no political virgin. What do you imagine she was doing in Berlin all that time, nearly a year after war'd been declared? She was a "stay-behind", wasn't she? A lot of people were persuaded to stay abroad when war looked increasingly likely. God knows who she was working for by the end of the war. I don't suppose she knew herself. I'll never know how much she had to do with us, at the end, with all of it . . .' His voice trailed off and his head sank sideways. In alarm, Greg looked towards Ivan, back on the floor by the door. Ivan shrugged, nodded towards the door.

'Come back tomorrow,' came Pym's slurred voice. 'Might as well get it straight . . . shtraight.'

Greg got up and went quietly to the door. He said goodbye to Ivan, who was on his feet now and moving towards Pym. 'He said I should come back tomorrow,' he said to Ivan, trying to speak clearly.

'Yes, sure. Tomorrow. You phone – OK?'

'OK,' said Greg, handed him a few dollars and left him bending over Pym's frail and shrunken form. He went, unsearched, down the stairs and out into the cold, grey, darkening Russian afternoon.

Later he met Alistair for dinner in one of Moscow's new luxury restaurants. The short walk through the darkness from their hotel had been disconcerting due to the beggars, buyers and sellers, lurkers in doorways. Now, warm and well seated, as a girl in traditional dress went from table to table playing the balalaika, Greg looked across the restaurant to see a gaunt face peering in through the window, and said, 'It's like a Muscovite New York.'

'They always said the USA and the Soviet Union had more in common than anyone thought,' Alistair remarked comfortably.

'There's a lot of poverty,' Greg ventured, although he knew that this was not a word men like Alistair wished to hear.

'Of course. Teething troubles of capitalism,' he said.

'It looks more like a serious illness.'

'Well, that's not for us to comment on, is it?' Alistair said. 'Internal problems, not our affair. We can only do what we can to set them straight, get them on board. So how did your meeting with Pym go? What's he like?'

'Old and frail but still very bright. He's attended by a devoted young soldier.'

'Not the first young soldier Pym ever met, I suppose.'

'Maybe the last, though.'

'Well, if he dies in the arms of a soldier I suppose you could say that's how he would have wanted to go. He tell you anything good?'

'He started, then he got drunk and sent me away, said I could go back tomorrow.'

'Not a bad beginning, though,' said Alistair, loading a piece of thin toast with caviare. 'Yum, yum, yum,' he said. 'God, I love caviare. Have some?'

But Greg had decided to skip it. He had a bad head after his afternoon's drinking.

'So, you asked him a few things,' Alistair continued. He took a swig of vodka. 'Did he ask you anything?'

Greg stared at him. The question seemed to indicate that Alistair was a jump ahead, but he decided not to reveal that Pym had asked for help in his campaign to be repatriated. He told Alistair, 'I was supposed to be interviewing him.'

'I know,' said Alistair, 'but Hugh told me he was wondering if the old bugger was going to reopen his bid to spend his last years under an apple tree in Kent, kindly provided by the British Government. It's obvious he might approach you to help fix it for him.'

'Yeah?' said Greg. 'Well, it's an interesting thought.' Just because you're paranoid it doesn't mean they aren't out to get you, he thought. In these days of economic warfare whose side was Alistair on, apart from his own?

'Only I wouldn't get involved,' Alistair went on. He looked up, 'Goodie, here's the food. Look,' he said, 'I'm sorry about this but I've only got time for one course. Something came up unexpectedly this afternoon and I have to go back to the hotel to see a man. It's a bore, but tonight's the only time I can catch him. He's leaving Moscow early tomorrow.' He began on his Stroganoff. 'You stay, of course. I'll take care of the bill.'

'No,' said Greg, who had ordered the same dish. 'This'll do me. I'll go when you do.'

'Nonsense! Get stuck in, enjoy the experience.'

'I'll go back to the hotel and do some reading.'

'Just as you wish,' Alistair said, not pleased.

'Business going well?' Greg enquired.

'So-so,' replied Alistair. 'Everything's clogged over here. It's like ploughing a swamp. I'm only here to open the conversation and try to assess the risks against the advantages.'

'Do you really think you'll set up in Moscow?'

'God knows,' Alistair said. 'I wouldn't like the job, that's for sure.'

'I should say it would be like opening a branch in Dodge City.'

'That's about right,' Alistair agreed.

'But people did it.'

'They certainly did.'

Back at the hotel Greg left Alistair in the bar and went upstairs. First he lay thinking, his arms behind his head, then fell asleep. He was awoken later by a dispute outside his door. He got out of his clothes, put on his Walkman, went back to bed and fell asleep again. At some point in the night he got rid of the headphones and woke early next day to see snowflakes drifting thickly past his window, like a moving white curtain.

Alistair was not at breakfast, had perhaps not been in the hotel overnight. Greg spent the morning sightseeing in the snow, ate lunch, smoked fish, in a basement café, then went to Pym's flat.

Upstairs Ivan, still in his threadbare uniform, barred the door, looking big.

'I've come for my appointment with Mr Pym,' Greg explained, pointing towards the interior of the flat.

'No, he is sick.' Ivan touched his Adam's apple and

coughed, to indicate the nature of the illness. He produced a sheet of paper and handed it to Greg. 'From Mr Pym,' he said. He waved a hand dismissively. Greg stood still. Ivan repeated the gesture. 'Go.'

With no Russian and no alternative, Greg went out into the snow. Outside the building he leaned against the wall and opened the piece of paper. 'Dear Mr Phillips,' it read, in a clear, though weak, hand, 'I regret I'm unable to see you at present. I will telephone your hotel at four.'

It was three thirty. Greg floundered away, peering through the stinging snow. The street was wide, with only a single car crawling by and a few pedestrians, heads down, forcing their way along. As he found himself at the verge of the park two men, stale-smelling, arrived suddenly, one at either side of him. At the same moment each of them grasped one of his forearms. Since he was almost opposite the house containing Pym's flat, Greg considered wrenching himself free, and getting into the lobby. Then he saw himself being murdered there, out of sight of the street.

He saw headlights in the road, slowly approaching on his left. Greg, who had been designated the most valuable player of his college football team for two years, knew how to move forward under restraint. He walked, boots and trousers soaked and freezing, heaving both men into its path. They were strong but surprised by the sudden movement. The car approached, ludicrously slowly, as in a dream. Greg reckoned the men had a few seconds, no longer, to bludgeon him down and rob him before the car was forced to pull up. Or would it steer round the episode? Why not? To his right, now, he heard the engine of another car, the swishing of tyres in snow. Trapped between the two approaching vehicles, he guessed the muggers were uncertain what to do. He wrenched his shoulders forward, sending one of his attackers lurching away. He turned his head and saw him blundering slowly through the snow, in the direction of the park. Then the other released him. The car pulled up in front of Greg and the driver, scarcely visible behind a windscreen where the wipers cleared, then cleared again, the snow driving against it, put his finger on the horn. Opposite Greg the other car slowed. He made out a sign on it that indicated it was a taxi. He went over, opened the door and got in.

A few minutes later, still a little shaken, he went up the hotel's stairs, and entered his room. The phone was ringing. He grabbed it. 'Mr Phillips, Greg, dear boy,' came Adrian Pym's voice, unaffected by any cold or fever as far as Greg could hear, 'I'm afraid it's a little inconvenient to see you now. Well, actually – ever. I don't want to go into details but it's been mentioned to me that I shouldn't talk to you. I feel it would be inadvisable to ignore the advice I've received. Things are very different here, as I'm sure you'll appreciate. I'm terribly sorry, after you've come all this way, but then, of course, you didn't warn me of your arrival . . .'

'Yes, sir,' Greg said, who had done this deliberately. 'What I can't understand, though, is who or why—'

'It's better if you don't know,' Adrian Pym said. 'As I say, Russia is different. And, these days, ever-changing. All is flux, dear boy. I really must ask you not to demand anything of me. The consequences could be quite serious, believe me. But that other matter . . .'

Greg sighed, depressed. 'Trust me,' he said wearily, struck that he was still exchanging the word 'trust' with Pym, the traitor.

'I hope I can, dear heart,' Pym said, then broke the connection.

'Shit,' said Greg. He looked round at his luxurious room, steaming hot, at the reproduction of a painting of a group of tough-looking medievals in furs and jewels on the wall. 'Shit,' he said again. He hadn't even had the chance to ask Pym what he had meant when he called Sally a 'stay-behind'. What was that?

He was stripped and standing in a pool of his soaking clothes when Alistair came in, in a thick coat and fur hat, snow clinging to him.

'Hi,' he said cheerfully, sitting down on an upholstered chair by the window. He took a bottle of Scotch from his pocket. 'You look cold. Drink?'

'Why not?' said Greg. He got dressed and Alistair handed him a glass.

'I'm happy,' he said. 'What a good day. What a good night as well. Russian girls, Russian girls. She had long, thick blonde plaits, like bell-ropes. Reminded me of my sister's schoolfriends – early stirrings – "Oh, Alistair, you beast."' He paused, then said, 'What of Pym?'

'He's been warned off, couldn't see me,' said Greg. 'Who the hell would be doing that?'

'Secret service,' said Alistair. 'They're still in work, even getting paid, unlike nearly everyone else. They know where the bodies are buried and knowledge is power. It could be very complicated, Greg.'

'Lay off?'

Alistair said, 'That would be my advice.' He sounded grave.

'Some guys tried to mug me, or worse,' Greg said, and told him what had happened.

'I don't suppose it had anything to do with Pym,' Alistair said, 'though it might have – this place is a minefield. I suppose we'll never know. So what now?'

'I'll try to rearrange my flight and go back,' Greg said. 'There's no point in hanging around here spending more money. I'll cut my losses. I got something, even if it was only confirmation of what Bruno, my other contact, told me. And I saw Pym. I guess that's not bad.'

'I suppose it isn't,' said Alistair. 'This is getting quite interesting, isn't it?'

Greg was able to bring his return flight forward a day or two, but still had time to kill in Moscow. He spent the next few days in solitary contemplation of paintings, icons, churches, great buildings. All was bold, wild and strange.

30

At La Vie the sound of the bombardment silenced the band. The basement walls shook. Cora was sitting at her table, drinking brandy imperturbably with a venerable politician in a wing collar. 'I can hear my poor old hotel up there shaking like a jelly,' she told him. 'It's high time it stopped.'

'I've been meaning to mention it to Herr Hitler,' said her companion.

Vi was under a table, clinging to an air commodore and gripping Sally with her free hand. She said, 'Jack's at home with Ted, but Ted's got to go off on early shift.'

'He won't leave Jack in the middle of a raid,' Sally said. 'They can't keep it up that long, anyway.'

'Can't they?' said Vi.

'They only have so much fuel,' the air commodore said, 'then they have to turn back. Of course,' he added, 'they can send a second wave.'

'And a third,' said Vi grimly.

'We'll drive them off, never fear,' he told her.

'It's all right, dear, you don't have to try to cheer me up,' Vi assured him.

In Pimlico Ted Simcox was on the stairs with his arm round the young woman from one of the two flats downstairs. His little brother Jack was asleep on a pile of blankets at the foot of the stairs. An elderly woman, who had come up from the basement holding a tin tray with a teapot, milk, sugar and cups on it, stepped past him and said, 'Here we are.'

There was a whistling sound, very close. The young woman stiffened in Ted's arms and buried her head in his shoulder. The woman with the tea froze.

There was an enormous crash, the walls and floor shook, glass shattered, as if every window in the house had been blown out. The coloured panes at the top of the front door cascaded on to the tiles below. Through the gaps, smoke and fire were visible. The woman with the tray walked up a few stairs. 'I think that was a direct hit on the house opposite,' she said. 'They're Poles, mostly.' The eyes of the other two were on the gaps in the window frames of the front door. She turned, 'Oh dear,' she said. 'That's number forty, all right. Don't you start rushing over there. Let the firemen handle it.'

'I wasn't going to,' Ted said. 'No point in being a hero and getting killed with Jack to look after.'

'Better a live coward than a dead hero, that's what I say,' she remarked, putting the tray on the stairs. 'Not that I'm calling you that, of course.' She poured the tea, with a slightly shaky hand, then glanced back. 'Pity. I liked them coloured panes. Never be able to replace them now.'

'I'll see if I can get some glass tomorrow. It'll only be plain, of course,' said Ted, taking a cup. 'Here you are, Mrs Hedges. Have a cup of tea.' The young woman straightened up and took the tea, but as she did so another bomb, further off, fell and her hand wobbled so that half the contents of the cup spilt in the saucer and on to her lap. The older woman listened. 'I think they're going back,' she said. 'Here – drink your tea. It'll calm you down.' She poured more into the cup.

'I'm sorry,' said the young woman. 'It's my nerves. They're getting worse.'

'It's not surprising, in your condition,' said the older woman. 'My goodness, you do look pale. Try to keep calm. Where's your husband now?'

'Africa – they call it Syria.'

'You can say that for this war – you certainly catch up with your geography,' the woman said. There was a chorus of crashes.

'I reckon I ought to go and wake the woman upstairs,' Ted said.

'She won't be pleased. She don't want to talk to anybody, air-raid or no air-raid. She's a bit peculiar.'

'You said they were going away, Mrs Brown,' the young woman said.

But the bombardment went on. 'That's Victoria Station,' said Ted. 'It'll be chaos in the morning.' Mrs Hedges was hiding against his chest once more.

'Your old man'll get some leave soon, I expect,' Ted told her. 'Maybe you'll have had the baby by then. Think of the look on his face when he sees you both.'

166

'Then you'll be able to sleep in the hall, with the rest of us,' Mrs Brown told her.

There was another loud screaming whistle. She spoke on, to cover the noise, 'Romantic, eh? You and your husband, the baby, me, this gentleman here and his sister—'

There came another horrendous crash, followed by a vibration.

'Bloody hell,' said Ted, looking at Jack's sleeping form, huddled in blankets. 'It beats me how that boy can sleep through all this.'

'Used to it,' said the older woman. 'Kids can get used to anything.'

They could hear bombers overhead. There were more explosions.

'This is the worst raid I've ever been in,' said Ted. 'If it's like this all over, there won't be much left of the docks tomorrow. I'm still worried about that woman upstairs.'

There was a loud hammering on the door. 'Anybody in? Open up!' Mrs Brown went to the door. A black-faced fireman stood in the entrance. Beyond him others were playing hoses over the flaming house opposite. 'Someone's seen an incendiary land on your roof,' he said.

'Bloody hell!' cried Ted. He let go of the young woman and swept Jack into his arms.

'We'll put it out, mate,' the fireman reassured him. 'Just let us get the hose upstairs.' He and another fireman ran up with it.

'There's a woman asleep in the top room,' called Mrs Brown.

'Don't worry, we won't wake her!' one of the firemen cried.

And the raid continued. The firemen came down. They quickly drank a cup of tea handed to them in the hall by Mrs Brown. One observed, 'That woman upstairs wasn't pleased. You'd have thought we'd come to rob her. We're on the roof, she's down below the trap-door, swearing at us and all sorts. There's a bit of a hole in your roof now. Could have been worse.'

'What about . . . ?' Mrs Brown asked, nodding at the house opposite, where firemen were still working on the blaze. Rescuers were already digging in the rubble. One stood by, holding a mongrel dog.

'Looks bad,' he said. 'Soon as it cools down we'll get Spot the Wonder Dog on to it. He can find anybody who's buried but it's too hot for his paws at the moment.'

This cheered pale-faced Jack. 'Can I watch?' he asked.

'Better not,' said the fireman, with a warning look at Ted. 'Well, time to go. Thanks for the tea, missus.'

Overhead the moon shone brightly, a bomber's moon, gleaming over the burning house, the firemen, the digging rescuers and the man with the dog, which strained at its leash. Planes sounded overhead, flashes shooting from their guns. Golden ack-ack fire pierced the dark sky. The horizon was orange.

Mrs Brown, Ted and Jack, hand in hand, stood near the front door, Mrs Hedges behind them on the stairs.

'You bastards,' said Ted, looking up. 'Pardon my French, Mrs Brown.'

Mrs Brown had lived for thirty years in the house,

which had been emptied of its established inhabitants in the course of a year. She liked the Simcoxes. 'It's excusable,' she said.

'You said bastard, Ted,' Jack said. 'And you said the Germans was only the same as us – fighting the bosses' war.'

'Yeah, the bastards,' said Ted.

And as if on cue the All Clear sounded.

'I can't believe it's over,' said Mrs Hedges weakly, from the stairs.

'It's been a night and a half,' Ted agreed. 'Better get some sleep, I suppose,' he said to the younger woman. 'Will you be all right, love?'

'Yes, thank you, Mr Simcox,' she said.

'You'd better call me Ted, seeing as we've spent the night together.'

She gave a wan smile.

'Still no sign of the mysterious lady upstairs,' he said. 'How can she be managing, with a hole in the roof?'

'She's a funny one,' said Mrs Brown, and they all went to bed, to sleep for a few hours until morning.

Vi and Sally came arm in arm through the dawn as the firemen were still putting out the last blazes. The silent streets were dusty and blocked with rubble, warm from the fires. Curtains still hung at the windows of roofless buildings, a bed hung half-way out from the broken floor of a house. Ambulances passed. A soldier, with a kit-bag over his shoulder, walked up the road, his arm round a woman with a pram.

Here and there was the smell of fire. Elsewhere was the

acrid yet stale odour of old buildings suddenly destroyed, as though the stench of years of food, sweat and breath had been released from the brickwork.

The sun was rising into the blue summer sky. As they turned into the corner of Vi's street, Sally grasped her friend's shaking arm, but although two houses in the road had been destroyed and several others damaged, Vi's was intact.

Vi stopped in the road outside. 'Thank God,' she said, looking up at the house. She grasped Sally's arm. 'My knees have gone. I can't move.'

In the silent house Ted and Jack were asleep in the same narrow bed in one room. Sally and Vi made themselves as comfortable as possible in the other, which contained the curtained-off kitchen. Vi was on the divan she normally slept on, Sally on the couch.

Next morning, Vi was sobbing. Most of a week's rations for the three of them – butter, bacon, tea, a bag of sugar, three eggs and a jar of jam – had gone from the food cupboard. Her winter coat had also disappeared. After they had discovered that the mysterious upstairs tenant had vanished – there was a view of blue sky through a hole three feet across in the roof and the carpet was soaked with water – they decided she had crept down after all the others had fallen asleep, stolen into the Simcoxes' rooms, put their food and Vi's coat into one of her suitcases, and left.

For Vi, somehow, this was the last straw. Crying, she said she couldn't go on. Mrs Brown made them all a cup of tea and they drank it round her big polished table in the basement flat. At last Vi calmed down and said, 'How could she? How could anybody be so rotten? I tell you, though, any more of this and our Jack's going to be evacuated again. There's no way we can go on like this – bombed every night, people's homes being destroyed, gas and electric mains shattered night after night. We'll all end up sleeping under the stars and cooking over open fires in the street. That's what'll happen. That's what it'll be like.'

'I don't want to go back to that vicar,' Jack protested. 'It was horrible.'

'You'll do what you're told,' Vi told him grimly. 'There's a war on. As for you and Sally and Joe Stalin,' she said to Ted, 'what's Russia doing for us? Helping Hitler out in case there aren't enough Germans to do the work, that's what.' Now she turned to Sally. 'Don't talk to me about Russia.'

'They'll fight if they have to,' said Sally.

'Well, they aren't going to have to, are they?' Vi cried impatiently. 'No one has to, only us. That's who there is – us British, and the Canadians and Australians and so forth and the Indians and several Africans and Jamaicans and a few people who managed to escape Hitler.'

'We've got the Gurkhas,' Jack said.

'Gurkhas! We'd need a million Gurkhas,' she said. 'It's like a horrible nightmare – all of us crowded on this little island with all the Germans throwing themselves at us.'

'Don't spread alarm and despondency, Vi,' Ted told her.

'It's the truth, though, isn't it?' Vi demanded.

'Something'll turn up,' Sally said.

'Oh, shut up,' said Vi, crying again.

But after that last, shattering night the raids diminished. Hitler had attacked Russia and needed much of his air force for the war in the east.

31

After less than a week in Moscow Greg returned with his head full of the images of domes against dark skies filled with swirling snow, the great river – and the wasted, lined face of the old traitor in his great carved chair in the gloomy flat.

Alistair Bradshaw, bright-eyed and fresh-faced under his fur hat, had seen him off at the airport, bidding him goodbye with a firm handshake and a friendly, 'Just as well to bail out, Greg. Frankly, I was worried about you and Pym from the first. Then, a couple of days ago, your name came up in discussions I was having with a trade guy here.'

'What? A Russian? What did he say?' asked Greg.

'He knew we were together. They've still got eyes everywhere. It's an old Russian custom.'

'What did he say?' insisted Greg.

'He just said he'd heard a friend of mine was visiting a long-standing guest of theirs, an Englishman. And that he didn't think it was a good idea. Would I have a word?

By that time Pym had backed off and you'd decided to return to the UK so I didn't think it was necessary to mention it to you. But maybe you should know. I wouldn't worry about it,' he reassured Greg. 'It's all meaningless paranoia. Russia's not a happy place. But there might be some repercussions, that's why I'm telling you now. I'd forget all about Pym, if I were you. You wouldn't want to get stranded between whatever two or three parties he's manipulating for his own purposes.'

'Is that what this official said?' asked Greg.

'Don't worry,' Alistair said. He smiled his broad, deceiver's smile and clapped Greg on the back. 'Goodbye – it's been fun.'

'Thanks for bringing me along,' Greg said, picked up his bag and made for the departure gate, feeling much like a child forced to leave a birthday party knowing that once he has left the others will go on playing games and eating cake.

On the long return flight he thought about Pym and his request for assistance in getting back to Britain. It was probably no more than the age-old Russian instinct for repression and secrecy that had caused the authorities to ban Pym from talking to him. Alistair Bradshaw's part in this was obscure. Had he informed the authorities about Greg's visit to Pym? Greg would not have been surprised at such collusion, designed to create a favourable atmosphere between Alistair and those with whom he was trying to trade. Had he got stuck between Russian bureaucracy and Western capitalism? But what about Pym? And would he ever manage to write the book? But at least he'd done it, he thought, gone to Moscow, met Pym, however unsatisfactorily. He'd done it!

However, by the time he was putting his bags down in his cold, lonely little flat he had begun to feel depressed and rather confused.

There was a message from Katherine – 'I think I'm going to be able to get to London for a week. Do ring, lots of love.' There was another from his head of department, asking him how he was getting on and saying he had some material Greg might be interested in. Had Greg a fax machine? His mother had called but, thanks to a meandering message from a distraught woman Greg did not know, his tape had run out and her voice on the machine stopped suddenly.

He talked to his mother and was on his way out to hire the cheapest fax machine when his phone rang. It was Bruno Lowenthal, with a heavy cold.

'Why don't I come over?' Greg asked. 'I can bring you in anything you need.'

'No, thank you. Fiona's helping me.'

'Look,' said Greg, on an impulse. 'I think I really need to talk to you. I've been in Moscow. I've seen Pym. He wants to come back. He wants me to help him fix it.'

There was a silence. Then Bruno said flatly, 'You'd better come over. Bring some oranges and lemons.'

Greg made his way down Holland Park Avenue and turned into the street where Bruno lived.

As he waited for him to answer his door, a woman in a mac and headscarf was putting something in a dustbin in the basement. She turned and went inside her flat, followed by a huge black cat, which had bounded down from the pavement through her railings.

Bruno, wheezing, opened the front door. He was wearing a long, elaborate red dressing-gown with black frogging. He led the way slowly upstairs and, on gaining his sitting-room, sat down heavily in his chair.

'Can I get you anything?' Greg asked.

'Can you make a hot toddy?' Bruno asked.

Greg went into the immaculate small kitchen next to the room where Bruno sat. He returned to the room with a steaming jug of whisky, lemon slices, sugar and honey.

'You'll join me?' Bruno said.

'Just a small one,' said Greg.

Once again he was sitting opposite an old man, drinking at an unusual hour of the day, not knowing quite what was going on.

Bruno drank a draught of the toddy and then asked, 'So, how's Pym?' He was evidently hoping for bad news.

'Pretty sick,' Greg said. 'And frail. He lives in a dignified old building near the Pushkin Museum. He's attended by a Russian soldier in a worn-out uniform.'

'He'll have fallen on his feet as usual,' Bruno commented. 'Tell me, why didn't you say you were going to Moscow?'

'It was a sudden impulse. The brother of a friend was going. He had some influence in the visa department. It seemed too good to pass up.'

'So you thought you'd go and find things out for yourself?' asked Bruno.

'That's what I'm here for,' Greg said laconically. He

felt that Bruno was annoyed that he'd gone to another person for information, as if his puppet was getting out of control.

'And?' prompted Bruno.

Greg told him.

'You should have spoken to me first,' Bruno told him. 'There's a lot you don't know.'

'And some I might have known, if you'd told me,' Greg responded coolly.

'I'm keeping many secrets, yes,' Bruno said reproachfully. 'But not all mine – few of them mine, in fact.'

Greg opened his mouth to ask what he meant, but Bruno went on, 'I'm a little upset with you. You go without saying, now you're back, and Pym has conned you into agreeing to do something you should not do, which no one wants you to do and which will not advance your interests in any way. Believe me when I tell you that. And you, I suppose, have given your word so you must do as you promised.'

'Well, no, I don't,' Greg admitted. 'At first I thought I should. Now I see I've told a very tricky character I'll do something for him, without knowing exactly what the results will be. I don't know if I should go ahead.'

'You're here on a visitor's visa, I suppose. This could get you thrown out,' Bruno observed. 'Then where is your book?'

Greg looked at him steadily. 'The thought had occurred to me.'

'I'm glad,' Bruno told him. 'Luckily the Americans are like the Germans, direct and not ashamed to act out of self-interest and say so. Here, it is different.' He began to cough in a fit that moved his whole body and seemed about to tear him apart. It ended, and he lay back weakly.

'Have you seen a doctor?' Greg asked.

But Bruno, swallowing toddy, just shook his head. He recovered his breath and said, 'That fool? No. A cold is a cold. So – you've decided not to do what Pym asked?'

'That's right,' said Greg. 'But what I really wanted to ask him was if he knew where Sally Bowles was, if she's alive. There's no record of her death at Somerset House.'

'Why would Pym know, in Moscow?'

'I guess there isn't much Adrian Pym doesn't know.'

Bruno nodded. 'All right. Now you're here, turn on that machine – I suppose you have it with you – and we shall go on with our story.' The old man spoke for more than an hour, then declared he was tired and wished to sleep.

Greg said goodbye and left. He felt better for having decided to forget Pym's requests.

However, when he got back to his flat he discovered that Pym was still pulling strings. He had been transcribing what Bruno had told him, when his phone rang. He answered it, and heard a woman's voice say, 'Is that Mr Phillips?' When he agreed that it was, she informed him that Sir Peveril Jones was on the line.

Then came a man's voice. 'Mr Phillips? I'm Peveril Jones. I hear you've been abroad and come back with a message for me.'

'Well, yes, sir,' Greg agreed uncertainly. 'I've seen Adrian Pym and he did ask—'

'Good, good,' Sir Peveril broke in. 'Let's not discuss it over the phone, shall we? I wonder, would it be too much trouble for you to have lunch with me at my club one day? We could talk it over there. Are you free at all this week, perhaps?'

Greg, who was free of any social engagements and too off-guard to come up with a good excuse, agreed to meet him on the following day. He put down the phone, realising that not only had Pym outmanoeuvred him from Moscow but that Sir Peveril had railroaded him here in London. Very well, he thought, he'd deliver Pym's message. Then it would be over.

Seconds later, Katherine called. She had arranged to get away – could she stay at the flat? Could she ever! Of course, Greg told her. It was strange, though. It wasn't love any more. So what was it? Sex? Friendship? Maybe they were both lonely. He went back to Bruno's tapes.

32

'By nineteen forty-two America, thank God, was in the war. With that and the German disasters in the Soviet Union, the situation seemed less desperate. But still men died; still there were air-raids. At home we were getting shabby because, as clothes and household things wore out, we were not allowed enough coupons to replace them. We were short of food and fuel. It was dark. Singapore was taken by the Japanese and Malta withstood heavy bombing. Here we were tired.

'There were bad rumours about what was happening to the Jews. The transports to the concentration camps had begun.

'I got a job, driving an ambulance for St George's Hospital. They called up all unmarried women – they could join the services or take over the jobs the men weren't doing and Sally was delivering the post. There was soon a scandal when all the mail for the Belgravia district went out stamped with a crude hammer and sickle. Several residents, including a general from the Boer War and a relative of the King, complained. Sally was held to be implicated in this.

'Anyway, one day in the early part of the summer I had been on duty for thirty hours with one two-hour break. I came back dog-tired in the afternoon and there was Sally fast asleep in her uniform on a sofa, her bare feet with painted toenails dangling over the edge – and very dirty. I went upstairs to my little room, lay down and fell asleep. As I did so I anticipated Briggs coming in unexpectedly, finding me and complaining about my sleeping in my uniform with my shoes still on but, then, what did I care? We were all so tired. We would have killed, sometimes, for sleep.

'I remember thinking, what would happen if Hitler pulled out of Russia and invaded? What was there to stop him? Then I was asleep, but not for long because suddenly there was this terrible noise of shouting in the corridor outside. Now, Pym and Briggs were supposed to be away doing secret work in the country, Julia was in Egypt with Sir Peveril – so why was Sally shouting, outside the bathroom door, "Come out of there, you bastard! For God's sake, don't use all the hot water. We're filthy. Come out, you mean bastard, or I'll come in and kill you!"

'And I was so angry at being woken, at the thought that someone was in the bathroom taking all the hot water that I got up and ran out. There was Sally, hammering on the bathroom door and ordering me over her shoulder, "Break this door down! Just break this door down! He can't have all that water."

'I was so mad that I stood back and kicked the lock of

the door. And Sally shouted, "Bruno's breaking the door down!"

'And then, just as I was aiming another kick and asking Sally, "Who's in there?" a voice said, "Bloody hell," in an indignant way and the door opened. There was Theo Fitzpatrick, looking annoyed, dripping, with a towel round his waist. Behind him, a huge bath of water steamed – you were only supposed to have five inches of water in the bath, to be patriotic and save fuel.

'Sally shouted to me, "Come on!" and pushed past Theo. She started stripping off her clothes. I went past him too – he was astonished – and at the sight of all that wonderful hot water I took off my clothes too. She jumped in and I jumped in after her. Oh, the joy of it! The water, of course.

'Sally and I did have something in common. We both loved cold, clever Englishmen. It's true that in a close relationship Sally – even I – would have been what they called "too much" for them. But, Christ, Greg,' Bruno burst out, 'whether it was sex or love or whatever it was, anybody, everybody was "too much" for them. What the rest of the world called love, they called too much for them.

'Then Sally started grabbing about for the soap and wailing, "Oh, God, Bruno. I've thrown him out of the bath. He'll never forgive me. What do you think I should do? Oh, Bruno." She grasped part of me I might as well not name and said, "Oh, darling, so sorry. Just a mistake. Vast apologies. Please, darling, give me your advice. What can I do? Do you think he'll hate me now?"

'Theo's voice then called from the doorway. "I've taken a pair of Briggs's pants. Is that all right?"

'"Not the silk ones!" I shouted from the bath. I was afraid of Briggs.

'"Don't worry. I'll square it with him."

'"Oh, God, the man I love, in Alexander Briggs's silk drawers." Sally groaned. "I can't bear it – it's so erotic!" She plunged out of the bath. "Theo!" she cried, running naked from the bathroom. When I emerged, there were sounds from Briggs's bedroom. I was horrified – as I've told you, I spent most of my nights in the dressing room next door, unless summoned by my master, and even then he'd often send me back when he'd finished with me. And now this desecration, as you might call it.

'Downstairs the kitchen was in chaos. Breakfast had consisted of the last egg, tea and plum brandy, which Theo must have brought with him. And, of course, broken glass all over the sink, draining board and much of the floor. I set to work to clear up before going back on duty again, worrying about Briggs coming back without warning to find his silk underwear gone, and his bedroom occupied. Sally and Theo did not emerge.

'I went back on duty. That day from a flat down by the river they pulled out twins, dead in their cot, which had been smashed by a falling ceiling. The parents, who had survived, stood outside the ruined house sobbing. The woman had their cat, a big tabby, in her arms and her tears were plopping down into the animal's fur.

'Funnily enough, though it wasn't funny really, the raids weren't so bad after that for a week or two.

'And Theo was back. At that time he was officially in the Army, but only loosely attached. We knew, or thought

183

we knew, that earlier he'd been in Yugoslavia helping the partisans there. The plum brandy, with its Serbo-Croat label, certainly supported this theory. Now he was on leave, awaiting orders, he said. During the early summer of 'forty-two he courted Sally, not that he hadn't won her many years before – and again, and again – but still, he courted her.

'So there were a few weeks of another of Sally's honeymoons.

'The group at Pontifex Street became one huge party based on the Gargoyle Club, or La Vie, and ending up in the early hours back at the house with armfuls of bottles.

'That was about when Sally and Theo would often make an appearance. Sally had to get up early for her job, and was still performing at La Vie, but she and Theo spent a lot of the day making love in her room. Briggs didn't like it, but surprisingly he made few objections. I always thought he and Theo had a peculiar relationship. At the time I believed it was based on something from the past. Now I wonder if Theo was Briggs's spymaster, his controller.

'So Theo and Sally were there, laughing, talking and making love until the early morning, and then Theo, who needed little sleep, would be up again at nine or ten, ready for a good talk with Briggs or, more likely, Pym, who was always late in the morning with a hangover, and anyone else who had stayed overnight. Geoffrey Forbes was often there and Charles Denham, with a Bohemian sort of girl who was after him and often caught him when his romance with the American woman was even more on the rocks than usual.

'You'd get up in the morning, as often as not, fall over a

kit-bag left at the top of the stairs, bump into some confused soldier or sailor in only his trousers, who was trying to find the bathroom, walk down and find that the sitting room contained three or four sleeping figures, go into the kitchen and hear these extraordinary conversations between Theo, Pym, Briggs, Forbes and Denham going on, about rows in the cabinet, partisan activities in Greece, strikes in the coal mines. It was very indiscreet. It was a ferment. "One-word answers to this question please," Theo said once, to an audience of Briggs, Pym, a Polish airman who had shot down thirty German planes, and Sally, back from her early delivery. "What will you do when Hitler wins the war?"

'Pym replied, "Drink," and Briggs, "Organise."

'The Polish airman replied, "Return."

'"Sally?" Theo asked, turning to her.

'"Loot," she responded, adding, "The shops, darling, for clothes and shoes."

'As the latest Mrs Thing came through the door – her name was Wendy Buck – Theo said, "What will you do when Hitler invades, Mrs – er—?'

'From the sink, where she went immediately to start washing up, she said, "Turn on the gas, I suppose. Do myself in. Funny, we're out of Jeyes' Fluid."

'"I'm saving it up to drink when Hitler marches in," claimed Pym.

'Sally's eyes were on Theo – they almost always were. '"What will you do, Theo?"

'"Oh, run," he said.

'"Where to?"

'"America – where else?"

'"Can I come too?" she asked – silly girl.

'He went round the table and kissed her ear. "You'll have your looted fur coat to keep you warm."

'Sally smiled at him, but she wanted more, more than Theo would give – probably more than he *could* give. Funnily enough it was Pym who called him a bastard.

'"During these great movements of history there's no time for personal relationships," Theo remarked.

'"Which is all right for you because you've never had one," Pym told him.

'Theo gave him a nasty look and said, "Look who's talking, duckie."

'Sally went upstairs. She was upset. But she came down, dressed, made-up and smiling and made Theo take her out to lunch at the Ritz and soon they seemed happy again, happy enough. After all, at that moment everything was temporary and conditional, there simply was no future to plan. It's always so in war, I suppose.

'Sally was in love – she glowed, the sun shone, they went away for the weekend to stay in a castle in Scotland. It was a dream for her,' said Bruno Lowenthal's voice on the tape. 'Theo so handsome, so clever, so bold, Sally with her feeling of being loved and protected. Nobody mentioned the baby, of course.'

Here Greg, transcribing busily in the damp Bloomsbury flat with its hissing gas fire, looked up and thought, why not? Sally's baby was a very big blank in the story. And where was the baby now? He turned on the machine again and the harsh, accented voice continued.

'I remember them coming in one night from the Café de

Paris, where they'd been dancing, Sally in a sequinned red dress, very good cut, very low, Theo a fine figure in a dinner jacket. They stood in the doorway at Pontifex Street, he with his arm round her shoulder, and they glowed. A golden couple, they had come through the darkness on foot, with just a little torch, and it was as if they had absorbed all that darkness and worked it into light. They made everyone else in the room, the two Army girls, the air commodore, the aide to the exiled Yugoslav king, drab and dull and stiff, like shop-window models. Theo had that effect.

'Poor Sally, silly cow. He left two days later for an undisclosed place and she didn't see him or hear from him again for more than a year.

'All right,' Bruno had told Greg, 'I liked and didn't like Sally, but Sally in love – poor Sally – she wasn't like the normal English rose. Not like that bitch Julia, who seemed all cream but underneath was determined to make Peveril leave his wife. Sally lacked a skin. She was naïve. She thought Theo was like her, all for love, but, of course, he wasn't. Underneath that careless charm he was like a clever boy, ambitious, competitive, emotionally neutral. The perfect spy, in fact. He couldn't afford to get into any trouble.

'After he left, Sally was very depressed. Theo'd gone without saying what she wanted to hear. I came across her crying into her gin one night, still in her cabaret dress, makeup running down her face. "There's a war on," she told me. "None of us can commit ourselves beyond tomorrow." Then she broke down. "But it's a bit much, Bruno."

'What could I say? "Silly girl, pull yourself together. Theo's got other targets in his sights" – no, I couldn't tell her that.

'But you see, we'd all overheard Theo on the phone one evening talking to someone and saying, "If you're speaking to Blanche give her my dearest love. Don't forget."

'Pym had been lying in a chair, half drunk, but not too drunk to understand. "Theo's off to Washington," he told Briggs. "He had a fling with Blanche Mencken when her uncle was *en poste* here in London. The Menckens are stinking rich – steel, railroads and automobiles. She's a very pretty girl, too."

'"If he's going to Washington, he'll be keen to find out what the Menckens are up to," Briggs said.

'"Do you think so?" Pym said. "It's not information about the US war effort our hero's after, believe me."

'Then Theo came back into the room. "Washington?" Pym queried.

'Theo didn't deny it. "Nice over there," Pym said. "Fridges, steaks, no rationing, no bombs, all those little inconveniences we're used to."

'"One goes where duty calls," Theo observed, cool as a cucumber.

'Sally came racing in from outside complete with tin hat, gas mask and wearing a soldier's coat. It had been raining. Theo went over and embraced her. "Shall we go out for a dance, darling?"

'"Let's," she cried. It was touching, her open face smiling up at him. They went off, into the darkness, leaving us sitting there like three sad old bachelors. Then, of course, the place began to fill up, as it always did.

'The day after that Theo left.

'Sally plunged,' Bruno reported gloomily. 'After that, she didn't care. It's not that she knew where Theo was. She went on thinking pathetically that he was in some horrible field of war, fighting gallantly with partisans in sheepskin coats, sending messages back to London from caves in the mountains. But even that didn't seem to make any difference. He'd left without giving her any guarantees, or any reassurance that he'd come back for her if he could. She got very depressed.

'Pym used to go about the flat when Sally was there singing, in a fake Irish tenor, "Oh, mother dear, what a fool was I, To kill myself for the creamery boy." What a nasty man he was.'

33

'So for a month,' Bruno said, 'Sally left La Vie each night with a man who wanted her – a Norwegian seaman, a British official, a pilot, on one occasion a nursing sister, she didn't care, she was too drunk. She got good presents, though, a bracelet here, a ring there, little boys were always coming round with flowers, the phone never stopped ringing. The atmosphere in the flat was terrible. Pym and Briggs became very censorious. Pym! Who went through the blackout like Dracula, sinking his teeth into whoever he could find in the darkness. There was never a call or a note from Theo.'

Bruno reflected, 'That was probably what put paid to her chance of the medal she might have been awarded for heroism in France – the night she stood on the table, dancing naked, dead drunk, in front of the Minister of Food and the exiled King of Yugoslavia.

'Then she got very quiet. She went to Pym, Briggs and many others. She had to contact Theo. Was there any way? She was very pale and vomiting in the mornings.

Nothing was said, but we all knew she was pregnant. Of course, everyone had to pretend they didn't know where he was, but I know Briggs wrote to Theo in Washington giving him the bad news. There was no reply. It was a horrible episode. No one could stand it. I told Julia one day she should speak to Sally but all she said was, "My God, why on earth should I? It's got nothing to do with me." Finally I think the nurse helped out. Anyway, she and Sally spent a day or two in Sally's garret, after which Sally emerged, pale and shaky, and went back to work and we all went on pretending nothing had happened.

'She was pretty low during that autumn. She'd never had a voice, as I've told you, only what today they would call an attitude, and when that went, Cora thought of giving her the sack. I can remember her going round the flat in her pyjamas, covered in a soldier's great-coat she had got from somewhere, singing in a tinny high soprano,

> 'I'm going to meet him today,
> Oh, I'm in a tizz
> And the people that I meet
> When I'm going down the street
> Will say you are a bloody fool.'

She'd stand in the kitchen, knocking up the wartime recipes – unspeakable things, sheep's head broth, swede and carrot pie. She'd hung four thrushes in the larder for days. I came across her frying them. When I asked her what she was doing, because when our rations ran out at Pontifex Street we just went out or ate in restaurants – which was why at the end of the war Pym owed Briggs four thousand pounds in food bills – Sally just said, "It's for the war effort," and burst out crying. She lost weight, got paler and paler. Poor Sally.

'You see Theo, like so many so-called lady-killers, specialised in confusing women. He didn't know what he was doing, and didn't want to, so he made no vows, no promises for the future and, when he began to feel unhappy or uncomfortable, he ran. It was hard on Sally. He was her first love but she never understood him and she was never wise enough to decide she must forget him. If she had, he would have sensed it and arrived a week later – that's what those men are like.

'Anyway,' said Bruno, 'she was so depressed that when her father rang and asked her to go home for Christmas, she went. I don't think it was a success.'

34

The Christmas party at Glebe House in 1942 consisted of Harold and Geneviève Jackson-Bowles, Sally's sister Betty and her husband Gideon Cunningham, their two boys aged five and seven and Sally's old Nanny, Miss Adelaide Trotter, who had come back to look after Gisela. There was, of course, Gisela herself, now aged eighteen months, walking and talking.

Perhaps it was lucky that Sally had only a two-day break because she was needed back at the post office after Boxing Day.

She arrived for the family gathering late on Christmas Eve after one of those long war-time journeys, in a darkened train full of servicemen, which had stopped on a siding outside Reading for two hours while a munitions train made its slow way past them.

Geneviève Jackson-Bowles was unhappy. Before the war, the household had included a cook, two maids and a gardener-handyman. Now the gardener had been called up and the maids were doing factory work in Birmingham. Only the cook and Miss Trotter were there, and Geneviève's hitherto impeccable house was suffering from the staff shortage. It was generally held by the family that Sally's inconsiderate dumping of Gisela there was to blame for all difficulties and shortages. Gisela, dark, bright-eyed and volatile, spent much of her time in the nursery with Miss Trotter. She was asleep when Sally arrived. On Christmas Day, Sally gave her an inordinately large doll, acquired through one of Cora's mysterious back-door visitors, and spoiled the atmosphere of war-time misery and deprivation by producing, from the same source, two pairs of nearly new roller skates for her nephews. Such things were now unheard of. 'Black market, I'm afraid,' Geneviève was heard murmuring to her son-in-law.

On Christmas morning Miss Trotter, Sally and Gisela went out for a walk, Gisela trailing the doll, which was nearly as big as she was.

'You don't look very happy,' said Miss Trotter. 'Can't you at least try to look as if you're enjoying yourself?'

'Theo's left me again,' complained Sally.

'That might be the sixth or seventh time,' the woman who had brought her up commented remorselessly. 'I wonder if you're entitled to say he was ever really with you. I warned you about him when you were sixteen. Never mind,' she added, more kindly, 'one day you'll get fed up with him and settle down with someone nice.'

'I don't think so,' Sally said.

'I do,' said Miss Trotter firmly. 'But with the war on, and in London where things are so terrible, perhaps I shouldn't say this but I suppose the best thing you can do is get as much fun as you can, while you can.'

Sally grinned. 'You're a terrible woman, Trot.' She looked at the little figure running ahead of them down the lane. 'Thank goodness you came to look after little Geezer. She's a sweetheart and it's all your doing.'

It might have been expected that at this point Miss Trotter would have made some reference to the influence of heredity on temperament, but she did not.

'That's partly why I'm here,' said Sally. 'There's something I must tell you about Gisela. I daren't tell anybody else, but just in case I get hit by a bus—'

Miss Trotter looked at her calmly. 'You'd better let me know what it is then, hadn't you?' So Sally did.

There was a goose for Christmas dinner, and a Christmas pudding, and much talk of shortages. Sally smoked right through the meal. Her mother stiffened every time she lit up but said nothing. Over the port and nuts the argument broke out. The younger of Betty Cunningham's boys was being forced now to wear his older brother's outgrown clothes. 'I used to give them to the charwoman,' Betty mourned. 'Now I haven't even got a charwoman.'

'It's a bit easier down here in the country, though,' remarked Sally. 'There's more food, and so forth.'

'I feel I can complain at nothing when I think of the troubles of France,' Geneviève said.

'They're probably all right, Maman, unless something's gone very wrong recently,' said Sally, who had been drinking her father's whisky since she had come in from the walk.

'I find that remark a little curious,' said Gideon, Sally's brother-in-law. 'I can't imagine how dreadful it would be to think of your family under German occupation.'

'All I'm saying, Maman, is that the du Tours are all right. They go to and fro between Paris and the farm and old Jean comes up on a bike with provisions when they're in Paris and they've still got Célestine. The last time I saw Paris, all was tickety-boo in the *faubourg*.'

'I can't understand what you're saying, Sally,' said Geneviève. 'If you mean to be reassuring, I don't think such remarks are of help. In fact, I find them rather unsympathetic.'

'Perhaps Sally's heard something,' Harold Jackson-Bowles said. 'If you have, Sally, perhaps you could tell us exactly what it is.'

'I get news,' said Sally, who, since her coup of the previous year, had special privileges. 'They're alive and all right,' she continued. 'That's all they let me know.'

'You might have told me,' Geneviève said.

'It's very hush-hush,' Sally said.

'It can't be that hush-hush if they tell you,' Betty stated, expressing everyone's thoughts.

'They give me the information because a year and a half ago they dropped me into France by parachute.'

'Oh, really, Sally,' Geneviève said impatiently. 'How much have you had to drink?'

'Tell us, Sally,' her father said.

'I don't believe it,' said Betty. 'Why you?'

'Lots of people are doing their bit,' said Sally.

Geneviève now sat like a statue, her hand on her heart. 'Have you really seen them, Madeleine and Bertrand?'

'Just Benoît. I was only there for an hour. I wasn't exactly a visitor. Charles and Benoît were going out killing Germans on the quiet. Benoît broke his leg running away. Otherwise, everything was fine. And I heard recently Uncle Bertrand did a big operation on an important German and saved his life.'

'I suppose one must live,' said Geneviève, 'even in such terrible times.'

'You'd think he could have arranged for the knife to slip,' said Harold Jackson-Bowles.

'I still can't see why they sent you, Sally,' said Gideon Cunningham.

'I had to look up an old boyfriend,' Sally said. 'He's a Nazi now. I can't say any more – it's frightfully secret.'

35

'That put rather a damper on Christmas Day,' Sally had reported to Bruno afterwards. 'You'd have thought I'd done something dreadful. I think they felt terribly guilty, really, making all those complaints about food, when I know Maman has a man who cycles round with all sorts of things hidden in his bicycle basket. And Gideon had gone on and on about his bad knee preventing him from service. Poor old Daddy is the only active one, really. He's charging in and out of his factory all week, pumping out uniforms for the Army and Navy to go and get killed in, but there you are, darling, somebody has to do it. To be utterly totally honest, I got drunker and drunker and I distinctly heard Betty telling Gideon that if I was the sort of person they were sending out on secret missions no wonder the war was going on so long. Honestly, how foul. Little Geezer's very sweet, though – but, my God, I'm glad to be back. Even Pym's face cheers me up so you can tell how ghastly it was *chez* Jackson-Bowles.'

Bruno observed, 'I think that moment marked when she started getting over Theo's defection and the consequent abortion.

'Then spring was on the way – and it really was. The Germans had had to surrender in Stalingrad, the Russians were driving them back, and there were victories in North Africa. The RAF was bombing Germany instead of the other way about.

'There were still raids, though. One evening we were in La Vie when there was a bad one. The place rocked with the explosions. Few people were there – Pym, Briggs and Charles Denham were playing poker with another man at one table, Cora was sitting with an elderly beau, drinking gin, and a couple of American colonels. Nobody was very happy, and the musicians were slumping. However, at a certain point a young American corporal, coloured soldier as he'd have been called in those days, stood up and went to the piano. He started playing, "Bye Bye, Blackbird" above the sound of the bombardment. Sally came ducking in then in her tin hat. She'd run through the raid from Pontifex Street and grinned when she saw him. She went over and began to sing the words "Pack up all my cares and woes, here I go, Singing Low, Bye Bye, Blackbird". Then the All Clear sounded, Vi turned up to do her act and, without a word it seemed, Sally and the soldier left.'

Greg heard his own surprised voice on the tape. 'An American serviceman? Black?'

'Yes,' came Bruno's voice. 'Eugene Hamilton. A GI. He was an artist and,' came Bruno's voice, with gloomy satisfaction, 'black, *ein Schwarz*.'

Greg heard himself saying, 'Well, I'll be damned.'

And that was the point at which Greg's doorbell at Everton Gardens rang.

36

Katherine was in the doorway in a thick coat, woolly hat and scarf, her eyes and cheeks glowing. She leaped towards Greg and embraced him warmly in the gloomy tiled entrance. Greg, seizing her joyfully, was nevertheless a little surprised at her enthusiasm.

They took the lift, kissing, up to the flat. 'It's wonderful to see you,' she said, when they were inside. 'And, look, I've brought all this food.' And she produced from her holdall a plastic carrier bag. 'A lovely leg of lamb.'

She went to the kitchen and began to put away the food. 'It looks so *clean*,' she cried. 'It was life-threatening when Dominic was here.'

Back in the living room she looked round. 'It's a bit grim, I suppose. Dominic doesn't care.'

'Well, you brighten the place up,' he said, kissing her. 'I have a plan. Let's go to bed, then out to dinner. The lamb can wait.'

Greg's was the plan they adopted. Lying contentedly in

his narrow bed, Katherine said in his ear, 'Ooh, it's so good to be here. At this time of year Cambridge is so chilly and dull. I had to get away.'

'How's your research going?'

'So-so. You know how it is, nine parts slog. How's Sally?'

'It's good,' Greg said, surprising himself a little by his statement. 'I'm transcribing the latest batch of stuff Bruno Lowenthal told me. I know half the time he's putting me on, but the other half he comes up with some amazing tales. My problem's going to be cross-checking. I don't want to produce a novel by Bruno Lowenthal, which he's been slowly constructing for himself over fifty years.'

'Is that your impression?' she said.

'It's my worry.'

'Oh,' she said, tightening her arm round his shoulders, 'it's so good here. How will I ever make myself go back to Cambridge?'

They drank a lot over a cheerful Italian meal in Soho and Greg relaxed. Up to then he had not been aware of how loneliness and distance from home had affected him. This he told Katherine. He confessed also about his almost abortive trip to Russia with Alistair Bradshaw.

Katherine was impressed. 'That was a bold move.'

'I got tired of Lowenthal. He's helpful and he's fairly friendly, but it's always like I'm an animal he's keeping on a chain. He makes sure that as soon as I start feeling relaxed about things the chain goes tight again. And I needed to check his story. One source is not enough.'

'Perhaps going to Moscow with Alistair wasn't the best way. He's bound to attract attention and he's got some funny contacts.'

'His trip seemed straightforward enough. He was looking into setting up a Moscow branch of the bank.'

'Yes. But whose money will he be handling? Ask yourself – who's got any in today's Russia? It's not the Bolshoi Ballet's account he'll be looking for, is it? Part of his researches will involve talking to some very dubious characters. You must have been watched from the moment you got off the plane. That might not have helped.'

'He was all I had,' said Greg. 'Well, maybe I was deceived by the suit, and the cordial City handshake. You know that style. I guess I didn't expect a guy like Alistair to be hanging out with gangsters.'

Katherine laughed.

'All right,' he said, 'but I'm still a stranger here. I guess you're all desperate, trying to find a new empire to the east.'

'Not an empire. Just some loot.

'Let's go and see Hugh Bradshaw,' Katherine suggested. 'I'll give him a call.' She produced a mobile phone from her deep handbag and rang the number.

They found Alistair's brother Hugh in an immense house in Chelsea where he lived with Tamara, a bright-lipsticked brunette who worked as an account executive in an advertising agency. Hugh was writing a film-script, as he always had been since their student days. The films were never made. 'I'd like to move to the country,' he said gloomily, in the very smart drawing-room of the house, which belonged to Tamara's father. There was a Corot on the wall. 'But it's Tamara's job – she doesn't want to commute forty miles a day.'

'At least this house is free,' Tamara remarked, with an edge to her tone.

'So how was Moscow?' Hugh asked. 'Alistair said it didn't last long.'

'The old spy was warned off. I bought the T-shirt and left,' Greg replied.

They talked of old friends briefly, but Tamara, who had not been at university with them, grew restless, so they departed.

'He's only a bird in a gilded cage,' Katherine said of Hugh, in the cab back to Everton Gardens. 'Their father took him and Alistair aside when they came of age and gave them a piece of sage paternal advice. Marry money.'

Hugging her to him, Greg said, 'Very wise. Have you got money, by the way?'

'Not a sausage. I have to live on my pay. How about you?'

'My father advised me to do an honest day's work for a day's pay. That way I could always hold my head up high. I'm not sure that's what I'm doing,' he added.

'Never mind,' she said comfortingly.

Next day, in good spirits, Greg went off to his date with Sir Peveril. He entered the imposing portals of the Athenaeum Club with all the confidence of a man in love, or something like it at any rate.

The porter directed him to the dining room where Sir

Peveril, a thick-set man, awaited him at a table. They shook hands and Greg sat down.

'So good of you to come,' Sir Peveril said.

'Not at all, sir,' Greg said. 'It's a pleasure to see the inside of this wonderful place.' However, he felt wary of this old man, of his charm, of his experience, of attitudes Greg felt he could only guess at.

'Tell me about your book,' Sir Peveril requested.

When Greg mentioned Bruno Lowenthal he got the distinct impression that Sir Peveril found the name unpleasant.

'I don't remember very much about Bruno Lowenthal. I was away from London for most of that period, but I'd take what he says with a considerable pinch of salt. From what I heard, he was ever a romancer, something of a hanger-on too. However, even fantasists can be enlightening, if you sift what they say intelligently.'

Greg nodded assent, but thought that if both Pym and Sir Peveril suggested that Bruno was a liar it didn't have to mean he was. Sir Peveril regarded him steadily from red-rimmed blue eyes. Plates were brought and taken away around them. The harsh, dry voice asked, 'So you saw Pym? And did he seem well?'

'Not really,' Greg told him. 'He's a little weak. He says he's ill.'

'He's not a man who ever looked after himself, to put it mildly,' Sir Peveril said. 'It's a miracle he's still alive, I'm inclined to think. Still drinking, is he?'

'Yes,' Greg told him. 'He's got a soldier looking after him.'

Sir Peveril smiled.

'His message went,' Greg went on, keeping his voice low, 'and I quote him, "Tell Peveril he must get me back to England, with no charges against me. I have copies of documents from Russian sources relating to the whole period during which I was an agent for the Soviet Union. Individuals in Britain never before officially connected with the activities of the defectors are named in them." He told me that with the situation as it was in Russia it had been possible to bribe someone from the old security services to obtain the documents. He said, sir,' Greg reported uncomfortably, 'that he would release this information to the press in Britain and the USA if you did not act to ensure his return to Britain as a free man. He said he'd also require money.'

Sir Peveril frowned. 'Did he show you any of these documents?' he asked.

'He was going to do that on the following day. Of course, I couldn't have read them. Actually, he was going to give me some pages to bring back, as proof. But then he was warned off. He cancelled our appointment and I came home. I had the impression he's dependent on those in power in Russia for everything so I suppose he had no choice.'

'He gave you no information about what he had in his possession?'

Greg shook his head. There was a long pause. Then Sir Peveril said, 'Well, I suppose it shouldn't be any surprise.'

'You do understand that I'm only a messenger, sir. I still can't see why he asked me to represent him,' Greg said. 'He could call you any time.'

'He did. That's why I rang you. But obviously what he originally wanted was to give you something to bring back here, which would make it absolutely clear what he had. He didn't dare send it openly, in case it was intercepted. He gambled that you would not be searched. Of course, if you had been, you would have been in serious trouble.'

'I doubt if I'd have agreed to carry any documents for him,' Greg said.

'He would have offered you something,' Sir Peveril said calmly. 'Something you wanted very much. For example, I take it that you'll be anticipating the book you're about to write will enhance your career. Pym might well have offered you some information, some details that you could not have found elsewhere. That would have been the arrangement – his information in return for your co-operation in carrying the documents. I just use that as an example, it would have been a possible tactic. Pym is a very clever man – they were all very clever. That is how they eluded detection for so long.'

Greg nodded in agreement but said nothing. He was beginning to feel uncomfortable about this meeting. He saw Sir Peveril as part of an old world governed by rules he did not know and did not want to know.

Sir Peveril instantly saw his mood. 'Well,' he said, 'let's eat. I hope your fish is good.'

'Excellent,' said Greg.

'One more thing, though. I doubt if Pym let you go without some personal message to me.'

'That's so,' Greg said awkwardly.

'Spit it out, Mr Phillips. My back is broad.'

'I'm afraid he said that you mustn't think that you personally would escape unharmed if he released the documents in his possession to the world's press.'

Sir Peveril took this in, though his expression did not change. 'He's an old man and he's desperate,' he said. 'Russia can't be a pleasant or comfortable place for a man in his position. The old regime owed him a debt. This one does not. Personally I doubt if he has anything important to communicate. It's a weakness of old men to think the minutiae of the past will excite people. In fact, for a later generation there is nothing more boring than the details of old battles.'

His manner was so easy that Greg half believed him. But he couldn't help thinking that if Pym had hard evidence from the Soviet side of wider involvements in pro-Soviet espionage by the great and the good of Britain – even down to Sir Peveril, a man who sat on many boards and public bodies, who had been a trusted adviser to a previous prime minister – then there was likely to be a big scandal. Pym and Forbes had fled in the fifties, Briggs's early Communist affiliations and war-time work had been mentioned much later, just before his death. And he, Greg, had just heard Bruno Lowenthal say on tape that he thought Theo Fitzpatrick had been running Pym as a spy, which meant that he, Fitzpatrick, could have been acting as a double agent during his posting in Washington. It all sounded seedy and suspicious. Of course, it was all over, as dead as the Gunpowder Plot – but there had been a nest of spies at Pontifex Street, in a house owned by Sir Peveril. Sir Peveril's girlfriend, whom Bruno had said later became his wife, had lived there during that era. If Sir Peveril had known nothing of the activities of his tenants he had been massively deceived. If he had known, and had chosen not to say what he knew, then he'd been either stupid or a traitor. This, Greg concluded, was an affair over but not over. It could not be unimportant to everyone or he wouldn't be here, having lunch at Sir Peveril's invitation. He ventured a question: 'Do you think in the end Pym will be able to return?'

'It's been discussed,' Sir Peveril said. 'It might be possible on purely humanitarian grounds. He's a sick man, after all. And perhaps there have been enough old Nazis living here since the end of the last war to make an old Russian spy, in the present climate, seem more acceptable. History's taken a new turn since Adrian Pym thought he could make a difference.'

'Didn't he betray a lot of people, though?' Greg asked. 'Whole networks were rounded up in Eastern Europe and he was responsible for quite a few deaths and deportations. Wouldn't there be an outcry?'

'The dogs bark but the caravan moves on,' Sir Peveril remarked comfortably, yet he eyed Greg a little coldly.

Greg backed off. 'I guess so,' he said. 'I guess now no one will care much.'

'Of course,' said Sir Peveril, 'he may not get through the winter – I may not. We're all in the hands of the gods.' He smiled, but with no real pretence of friendliness. 'All this is a far cry from Miss Bowles, eh? To whom you're trying to get back. Tell me, have you fallen in love with her yet?'

'No, sir, I haven't.'

'Biographers generally end up loving or hating their subjects, so they tell me.'

'I wonder which is best?' Greg said, and sensing that Sir Peveril was bored with him, he finished his meal, declined coffee and stood up.

Sir Peveril saw him down the steps of the club and Greg headed for the Mall then into St James's Park. There were few people about and he stood under a tree looking out towards the lake. Sir Peveril had gone back for coffee, brandy and then, if Greg knew anything, to make a few strategic phone calls in the matter of Adrian Pym.

'A far cry from Miss Bowles,' Sir Peveril had said, and Greg hoped to God it was.

He did not know that he was standing under the same tree where, so long ago, back in 1943, a girl and a soldier had been alone together for the first time.

37

They sat on Eugene's greatcoat under the tree, looking up at the stars, the weaving beams of searchlights, the huge white barrage balloons moving gently in a warm, early summer breeze.

'I've never been so conscious of the skies,' Sally said.

Eugene propped himself against the tree. 'Well, here I am leaning against a mighty British oak.'

'I think it's a beech,' Sally said.

'I'm from New York, how would I know? Right. A mighty British beech, at the heart of the great British empire, with a very pretty girl.'

'Now you're in, we'll win,' Sally said.

'I wouldn't be too sure,' Eugene told her. He was a clerk on a US Army base in Norfolk. 'They sent us five hundred left-foot boots last week. It looks like we're planning to surprise the enemy into surrender by hopping into battle.'

'I don't think you should be telling me these military secrets,' Sally said.

A drunken soldier fell over Eugene's foot, got up and said, 'Sorry, mate.' He peered at him. 'I couldn't see you in the darkness,' he added, and went off laughing.

Eugene said to Sally, 'I wish you people wouldn't keep on saying that. At first it has a certain charm, then it gets tedious.'

'It's true I can hardly see you,' said Sally.

'I can see *you*,' said Eugene, looking at her.

'Well . . .' said Sally.

'OK,' said Eugene, taking her hand. 'Tell me about yourself.'

'You first.'

'Eugene Clark Hamilton, named Clark after my late uncle, my mother's only brother, who suffered an ugly fate in Georgia. We live in Harlem, in New York. I have a brother and sister. My father is a historian and my mother trained as a singer, but gave it up when she married.'

'What did you do before you started collecting left boots in East Anglia?'

'I was an artist. I keep the rent paid by illustrating books, mostly children's books.' He added, 'I'm twenty-eight and unmarried, though I've had my moments. And you?'

'I've had my moments too,' Sally admitted. 'Quite a few.'

'That's strange. I thought night-club singers led quiet lives.'

'I'm in love with a man who's a hero,' Sally declared.

'Where's the hero now?' Eugene asked calmly.

'No one knows. It's too secret.'

Eugene laughed.

'Don't mock,' Sally cried, off her guard. 'Everybody always laughs.'

'Who laughs?'

'The people I live with. They're all very brilliant people in intelligence.'

'Well, I only deal with the stores,' said Eugene. 'Your story's turning into one of those complicated British ones, which you're supposed to understand by being something brilliant in intelligence. Does it get any clearer, or shall we find a place to have coffee?'

'It's so nice here. I wish they'd bring it,' said Sally, standing up. 'Still I suppose it's a bit damp. I'm a Communist, by the way. Do you mind?'

'Some of my best friends are Communists,' said Eugene.

'Did you know Harry Saunders?' asked Sally.

'Sure. He wanted to marry my sister,' said Eugene.

'No!' Sally exclaimed. 'I met Harry in Spain.'

They began to walk out of the park, still hand in hand.

'What were you doing in Spain?'

'I wound up trying to nurse. I was hopeless at it, though.'

'Like you are at everything?' Eugene asked her.

'Sort of.'

'That's what I thought.'

They walked through the silent streets, looking for a taxi. Eugene was staying in a low-grade hotel near Paddington Station. But when Sally invited him back to Pontifex Street he said no, he had to start back at five a.m., adding, 'I don't think I'm brilliant enough. I might walk in and they'd challenge me to a game of chess.'

In Piccadilly Circus Sally ran into the road to stop a

cab, but the cabbie, looking from Eugene to Sally and back, refused to take them. 'He's over here to help us, you know,' Sally told him indignantly.

'Help himself to our women,' the cabbie said, and drove off.

'You bastard!' Sally cried after him.

'I guess I'll walk,' Eugene said.

'Are you sure you don't want—'

'Yes,' he said. 'It's been a pleasant evening. I hope we'll meet again. Look, there's a taxi. Get in and go home.'

Sally did, feeling stronger and more hopeful than she had for a long time, though the feeling ebbed during the next few days. She did not see Eugene for a month and then, one day, he was at the club again.

38

When she came in that night Briggs, Pym and Bruno were sitting with Sir Peveril Jones – and at the table with them, looking quite at ease, was Eugene. She stepped straight up and struck a pose, hip out, '*Salut, les mecs*,' she growled.

'*Et merde à tout le monde*,' Pym growled back, louchely. He stood up unsteadily and they moved to the space in front of the band, which was tiredly playing a Latin American number. It was as if they were all asleep. Pym and Sally swung into an Apache dance. Pym, with the genius of the drunkard lifting his stride in the part of a Paris gangster, flung Sally about with skilled abandon, pushing her away then hauling her to him in a firm and sexual embrace. The band livened up and moved into a more suitable tempo.

Briggs looked on, his face expressionless. Bruno glanced at Eugene, who was smiling.

On the dance floor Pym swung Sally right round and then clasped her to him, where she remained, body to body, as if glued there. Then he staggered and nearly fell over. 'That's me done for. Besides, people will start talking,' he said. Then he put his face close to hers and said, 'What are you playing at, dear?'

Sally snapped at his nose, which was dangerously close, and he reared back in alarm. She laughed.

Back at the table Sally said, 'Hello, all – hello, Eugene. What are you doing here?'

'I came to see you,' he said.

'That's awfully nice of you,' she replied crisply. 'But I'm afraid I'm working. I'm on in about two minutes.'

'I guess I can still watch you.'

'That's what they pay me for. Well – here I go.'

She went to the stage. As she sang, more people began to drift in. Cora came over and said to Pym, 'I hear you got the sack, dear. Bad luck.'

'I'm fixed up again now. Thanks.'

'That's right, dear. I'm sure you'll always bob to the surface like a cork.' She turned to Eugene, 'You're an American soldier, are you? Jolly good. What do you do?'

'I'm making a fortune selling off Army stores,' he told her.

'You'll soon be in action, dear,' she encouraged him. 'You look able-bodied enough to me. Gawd,' she said, 'Sally's rotten tonight, though. I thought we'd touched bottom months ago, when she was so depressed, but this is worse.'

It was true, alas, that Sally's voice had deteriorated even further than usual that night and her manner was both lacklustre and aggressive. Even her timing was off.

Where music and art were concerned Briggs was a man

of sensitivity. Now he agreed, wincingly, with Cora that Sally did not seem to be on form that evening. 'Something on her mind, perhaps,' Cora said. She turned to Eugene. 'I suppose you've heard the best, really. Billie Holiday, Ella Fitzgerald, the trumpeter fellow.' What had carried Cora through fifty years of successful meetings with all kinds of people was natural good nature and a brilliant, erratic capacity to pick up information and apply it socially. Eugene appeared to understand her. He said 'I've heard some of them, yes. This is a different style, cabaret. I don't know too much about that.'

'Well, you won't learn it here, tonight,' Cora said bluntly. 'And the other girl, Vi, she's off because her little brother's got chicken-pox. I ask you! Oh,' she said, standing up, 'excuse me. There's Hugo de Belvue. I'll bring him over. He needs cheering up. They're very stiff, these Frenchmen.'

Even before Sally's set had ended, a small party had got itself together. Charles Denham had turned up, with his American mistress, and the stiff Frenchman had seated himself, though he was rather pointedly not speaking to a French sailor whom Pym had resourcefully pursued into the gentlemen's WC, and brought back, smiling, to the table. Vi had also appeared, having arranged for her neighbour to look after Jack. With Charles Denham's delight at the presence of his elusive mistress, and Pym and the sailor's satiated pleasure, the atmosphere round the party's two tables was genial and sexy. Other factors contributed to the good mood. The war was going better; there was plenty of gin; Cora was in a good mood.

Only Sally was at odds. She sat as far away as possible

from Eugene, between Pym and Bruno, and said loudly, 'It's hardly worth bothering tonight. There's nobody here. I think I'll go home in a minute. Vi, you can do the songs.'

Vi, though, got from Eugene the information that he could play the piano and persuaded him to accompany her in a couple of numbers, 'A Fine Romance' and 'Alexander's Ragtime Band'. This gave the musicians a rest and the clientele a much-appreciated change from them. Eugene and Vi sat down to genuine applause and requests for more. Sally stood up abruptly and said, 'I'm going home. I've got a terrible pain in my stomach.'

'Bile, I should think,' Briggs was heard to say.

Sally, retreating fast, was also heard to say, 'Miserable old queen.' But Eugene, who had taken up her abandoned gas mask, which she was using as a handbag, had risen and was after her.

He caught up with her in the street outside and said, 'I'll see you home.'

'I'm all right on my own. I'm not a baby.'

'What are you going to do when you get there anyway? Slam doors and shout, "I hate everybody, especially myself"? What's the matter?'

'What do you care what's the matter?'

'I like you. You're nice.'

'Oh, God,' cried Sally, stopping in the middle of the street. 'Why? I'm horrible. What's the matter with me? Why am I such a bitch?' And she burst into tears.

Eugene held her. 'Don't worry. It doesn't matter. It's all right.'

They kissed. He led her back to Pontifex Street, where they went to bed, and so Sally's affair with Eugene began.

'I'm still in love with Theo,' she told him, in the middle of the night. 'He's the only man I've ever loved.'

'That's all right,' Eugene said.

'He loves me, too,' she said.

'Why wouldn't he?' Eugene told her.

'As long as that's clear,' Sally said warningly.

'It's perfectly clear.'

'That's all right, then.'

In the kitchen next morning Eugene, usefully making coffee, asked Bruno, who was scrambling one egg with flour to make it go further, asked, 'Who's this Theo?'

'Theo's a bastard,' said Bruno, arranging Briggs's breakfast tray.

'That was the impression I got,' Eugene responded.

Bruno poured some of the coffee into Briggs's cup. 'Do you want a spoonful of this egg?' he said generously.

'No. I'm an overfed American,' Eugene answered.

Bruno picked up the tray and in the doorway turned and said, 'Don't let her make you give her up.'

'I wasn't planning to,' Eugene said firmly.

39

'He loved her, you see,' said Bruno on Greg's tape.

Greg and Katherine were sitting in front of the gas fire at Everton Gardens, silently listening to Bruno's version of Eugene and Sally's affair. Katherine sat on the floor, her brown hair against Greg's knee.

'But I don't think,' the voice went on, 'that Sally could understand that kind of relationship. She'd come from a cold home. She lived among those cold, clever people at Pontifex Street. She'd known a lot of men, probably too many, and given them what they wanted, taken what she thought she wanted. Her heart was another matter. I don't think her heart had ever been involved – I don't think she knew what that was. Greg, you have to live a long time with those kind of people to understand what isn't there, the vacuum, the heart of darkness. That's a phrase from Conrad, you will recognise it, you are an educated man. Conrad was a Pole, you will know that too. That is how he could see that void. Poor Sally. Eugene drew her, you know. I have the picture somewhere. When I find it I will show you.' The tape ended, with a click.

'Phew!' said Katherine. 'He is opening up, isn't he?'

'He opens and shuts like a clam,' Greg told her.

At that moment the phone rang. It was Bruno. He had more to impart. 'Can you meet me at di Angelo's, near the park – say, tomorrow? I'll buy you lunch.'

'You must let me—'

'No, no.'

'Di Angelo's, tomorrow then.' Greg put the phone down. 'Tomorrow! That's great!'

'You're hooked, aren't you?' Katherine observed.

'He makes sure of it,' Greg admitted. He ruffled Katherine's hair and she moved her head under his hand, like a cat, he thought, an expensive brown cat, a Burmese. 'I wonder if he found the picture he mentioned. I guess I'd be one of the first people, maybe the only person, who's seen it since the Second World War.'

'I'd love to see it, too. Will he let you photograph it?'

'Who knows? He makes all the rules.'

They met at the Italian restaurant, which was not far from where Bruno lived. They ordered their food and Bruno said, 'So, you've seen Pym and now Sir Peveril.' He took a sip of wine. 'The cast is growing bigger – yes?'

'It's not making the story any simpler,' Greg told him.

'And what did Sir Peveril say?'

Greg looked at him carefully.

'Come,' Bruno urged. 'I'm an old man, harmless, curious – indulge me.'

'Sir Peveril's an old man,' Greg said. 'But I have the

221

impression he's not harmless. Any more than you are. Look, Bruno, I keep thinking I'm getting into the wrong areas.'

'Sir Peveril is old. He wants to keep old secrets. He has nothing to do with you or the world you live in. He is living in the past, which has changed, and changed again, and will go on changing while he sits in his comfortable country house, thinking and brooding and counting his medals and honours.'

'He thinks Pym can disgrace him,' Greg said steadily. 'Tell me, Bruno, why do I keep on imagining I'm being sucked into something?'

'Don't worry. Or do you see the book you will write as a passport into the CIA?'

'God forbid,' Greg told him, tucking into his pasta.

'You seem different,' observed Bruno. 'Has something happened to you?'

'No. Well, my girlfriend's with me.'

'That always makes a difference. Is she an American?'

'No – Katherine's English. I met her when I was at Cambridge, six years ago.'

'Oh, yes?' said Bruno encouragingly. But Greg told him no more.

Instead he said, 'Pym's saying he has papers concerning relationships between the Soviet authorities and British spies which he's obtained by bribery from Soviet secret files. This is what Pym told me in Moscow to tell Sir Peveril. Now, he phoned Sir Peveril and Sir Peveril phoned me and when I passed on the message Sir Peveril didn't like it. Sir Peveril hinted that Pym would be brought back home, that the process had already been started, regardless of his threats.'

Bruno's fork stopped half-way to his mouth. He was silent, thinking.

'Screw it, Bruno,' Greg said. 'What is this? You know, don't you, what this is all about? Are you involved? Does Pym know something about you? Could he hurt you?'

'Thank you for your concern but no,' Bruno replied, in a formal, dismissive tone.

Greg looked at him for a moment, then said, 'Dammit, Bruno, you're not being frank with me. How do you think this makes me feel? I see Pym, Sir Peveril sees me, I tell you, then I guess you're involved, but you won't say how. What am I supposed to feel? Foolish or what? I'll tell you I do feel foolish, very foolish.'

'If it comes to an exchange of information,' Bruno pointed out, 'you're still in my debt. I'm telling you about Sally, a lot about Sally. You've told me one little thing about an old spy and suddenly you're angry. I have the picture of Sally I told you about. The picture Eugene drew.'

'No!' Greg said.

'But yes, here it is. I'm going to take it to the framer's this afternoon.'

He bent down, picked up the briefcase beside him, opened it and handed Greg a picture about a foot square, drawn on cartridge paper, mounted on cardboard, with a protective sheet of tissue paper over it. This he handed to Greg.

Greg lifted the tissue and found himself staring down at the face of Sally Bowles in 1943. It was a simple line drawing in black ink of a young woman in thick trousers and a long coat, with a vaguely military cut. She had a sack on her back, held by one hand and was looking half over her shoulder, as she must have been looking at the artist as he drew her, irate, but laughing in spite of herself. Her three-quarter face was a pale oval, she had strongly marked black eyebrows, frowning, a short nose, a wide slash of lipsticked mouth, a heavy dark fringe.

Greg felt as if he'd been kicked in the stomach. 'She was a beauty,' he said, awed. Here was the woman about whom he had been researching, drawn by the man who had loved her, so long ago. 'Oh, God!' he said.

'She was a postwoman then. The picture looks as if she didn't want to be represented so,' Bruno said steadily. 'She would have preferred, no doubt, a glamorous image, something like the woman Marlene Dietrich came to represent eventually. But Sally wasn't like that. Not even beautiful, really. She was, in any case, more attractive in motion, Sally, that was the point. You like it?'

'I love it,' Greg told him.

'Good. When it's framed, I'll give it to you.'

'No,' Greg said, shaking his head. 'No, Bruno. It's too good to give away.'

'It means nothing to me,' he said. 'But I think it does to you.'

'You can say that again,' Greg said. 'You certainly can.'

'I'll give you the appropriate papers, the provenance,' Bruno told him.

'Do you think he had talent, Eugene? I'm no judge of these things.'

'Oh, yes, I believe he did,' Bruno replied. 'Briggs certainly thought so. He knew Eugene's work, you see. There were some paintings but more book illustrations. That was why he was so quickly accepted by the Pontifex Street set. When Eugene came to the club Briggs had already heard of him.'

'What happened to Eugene?'

'Oh, I don't know,' Bruno said.

'I guess the US military could help me there. There could be records.'

'There could be,' Bruno agreed. 'Give me the picture,' for Greg was still holding it. Reluctantly he surrendered it.

'So, a little more of our story. We must speed it up now,' Bruno declared.

'Why's that?'

'I'm an old man,' Bruno said, which sounded to Greg like an evasion. 'Let's talk a little more of Sally, then I must go to the shop. Some of Fiona's silly mistakes still need attention.

'Eugene managed to get to London quite a lot that summer, to be with Sally. But he still kept on trying to get posted.'

40

'It was difficult for the black troops, always. They were in separate regiments, obviously, and commanded by white officers. Many of the white troops resented them. When they were posted near small towns they had to go into town on separate days, the black and white units. There were many fights. The sight of British girls going around with black soldiers drove some of the other Americans mad, especially the Southerners. And Eugene guessed right when he said the policy was to keep the black regiments away from combat, in case they came out as heroes. Different from Vietnam, eh?'

'Pretty different,' Greg agreed. 'So Eugene wanted to be a hero?'

'I don't know. As he saw it it was a fight for democracy. That the US Army was not democratic he had to accept. Anyway, that summer was Eugene and Sally's time. There were raids, yes, and the war went on. But it *was* summer, and that matters a lot when you've no fuel and clothing is scarce and you can't light the streets. Summer, I suppose, became as it must have been in Elizabethan times, a time of sunshine, warmth and freedom.'

'Time for lovers?' Greg said.

'That, too. Of course, the bombing intensified because of the long, light nights.'

41

Eugene and Sally went to stay at an old manor house in a village near Cambridge. This belonged to someone Sally knew who was at that time code-breaking at Bletchley.

In the four-poster bed one morning Eugene stretched and murmured, 'Why isn't this place filled with evacuees?'

'Hunter must have pulled some strings,' Sally said.

'Yeah.'

They got a punt and drifted down the Cam. Sally lay with her arms behind her head while Eugene, in uniform, got the hang of the punt pole. Later, he made her punt, while he drew her. There were some disapproving stares at the tall, fit-looking American soldier drawing the short woman in a straw hat and cotton dress, who was punting them along.

On a bank they lay down. 'Ah,' said Sally lazily, under a tree. 'This beats delivering the post to houses that were bombed the night before.'

'It certainly beats life as a clerk under Captain Smith.'

'Think you'll ever get into the war?'

'Not if the US Army has got anything to do with it. The military plan is to have the Negro troops spend the war fighting the Dixie boys on our side. Same enemy, only in uniform in a different country. If there's a spot on the battlefield where some garbage needs cleaning up, that's where we'll go. What will you do after?'

'After?'

'After the war.'

Sally looked up, through the leaves, at the blue, blue sky.

'Continue the struggle?' he suggested.

'I suppose so. The struggle goes on.'

'And on – and on. What about a little private life?'

'What's that?'

He laughed. 'You don't know? Maybe you really don't.'

'I'll become a celebrated cabaret star and come to New York to visit you. You'll be a very, very famous artist. We'll both be very, very sought-after.'

'But still simple and unaffected?'

They kissed.

On the dark train back to London they held hands secretly under Sally's coat. 'I nearly love you,' Sally whispered in his ear.

'Ssh,' warned Eugene. He pointed at the notice on the carriage wall: 'Careless talk costs lives.'

When they got back to Pontifex Street Pym was there, alone, drunk and in a bad mood. Eugene, about to leave, stood near the doorway. 'They've all gone out to hear Vi at La Vie. She's got a new song and the old saxophonist's disappeared and there's a new chap, an invalided-out soldier. He's lost a leg, but he used to play the saxophone with one of the big West End dance bands. And he's still got two arms.'

'Cora never told me.'

'You haven't been around much, have you, Sally? And there's a bit of news about Claudia Stein,' Pym added.

Suddenly Sally became very pale. 'Is she alive?' she asked.

'Oh, yes. She's working outside Berlin at Kummersdorf-West. It's a research institute.'

'What sort?'

'Find out for yourself,' Pym said suddenly and aggressively.

'I must go, Sally,' said Eugene.

'By the way,' Pym said, 'Theo's back. He's in La Vie with the others.'

'What?' cried Sally. 'I'll go there.' And she pushed past Eugene and was off. He stared after her.

'Don't worry, old man. She probably wants to see him about the baby,' Pym remarked from his chair.

'What baby?' asked Eugene.

'Oh,' said Pym luxuriously. 'She hasn't told you about the baby?'

42

'Why the hell didn't you tell me you had a baby?' shouted
Eugene. 'A baby, for God's sake. How come you didn't
mention your baby? A baby!' he continued disgustedly.
'Theo Fitzpatrick's baby, whoever and whatever the hell
he is!'

'Don't you talk like that about Theo,' yelled Sally.

They stood in darkness outside a dance-hall in the
Strand, from which came the sounds of music. Nearby, a
couple were embracing against a wall. Two soldiers passed
them, hurrying into light and clouds of smoke.

'To hell with Theo. What about the baby?'

'Shut up about the baby,' cried Sally, who was very upset
about Theo.

On getting downstairs at La Vie she'd searched for
him with her eyes – and found only the usuals, including Briggs and Bruno, in his ambulance-driver's uniform.
There was no sign of Theo. Briggs had explained he'd
gone to Chequers, for a high-level secret conference, and

231

would be leaving immediately afterwards. A plane had been laid on.

'Going where?' Sally had asked.

'It's hush-hush,' Briggs had told her, tapping his nose.

'Did he leave a message?' she'd been forced to ask. Briggs had just shaken his head.

'Well, if you don't care about this baby, I guess I don't have to,' Eugene declared.

'Let's go in and dance,' said Sally. So they did.

The band was loud, the crowd of dancers huge. There were women in bright frocks, though some wore ankle socks due to the lack of stockings. There were soldiers, sailors, airmen and uniforms of every description and nation. There was a haze of smoke above the dancers. Under a notice sternly saying 'No Jitterbugging' couples flung around, jitterbugging.

Then Eugene and Sally were dancing. But Eugene kept saying, 'What upsets me is that you didn't tell me. What did you think I'd say? That it was wrong that you had it? Didn't you trust—'

And then there was a big hand on Sally's shoulder and a Southern American voice said to Eugene, 'Mind if I cut in?'

'Not if the lady doesn't object,' said Eugene, expressionlessly.

'I do, actually,' Sally said. 'I'm dancing with this man. And I don't know you.'

'I think it's better if you dance with me,' he said politely. He was a tall man, with a lieutenant's stripes. 'Don't you, boy?' he said to Eugene.

'Like I said, it's the lady's choice,' said Eugene, but his eyes told Sally to dance with the lieutenant. Sally wouldn't.

'I don't think so,' she said. She moved a little closer to Eugene's rigid body.

'Dance with him,' he muttered.

The eyes of ten soldiers who had massed behind the lieutenant were on him. Immediately a dozen black soldiers came from all corners of the hall. The band stopped playing. Couples scattered to the edge of the floor.

A British soldier observed, in a disgruntled tone, 'It's about time these blokes thought about fighting the enemy once in a while, instead of each other.'

'Ain't that what I'm always telling them?' said a vast white-helmeted military policeman, pushing past him. He grabbed a soldier and fielded him into the arms of the MP behind him. 'Do you guys from Dixie never learn?'

Meanwhile Eugene had dragged Sally away from the core of the fight. A man in a red jacket beckoned them down a passageway at the back of the dance hall where he pulled up a bar and opened the door into an alleyway. They ran up it to a deserted street with another black soldier behind them. An exchange of nods between Eugene and the other man established that one would go right, the other left. 'Same old story,' said the other soldier. 'Feets, do your stuff.' He took off and Eugene and Sally found themselves back in another part of the Strand. They pulled up, panting.

'You could have explained,' Sally said. 'It wasn't your fault.'

'Yeah. Those white boys would have up and confessed to everything,' Eugene said harshly. '"Sorry, officer. We all apologise that we launched an unprovoked attack on our fellow soldiers."'

A bus came crawling along and Eugene and Sally got on. All the seats were full, so they stood.

Sally went on with the argument. 'What did you want me to do? Give in and dance with a perfect stranger?'

'Didn't you see the guys crowding up behind?'

'No, actually.'

'I did. And you wanted to know whether I wanted you to give in and dance with a perfect stranger. I told you then and there – yes. It wasn't just me, you know. It was all the other guys.'

'Look,' she said, 'this is England.'

'No, Sally, it is not England. The US troops are under US military law. If you are a US enlisted man they will try you and if they want, they will hang you.' He paused. 'This just isn't working out.'

'OK, Eugene. If you want me to say I'm sorry, I'm sorry.'

'It's not only that.'

'What?' she exclaimed.

'The baby – the fight – the baby,' he said. He told her, 'I'm going. Just for a while, to clear my mind. Just for a while, Sally.' And he pushed his way down the bus and got off, leaving Sally, bewildered, still clinging to the strap. She looked back to see if she could spot him on the pavement, but there were heads in the way. Her eyes filled with tears. People who had been pretending not to listen to their conversation, pretended now not to notice what had happened, except for one old lady, sitting under Sally's elbow.

'You should have stuck with your own kind, girl,' she said, though it was not clear whether she was referring to Eugene's colour or his uniform.

'Shut up,' Sally said venomously. Listeners were shocked, faces set in disapproval. First, she'd been going out with a Yank, then there was something about a baby, now she'd turned on a poor old lady. It was all due to the war. It was disgusting.

'Eugene didn't get in touch again. Sally wrote to him at his base but he did not reply.

'They would probably have made up the row if there had been time,' Bruno said. 'But it was war, there was always too much time or too little. Eugene got posted, so that seemed to be the end of it.'

43

Greg said goodbye to Bruno in the restaurant and, thinking hard, went down the tube station steps, planning to go back to Everton Gardens and write up his notes, perhaps do some reading. Instead, on impulse, he went to the Tate Gallery. At a desk he asked for information about an artist, Eugene Hamilton.

He half expected some heavy delving and then, possibly, instructions to visit some remote gallery or archive. He was surprised when the young woman he had asked answered briskly, 'We've got one. I'll check exactly where it is.'

'You mean you have a painting here by Eugene Hamilton, an American?'

'Yes,' she told him. 'The Metropolitan in New York has more, two or three, I think.'

'This would be a black American, around the time of the Second World War,' persisted Greg.

'That's right,' she said. She pulled out a book. 'Here we are – Eugene Hamilton, born in New York in nineteen fifteen, illustrator, painter, relationship with the Harlem Renaissance. There's nothing after the fifties, though he was certainly painting immediately after the Second World War. In fact, that's the point.' And she told him how to find the painting.

The picture was largely in blacks and browns. From the light, it was dusk and at the centre of the canvas was a glow of red, a small fire around which six figures sat – three men, two women and a child. All were emaciated and in rags. One of the men, gaunt and shaven-headed, wore a tattered uniform of some striped material. A woman, a shawl over her head, looked out at Greg with huge, blank eyes, eyes that chilled and sobered the viewer. Behind the group was a long wooden barrack block. The child, a wizened dwarf hunched over an enamel mug, was gazing, plainly in fear, at something or someone invisible to one side of the picture. All the others looked into space or at the fire, incapable, it seemed, of any thought, movement, reaction.

There could be no doubt of what the picture showed.

Greg gazed at it in awe for some minutes. Then he ran downstairs and spoke again to the woman at the enquiry desk. 'When you said the Second World War was the point, did you mean that all he painted were war pictures?'

'Pictures of the Holocaust,' she said. 'Just a few, perhaps four, and some drawings, and then nothing more. I've just looked it up. His regiment, or part of it, was stationed at Dachau to guard the camp after it was liberated.'

'My God!'

'Yes,' she said. 'Terrible.'

'Is he alive?'

She checked her book again. 'It looks as if no one knows. He disappeared.'

'Disappeared?'

She nodded.

'Can I get that book you have?' he asked. She wrote down the title for him.

Greg crossed the road and stood looking down into the swirling water of the Thames. He felt very sober. Now his story included a young American, much the same age as himself, first an inheritor of that bygone world of the Harlem Renaissance, then a guard in the terrible Dachau camp. And it seemed the young man had shown what he had seen, then ceased to draw or paint.

Shaken, he made his way back to Everton Gardens and Katherine. When he came in, her voice seemed to come from a distance as she said, 'I've been wondering what to do at Christmas. I thought of going to my uncle Simon's. Will you come with me?'

Greg, his mind still full of Eugene Hamilton, said, 'Christmas? Oh, yes, sure. I haven't any plans. Who is your uncle? Where does he live?'

'In a little village in Dorset – very pretty. He's my great-uncle, really, my grandfather's brother, but he's only about ten years older than Dad. The only reason I can give my parents for not spending Christmas at home. And it'll be much more fun at Simon's, more still if you come. I know he'd be pleased to meet you.'

'I'll rent a car,' Greg said. 'It'd be good to get out of London.'

'Great,' she said. 'Any more news of Pym?'

'Why should there be?' he asked. And then told her eagerly about the picture of Sally, and Eugene and Sally's row, and of his discoveries at the Tate. He said also, 'I've asked Bruno to dinner here tomorrow and he accepted. I thought you'd like to meet him.'

'Bruno Lowenthal, coming here!' she exclaimed. 'Oh, Greg, what a disappointment! I've got to go back early to Cambridge tomorrow. It's an emergency – a sudden funding crisis, a half-million shortfall just discovered and consequent staffing and curriculum changes. Don't ask how they mislaid half a million. But you know what it's like, these days. You have to be there when these things are discussed. My professor's demanded my presence. Or else.'

Greg was disappointed and a little upset that she did not seem more sorry to go. The evening was dull. They ate, and opened a bottle of wine of which Katherine drank more than her fair share. Greg phoned the Metropolitan Museum in New York and confirmed that they had several Hamiltons on their walls. They agreed to fax him any information they had about the artist, but said that they had no current address for him. Any business connected with the paintings was done through his late brother's lawyers in Atlanta. This address they agreed to send to Greg. He went back into the living room and opened another bottle of wine. As soon as they got into bed Katherine fell asleep. Greg lay awake, feeling lonely.

Next day he said, as she packed, 'I guess you'll be stuck

in Cambridge pretty much up to Christmas now. Shall I pick you up?'

'Mm,' agreed Katherine, trying to zip her holdall.

By now he was wondering if Katherine had suddenly gone off him, and asked, 'Is the visit still on?'

'Of course!' she exclaimed, finally closing the zip. 'It'll be wonderful. It's a beautiful house, called Chapel Manor Farm, stuffed with paintings and china and all the rest of it. Simon inherited it from some 'relative'. But we think his benefactor was more a lover. The family connection was pretty tenuous. You'll love it – it's so English, fields, village green, incredible views. Can you pick me up on the twenty-third? Sit on this little case, darling. I can't close it. I don't know why. I haven't bought anything extra.'

It was on the bed so Greg sat on it and asked, 'You're not going just to avoid Bruno, are you?'

She looked at him incredulously, 'Don't be daft. Why should I? I told you the reason I had to go. To be honest, I think my job may be at stake.' She fell on him and they made love, beside the little suitcase, one last time.

44

After Katherine's departure Greg was feeling low and lonely but pulled himself together and fixed a careful dinner for Bruno: a plate of antipasto from a nearby delicatessen, to be followed by meatloaf and tomato sauce, his speciality, then pastries, fruit and cheese. While he was tending the tomato sauce he received the material from the Metropolitan Museum, along with the address of Eugene Hamilton's brother's lawyer. He wrote a letter of enquiry to them and faxed the letter as well as posting it. Later Bruno arrived and they ate in front of the gas fire in the little sitting room. That was when Bruno produced the picture of Sally, nicely mounted. 'I have a man who does a lot of work for me,' he said, 'so he did it quickly. I knew how much you wanted to see it again.'

Greg did not mention his fear that Bruno would not, in the end, give it to him. He accepted and propped it on the mantelpiece where Sally, annoyed and laughing in spite of herself, her big sack on her shoulder, looked down at them.

'Be careful it doesn't fade,' Bruno said.

'I will. I can't thank you enough – really not. Do you think it would be possible to use it as a cover for the book?'

'Why not? It's yours. Eugene gave it to me. I'm giving it to you. Here's a document stating that.'

Overwhelmed at this generosity Greg spluttered his thanks.

'We must get on,' Bruno said firmly, between mouthfuls of his antipasto. And while keen enough himself to get Bruno's story as fast as possible Greg wondered again at the old man's sudden emphasis on speed.

45

'Sally was rather quiet and subdued after Eugene left,' Bruno said. 'She didn't have a leg to stand on, really, for during the course of the relationship she'd told everybody repeatedly, even Eugene himself, how Theo was the only man she'd ever loved. Once he'd gone, though, she'd lie around the flat when she'd done her postal deliveries, saying, 'I've got the blues.'

'There were other reasons for her depression. Pym was feeding her with secret reports about measures being taken against European Jews, the deportations and such. All Jews had had to wear a yellow star since September 'forty-one, and at the beginning of 'forty-two, though we didn't know it then, Heydrich had started organising what they called "the final solution". By nineteen forty-three millions had been murdered. This is the sort of information that Pym relayed to Sally and, of course, it made her unhappy. Not everybody was familiar with the details of all this, but as early as December 'forty-two the British Government knew enough about the exterminations to condemn them publicly. Few could have guessed how bad it was, though.' Bruno sighed. 'Not till the end.'

'Then, Ralph Hodd, who had escaped from his prison camp and gone back, unhurt, to Bomber Command, was killed in a raid over Germany. Sally's mother sent her the newspaper cutting announcing his death, without a word of comment.'

'Why would Pym have been trying to upset Sally with all this information about the Holocaust?' Greg asked.

'He thought it would be useful later,' Bruno said.

'Useful? I don't understand.'

'You will,' said Bruno grimly. He raised a finger. 'You must wait. You are irritated, but it will be easier by far, to take everything in order.' He smiled. 'I am a German, after all. Everything in order,' he said.

Greg produced his meatloaf and tomato sauce.

'Good,' said Bruno. 'Did your girlfriend help?'

'She had to leave. Budget problems at her college.'

'An intelligent young lady – yes?'

'She certainly is.'

'Will you have the pleasure of Christmas together?'

'Yes, with her uncle, in Dorset.'

'A charming place, Dorset,' said Bruno, with a nasty expression on his face. Then, 'Well, on with the tale. Sally was sad and then her mood improved a little. She was an optimist at heart. Things would get better – the struggle continues – we will overcome in the end. All that sort of thing she believed.'

'Not a bad philosophy,' said Greg stoutly.

'For an American,' Bruno said. 'A little foolish for a European. But never mind. She went on singing, and doing her day-time job.' Bruno broke into song in a cracked voice. '"Please don't talk about me when I'm gone – no matter how I carry on – please don't talk about me when I'm gone."'

Greg smiled.

'There was another song. I think she learned it from Eugene. "That don't bother me. You can see that I ain't free, but that don't bother me."'

Greg joined in and they both laughed.

'However,' Bruno went on, 'unlike when Theo dumped her, she said this time that she'd given up men. "I've given up men, darling,"' he quoted. '"From now on I'm going to be like a little nun and dedicate myself to the Party." But there were other things going on at Pontifex Street too.

'It was around that time that I got up one night – I couldn't sleep I suppose – and went to the kitchen for a glass of water. I found Pym and Briggs and Geoffrey Forbes poring over some blueprints they had spread out on the kitchen table. That wasn't so strange. They were all concerned with secrets and naturally new scientific developments in warfare were important to them. I think what shook me was the way they looked at me when I first came in – they covered it up quickly, but I saw they were very shocked. Just that I'd come into the room. They didn't want any witnesses, even me. I didn't know what they were doing and I didn't care, which they would have known well. So why the alarm? Why the secrecy? I went back to bed and forgot it as soon as possible.

'But not really, because the next day I came in to find Sally painting her toenails red with some paint from a child's painting kit – the red enamel used for the lead soldiers' tunics. She was quite proud to have discovered it in a shop somewhere in Soho. And then I asked her, "Sally, do you know anywhere I could stay? Don't tell anybody I asked."

'"You want to move?" she asked me. "I don't know anywhere. Sorry." So many houses had been destroyed and people were living in very bad accommodation, with relatives – anything. So I knew she probably would have heard of nothing and had to be content. Though, basically, I was not.

'Cora then did a strange thing. She banned Pym from La Vie. When he arrived one night she just said, like a pub landlady, "No, you're barred." He tried to argue, but it was hopeless. She said it was over his bill, which was enormous, but that wasn't it. Cora never cared about things like that. I think she smelt trouble. Pym had a good cover – his perpetual drinking and roaming around for sex masked everything. But there was a Russian sailor, for example, who spent two weeks at Pontifex Street before his ship sailed, drinking vodka straight from the bottle and singing all the time. Who was he, really? A pick-up of Pym's, or a messenger? Although the Allies were winning the war, things at Pontifex Street seemed more unpleasant somehow than during its worst hours. The atmosphere was bad. Cora had guessed something too, I'm sure of that now.

'Anyway, I stayed, for there was nowhere else to go. Not

long after, Sally too was looking around for somewhere else to live.

'That began one morning with the arrival of Sally's parents, Geneviève in a good pre-war suit, Harry looking worn out. I could see there was going to be trouble so I left the sitting room and went into the kitchen where I started to read the paper. Sally, with a gloomy face, followed me in to make some tea. "Storm clouds overhead," she said, picking up the tray. Later, I could hear voices in the living room.

'"Sally. Something really must be done," her father said.

'Then Geneviève. "It's too much, now Nanny's left, with all the shortages. Only an unpleasant girl from the village—"

'Then came Harry Jackson-Bowles's rumble again. "Too much for your mother," and Geneviève's, "Gisela's out of hand."

'Sally said something about the bombing and was rapidly interrupted by her mother more loudly. "Sally, we've done our best, but this can't go on for ever. What about the child's father? Can't he do anything? You've got to think of her future."

'Sally seemed to be pleading for time. I heard Geneviève say, "No, no, Sally. This must be settled now. What are you going to do?"

'Then her father's voice and then Sally's, rising, "I can't come home."

'Feet came upstairs, Briggs's step, which went past the kitchen door. The living-room door opened, and I heard

Sally's father's voice, which broke off. Sally must have pleaded, silently, with Briggs, for somehow he was invited to dinner at the Connaught, where the Jackson-Bowleses were staying, to serve as the buffer between them and Sally, I suppose.

'He came in later in the evening, took off his hat and neatly put his gloves in it. "My God, Bruno," he exclaimed, "Geneviève Jackson-Bowles is a bitch of the first water. I really can't understand why Sally puts up with it. How sweetly Geneviève denigrates her. 'Poor Clothilde,'" he mimicked, "'she's so ill. Sally wouldn't care, Mr Briggs. Family means so little to these modern girls, don't you agree? But, forgive me, I can't expect you to understand a mother's feelings when she sees a daughter so.' What a dreadful woman. I wonder why she doesn't like Sally?"

'"You ought to know," I said. "You dislike her enough yourself."

'"I detest her sloppy habits and her sloppy emotions. 'Theo – the only man I've ever really loved,'" he mimicked again, with cruel accuracy. "I can't bear her stockings in the bathroom, her muddles and messes. Well, I've never liked women, you know that, Bruno."

'"You've never liked anybody. You can't stand the disorder," I dared to tell him.

'He laughed. "The Jackson-Bowleses are determined to get rid of the child," he told me. "Well, Sally can't bring it here. Even she sees that. Of course," he added, "what Sally doesn't know is that Theo's on his way back from Washington. They want him for the Balkans. He's trying to wriggle out of it, but I don't think he'll be successful.

Poor old Fitzpatrick's coming from the brigh
London." And Briggs laughed again. "Woman tro
Eleanor Roosevelt took a dislike to him. Curtains fo
Fitzpatrick. I wonder what Sally'll make of that?"

'Well, we all wondered,' said Bruno.

46

Sally was at Vi's flat in Pimlico. Washing was stretched across a corner of the room, Vi's bed, neatly made up, was in another corner. Vi was putting carrots and potatoes into an enamel dish.

'I'm sorry, Sally,' she was saying, 'but I can't see any way. Ted's patched the roof and the landlord's let the upstairs flat again to some friends of Ted who got bombed out just last week. It's a mate of his from the docks, his wife and three kids under six. They'd been bombed out once before. They had to move in with her mum and dad and the wife began to go round the bend – I mean it, sitting on the edge of the bed all day, crying and ignoring the kids. Here they've only got two attic rooms, but to her it's Paradise. You know what it's like, Sal. There's nowhere to rent.'

Sally sighed.

'Look,' Vi said, 'They can't just bring Gisela down here and dump her, like an unwanted dog.'

'Trot's had to go down to Folkestone to look after her

250

sister who was a nurse in London, but she's collapsed under the strain. She's terribly ill. Mother says she can't manage and if Gisela doesn't come here I'll have to go back to take care of her.'

'You don't want to bring her back to the bombing. But going home doesn't sound too good.' Vi had her own opinion of Sally's mother. 'Can't you get Sir Peveril to wangle something?'

'I doubt it.'

Vi put the vegetable stew in the oven and turned on the gas. 'That'll have to do for Ted and Jack when they get in. I wish I could've got a sausage or two to go with it. Jack's downstairs with Mrs Brown. Ted'll be going to pick him up when he gets off shift. I think he's getting sweet on the woman downstairs, her with the kid and the husband with Monty in North Africa. Her husband hasn't seen the boy since he was tiny, hasn't had leave for a year. That'll be a nice surprise for him, finding his wife in love with another man when he gets back, won't it?'

'What are *you* going to eat, Vi?' asked Sally.

'A cup of tea and a fag, as usual,' said Vi.

'You'll cave in,' Sally said.

'We can't all afford to eat out in restaurants,' Vi told her.

'What've you got?'

'Two bob, till Cora pays me.'

'I've got a shilling. Let's go to Lyon's quickly.'

'You're on,' said Vi.

They hurried out, Vi carrying her flimsy evening-dress in her gas mask case while Sally's contained a torch and

Vi's make-up and shoes. In the street, there was a strong gust of wind and some leaves blew in their faces. 'Another winter coming on,' Vi remarked.

'Any news from Archie?' asked Sally, as they turned to the bus stop.

Vi's boyfriend's ship had been sunk off Norway *en route* to Russia and there was no news. 'It's so bloody long since I've seen him,' Vi confessed. 'Of course I want him to be OK, but who'll come back, eh? The same old Archie? To the same old Vi?'

There was a silence.

Then, across the road, Sally spotted two American uniforms, and Vi, noticing, said, 'You still haven't got over that darkie, have you?'

'There wasn't much in it,' Sally told her.

'No?' said Vi, sceptical.

'No,' Sally said. 'Are my eyes deceiving me or is that a bus coming?'

'It must be a mirage.'

Once on the parked bus Vi said, 'If this is winning, I wonder what losing's like?'

'A bloody sight worse,' Sally said.

47

Stretched out in a chair in the flat, with a glass of brandy in his hand, Bruno said, 'Theo got back just after the Jackson-Bowleses' visit. Geneviève had been ringing Sally regularly every Sunday morning, early, so as to disturb us all, to ask how Sally's search for a flat for herself and Gisela was going and Sally, for some reason, did not evade these phone calls. Each Sunday morning we'd hear her saying, "Yes, maman. No, maman. I'll do as you say, maman." When she'd put the phone down she'd head for the gin.

'Then one Sunday she turned round and there was Theo, in the doorway with his suitcase. She launched herself towards him and he embraced her. They went upstairs without a word. Julia, Briggs and Pym were all there, drinking coffee and reading.

'Julia looked up and said, "Oh, God, not again."

'Pym, bare-chested, in a pair of very dirty trousers, asked, "I wonder what our boy's playing at now?"

'Briggs just shook his head. "Whatever it is there'll be an ace up his sleeve as usual."

'"And he'll have his eye on the pot."

'"Sally's got no money," said Julia. "She's just borrowed ten bob from me." But Pym was right,' said Bruno. 'Money was involved. Although we didn't know it, that was why Theo married Sally.'

Bruno held out his glass for more brandy and Greg leaped to his feet. '*What?*'

'Yes,' said Bruno. 'Theo's confidence must have gone in Washington. The Menckens threw him over and something shocking must have happened to set Eleanor Roosevelt against him. Well, I suppose in his way Theo loved Sally – and she certainly loved him. And then,' said Bruno, 'there was the money.'

'Well, Bruno,' Greg said steadily, 'it might have helped if you'd said earlier that Sally had married, that her name became Fitzpatrick. But when I checked him out he was married to someone else.'

'That was later.'

'At least she got her baby's father on board, just for a time.'

'Oh, no,' said Bruno. 'She didn't.' He finished his brandy and said, 'I'd better go, I think, it's late.'

Greg looked at him in despair. 'Bruno, you must be the meanest, most annoying person I have ever met.'

'I hope so, I hope so,' said the old man. 'Help me down the stairs, dear boy.'

Greg assisted him into his coat and down to the street where he flagged down a taxi. 'I'll see you after Christmas,' Bruno said.

Immediately after the meeting with Bruno, Greg visited

Somerset House to see if Sally's death had been recorded under her married name. It hadn't. But then, he thought, she might have married again after the divorce – if there had been one, but as yet he didn't even know that.

And now he must wait until after Christmas to hear more.

48

Greg and Katherine sped down the motorway, past fields full of freezing fog on either side, then turned off on to a narrow hedge-overhung road. Two miles further on they reached the village of Norfield Fitzcrewe.

On its outskirts stood the traditional enclave of council housing, low red-brick houses with dustbins and bicycles in the front gardens, cars and motorbikes parked outside. Then they entered the old village. There was a green, covered in frost-spiked grass, with a frozen pond and a great chestnut tree. On one side of the green was a church; around it lay old houses, well tended and preserved, a shop, a post office and a pub.

Beside the church they took a road leading through trees for half a mile, then turned up a drive. In front of the house, a low, Georgian building of old red brick, was a half-circle, also of red brick, and there Greg left the car. As he got their luggage from the boot he heard Katherine cry, 'Mrs Chambers – so glad to see you're still here.'

He turned round to see her greet a short, plump woman in an overall. He got the bags and followed them in.

'Would you mind taking them straight up?' Mrs Chambers asked him. 'Mr Ledbetter's put you in your old room, Katherine.'

'Oh, goody,' said Katherine, 'the green room. At the top of the stairs, Greg. We'll be in the drawing room – that way,' and she pointed.

Greg struggled upstairs to a long landing with many doors and arched windows at either end. He opened the heavy, varnished door opposite him. He found a bright, spacious room, papered in green, containing a broad double bed with a carved modern headboard. Another door revealed a bathroom in what presumably had once been a dressing room. The windows looked out over the garden, with a line of trees at its end. Inside the room, radiators flung out warmth. Greg, who had suspected that Chapel Manor Farm might be a cold, run-down farmhouse inhabited by an elderly madman, was cheered. He put down the bags and went to meet his host.

In the drawing room Simon Ledbetter sat in a big chair in the long, bright room beside a roaring fire. Beside him stood an electric wheelchair. He was a thin, heavily lined man, with a shock of thick white hair. He wore a blue polo-necked sweater, and brown corduroy trousers covered his skinny legs. Katherine stood at a large window, which overlooked the garden.

Simon raised a hand in greeting. 'Greg,' he said, 'Kate will get you a drink. Lunch will be ready soon.'

Katherine went to a sideboard on which bottles stood on a tray and asked, 'Whisky, Uncle Simon?'

'Good to meet you,' said Greg, crossing the room and shaking hands.

He sat down opposite Simon.

'It's good to have you here,' Simon said to them. 'You've saved me from a long, lonely Christmas. It'll probably be rather quiet for you as I haven't arranged anything.'

'We can go to the pub this evening, then,' Katherine said.

'If you don't mind Julia Wells,' he said.

'Is she still after you?' Katherine asked.

'I'm afraid so. She seems undeterred at the prospect of marrying a cripple. Can you imagine us, her overweight in a bridal gown, and me in my wheelchair, advancing up the aisle at St Tim's? What a spectacle. She's always telling me how lonely I must feel. Of course, she's usually a bit drunk – been married three times already. You'd think she'd have learned.' He turned to Greg. 'Life's so hectic in the country, one way and another. I often think it would be more peaceful to return to London.'

'You'd never do that,' Katherine told him.

'I suppose not. I'm too comfortable. Potty old Adie Robinson and his wife have moved down here. They're coming to Christmas lunch. It's rather a bore but I owe them a meal and you know what it's like in the country. You have to get on with neighbours,' he explained to Greg. 'If you can't get the company you like you have to like the company you've got.'

'Has his wife still got those sheepdogs?' Katherine asked.

'Worse than that. She's breeding them. They won't bring them, though. I've explained I'm allergic to furry animals. I don't think she believes me but she has to accept it in case I swell up and choke. They do make me swell up and choke, as it happens, but with rage – noisy, brainless things. You must go up to the tor after lunch. It's an Ancient Britons' burial mound,' he explained to Greg. 'They're planning to excavate it next year.'

'Do you want them to?' asked Katherine.

'Not particularly. I've lived here for twenty years and never felt the slightest curiosity about it. Not my thing, really. I hear you're a bit of an historian,' he said to Greg.

'I don't go as far back as that,' Greg informed him. 'I'm only in the Second World War at the moment.'

'It's far more dangerous to dig about in the near-present,' remarked Simon. 'At least if one excavates old mounds all one finds are some bones, a torque and some mysterious cult objects which may never be understood properly.'

'Your interest must be more in art, sir,' said Greg, who had been looking about him and seen what he thought were paintings by Sidney Nolan and Lucian Freud. There were also some Chinese pots, one on a table, one on a long sideboard, and a glass cabinet containing smaller oriental items, some plates, a figurine.

'I have got one or two things,' his host told him, in a way that discouraged further comment.

Mrs Chambers came in and told them lunch was ready. Simon deftly shifted himself into his electric chair and set off through the door, across the hall and into the dining room. Mrs Chambers served cold salmon, hot potatoes and salad. A dessert and cheese lay on a side table. Then she said goodbye.

'Chambers died, caught something from one of his animals, they believe,' Simon said, after she had left. 'It makes you think.'

'Oh dear. Who does the garden now?' Katherine asked.

'Contractors,' he told her. 'They send round burly boys in shorts, and it all works rather well. They do exactly as you say because they don't know anything about it. I feel rather guilty, but I prefer it to having Chambers bossing me about. The roses have never been better. Now, tell me what you're doing, Kate.'

'Muddling on. I've got extra work next year. They've had to get rid of somebody, Peggy Corrigan, early retirement, so I'm taking on all her work.'

'Can you manage?'

'Got to,' she said.

'What about your research?'

'I'll have to keep it up somehow,' Katherine said, not very hopefully.

'Now I can see what's going on I'm glad I got out,' Simon said.

'What was your—' Greg asked.

'Medical research. I was working on enzymes when a relative left this place to me with enough to keep it up. I hesitated about giving up the job. I was at Churchill and only in my forties, but by that time this was happening,' he gestured below the table, at his legs, 'so I resigned.' He paused. 'It's a decision I'm still not sure about,' he said.

'It's the if-onlys that get to you,' Greg observed.

'I doubt if you've accumulated many of those yet.'

'He may be in the middle of one,' interjected Katherine, with a disloyal laugh. Her manner changed in the presence of her uncle, Greg noticed. He'd met her parents, a solid couple who lived near Birmingham, her father a doctor. With them she was meek and slightly subdued; with her uncle her tone was sharper, more worldly.

That afternoon they walked up a footpath to the tor, which stood in an empty field about a mile from the house. They paused, looking down at a composed vista of fields, hedgerows and trees. A small river ran peacefully through it.

'Is this part of your uncle's land?' asked Greg.

'It ends there. The boundary's the riverbank,' she replied. 'He's so lucky to have it.'

'Who was the relative who left it to him?'

'It was some kind of cousin,' she said.

'You said it was a lover.'

'Well, we thought he might have been both.'

'Ah,' said Greg.

'If we go back that way,' Katherine said, gesturing towards the river, 'we can stop for tea in Merricombe.'

They strolled along the banks, by willows. 'Was the reorganisation that bad?' asked Greg. 'Does it really mean a problem with your research?'

'Oh yes,' she assured him. 'I'm pretty sure the post we

lost might easily have been mine. 'It's an arena. Be grateful you're in a system where money counts, publication is a measure of your work and everybody knows the rules.'

Greg, who was all too aware of the academic's need to publish, asked, 'Did you mean it when you told your uncle I might be in a position I could regret later?'

'Don't say you haven't thought it yourself.'

'No pain, no gain,' Greg said bravely.

'What happens if it falls through?' Katherine asked.

'Well, thank you,' he said. 'That's a really encouraging thing to say.'

'It must have crossed your mind.'

Greg was silent for a moment, wrestling with anger. Of course Katherine was right to think he might have had doubts about his project. But it might have been kinder not to have mentioned it, especially in front of her uncle. He fought down a sharp response.

She continued, 'What have you got, after all? Just that old man, who may be potty or have some ulterior motive. You know what the old are like when it comes to distorting the past to make themselves look important or pay off some ancient grudge. And otherwise – nothing.'

'Why are you doing this?' he asked.

'What *have* you got, then?' she challenged.

'And why are you doing this?' he repeated. He wanted to walk away from her, but it would have been ridiculous and, in any case, where would he go? Back to her uncle's house?

'If we're going to argue,' she said, 'it'll be a rotten Christmas.'

They had reached a path leading off from the river by a little bridge. She tucked her arm through his. 'Sorry,' she said.

'That's OK. And you're right anyway. I do sometimes have doubts,' Greg told her, as they set off along the path.

'I'm sure it'll be marvellous. Have you got some new stuff?'

He thought of that line drawing of Sally, head turned, back bent under her mail sack, the slash of black that was her lipsticked mouth. He had brought it with him, in the bottom of his travel bag, he didn't know why. He thought of Katherine, whose arm was in his, of her lithe, thin body, her long, fine, pale face, the abundant, fox-coloured hair. He realised he was comparing the two women, the flesh and blood one he was with and the other, long dead, two-dimensional, a mere line on a piece of paper drawn by a lover. He almost groaned, realising he didn't want to talk about Sally Bowles to this woman who wasn't Sally Bowles.

After tea at Merricombe and a good walk back his mood improved. He and Katherine went upstairs then, to snooze before dinner and make love.

They lay, chatting, and he told her about Eugene.

'That's wonderful!' she exclaimed. He got up and found the picture. Katherine lay back, scrutinising it. 'She must have been really something.'

'That's the impression I have. Now I've got to find Eugene, if he's still alive.'

'I don't suppose he will be.'

263

'He'd be in his early eighties. But everyone else I've spoken to has been about that age. A tough generation. I've written to his family's lawyers.'

'Where are they?'

'In Atlanta. It looks like a respectable firm.'

'Well,' said Katherine, 'you *have* done your stuff.'

Supper had been laid out in the kitchen by Mrs Chambers and was heated and served by Katherine and Greg. Over the meal Katherine started Greg off on the story of Eugene. Simon appeared interested and asked questions. Katherine ran up to get the picture of Sally, which he admired. 'There's talent there,' he said.

Over coffee Simon said, 'Now, chaps, if we can drag ourselves into the dull present, will you wrap me up warmly and push me to the pub?'

'We could drive, if you like,' Greg offered, but Simon said, 'No, if you don't mind. I like to go out at night and see the stars and, these days, I don't often get the opportunity.'

And so they set out, Simon in his wheelchair, which did not really need pushing, Katherine and Greg walking on either side. The chair bumped slightly as they went down the drive between the trees. The sky above was big and clear.

The pub, quiet, well decorated and obviously very old, contained only two men in a corner and, by the fire, a well-preserved woman in her late forties, drinking gin.

'I'll bring them over, Mr Ledbetter,' the landlord said, as they settled down by the fire.

'Julia Wells, Greg Phillips,' Simon said.

264

'Wonderful,' she said. 'Another man. You'll all come over tomorrow, won't you?'

'Of course,' Simon agreed.

'Just a few local bores and my son and his girlfriend,' she said. 'Roger the Bastard's threatening to turn up, but I don't believe he'll make it.'

There ensued a brief conversation between Simon and Julia about the likelihood of Julia's ex-husband Roger the Bastard's arrival on Christmas Eve. To Greg, Simon's attention seemed strained. Then Julia began to describe her argument with the farmer next door to her, whose sheep had made incursions, again, into her garden. 'So what do you do for a crust?' she asked Greg suddenly.

'Just now I'm researching a book about the Second World War,' he explained. 'It's a biography, of sorts, called *Sally Bowles and her Circle*.'

'I'm very ignorant, I'm sure,' Julia said, 'but I'm afraid I've never heard of her. Who was she?'

Briefly Greg explained.

'Fascinating, isn't it?' Simon asked her. 'A bit before your time, I suppose, Julia.'

'A bit before yours even, Simon, I suppose. You'd have been – what?'

'I grew up with people telling me they were fighting the war for me,' he told her.

'It must be very interesting,' Julia said to Greg. 'Do you find it a problem being American and writing about English people?'

'Yes,' Greg told her. 'There's a lot I don't understand. I have to work at it.'

'I read such a wonderful biography the other day – Virginia Woolf,' said Julia, with an effort for she was by now a bit drunk. 'So interesting, all those people. You've got a picture by one of them, haven't you, Simon?'

'I think you may be thinking of Vanessa Bell,' he said.

'Something like that. One of Allie's, was it?'

'Yes, it was,' he said. 'But, Julia, we must be going. I'm so sorry, dear, but you know how tired I sometimes get.'

'It's only half past nine,' she remonstrated.

'I know, but it just sweeps over me. I'm getting on a bit and shortly I'll have to go to the lavatory – and between ourselves, I prefer my own to the one here. Katherine, would you help me put on my coat?'

And so they went back to the house, with Simon gazing up again at the clear, starry sky.

'Are you really tired, Simon?' Katherine asked, as they went.

'Well, Julia's getting drunker faster these days,' he replied, 'and she can be a bit of a bore when she's had one too many. It's not fair on Greg to subject him to hour after hour of the local divorcée.'

'She seemed very pleasant,' Greg said.

'Oh, she is – very pleasant.'

On their return Simon said, 'I'll leave you to it – I'm off to bed, I think.' He wheeled himself away to his room, which lay next to a small study on the side of the house opposite the drawing room.

'We might as well watch that film on TV,' Katherine said. She went to an alcove and moved an old screen to reveal a television set on a stand. 'It's the kind of screen they hid the chamberpots behind in the eighteenth century,' she said.

'You can't read Latin all the time,' Greg said, for he had noted that Simon's current book, which lay open on a small table by his usual chair, was Virgil.

'Or, in my case, any of the time,' said Katherine, and plugged in the TV.

But Greg fell asleep during the film and when he awoke he was alone in the silent room. Only one lamp burned. Suddenly he realised he was alert, almost watchful. Relax, Greg, he told himself. You're on holiday, and went upstairs and got into bed beside Katherine.

'Mm,' she murmured, and snuggled up to him, 'you looked so peaceful down there, I didn't like to disturb you.'

Next day they all drove into Dorchester to do last-minute shopping and some sightseeing. Simon's wheel-chair fitted quite neatly into the car's boot.

When they got back Simon said again that he was tired and would take a nap before supper. Katherine settled down with a book, while Greg went out to the kitchen to see if he could help Mrs Chambers, who was preparing that night's supper and the Christmas dinner. The kitchen smelt of roasting meat. 'You could do these sprouts,' said Mrs Chambers, 'if you don't mind. You do know how to do sprouts, don't you?' she added suspiciously.

'I'm an old hand,' said Greg, and sat down at the kitchen table. After that he prepared a salad to go with their supper.

'Just heat the soup,' she said, 'and everything else is

on this table. I want to get away to collect our turkey from the farm. Can you take Mr Ledbetter his cup of tea about six? The tray's laid. All the Christmas food is in the fridge. Katherine will know how to manage.' She picked up her bag and went to the kitchen door. 'Merry Christmas.'

'Merry Christmas,' said Greg, getting on with the sprouts.

Later, he made the tea and put it on a tray, which he took to Simon's bedroom. He tapped on the door and, getting no reply, opened it. The small bedroom was empty, though the curtains were still drawn. There was Simon's bed, and beneath the window a small, elegant table on which stood a lamp. There was an old, gilt-framed mirror on one wall.

Beside it hung several drawings. Greg walked over and looked at them. There was a Leonardo cartoon, or something very like it, a Beardsley sketch – and two black and white drawings he seemed to recognise. One showed a small child standing, blank-faced, by a ruined wall, the other a weary soldier, leaning against a tree-trunk smoking, his helmet, an American helmet, on the ground before him. Greg stepped up. Both pictures were initialled, as was his own sketch of Sally Bowles, with a small, precise EH in the bottom right-hand corner.

Astonished, but feeling he should not have been prying in his host's bedroom and that he certainly didn't want to be caught doing so, Greg left the room and took the tray back into the kitchen. There he leaned against the sink, thinking. When Simon had looked at his own portrait of Sally by Eugene, he had not mentioned that he had two sketches, very similar, from the same era by the same artist. Greg could think of no reason for that but decided it would be rude to challenge his host. He left the tray in the kitchen and went into the drawing room, where he found Simon and Katherine talking. He told Simon, 'Mrs Chambers left some tea for you.'

'Would you mind very much bringing it in?'

'Not at all,' Greg said, and returned to the kitchen, picked up the tray and took it into the drawing room.

Yet as they sat and talked, and over supper, he still found himself wondering about the sketches by Eugene Hamilton on Simon's bedroom wall, and why he had not mentioned them.

That evening they took the road down to the village again. Julia's house, explained Simon, was in fact the church's old rectory. It lay on one side of the village green, next to St Timothy's. Julia's father, he said, had been rector at one time and on his retirement had purchased the rectory from the Church commissioners, who were happy to relinquish ownership of the large, old-fashioned house.

It was big and comfortable, untidy and, Greg thought, more welcoming, though less grand, than Simon's house. A large sitting room was cluttered with small tables and pushed-back over-stuffed furniture. On the walls were various Victorian engravings, some nearly invisible oil paintings and a copy of *The Fighting Temeraire*.

The room was crowded. Simon appeared to know almost everyone there, Katherine knew a few people and Greg no one. Simon, in his chair, disappeared quickly into the throng.

'Jim Maclaren – vet,' said a big man beside Greg. 'You've forgotten me, Katherine. We met three years ago on another Christmas Eve.'

'Oh, yes. Greg Phillips, Jim.'

'Hi,' Greg said, shaking hands. 'So, what does one say to a vet at a party?'

'Usually that your dog's developed a funny tremble, or the budgie's hanging its head.'

'Can't help you there,' Greg told him.

'That's a relief.' They began to talk about sport; the vet was a keen American football fan who had been to the States for the Superbowl. A large woman then came up to talk about her basset hounds, and Greg was left alone, looking round the room. Charlie, from the pub, was talking to a clergyman; a thin woman with a huge string of pearls was holding forth to two men in tweeds by the fireplace; a girl in leggings with a ring in her nose was talking to a young man in jeans and an Arran sweater. Simon himself was engaged in a conversation with a woman in a tartan shawl seated on a sofa. They were laughing.

Katherine, by the window with a tall man, spotted him and beckoned him over, but he went to the kitchen and got himself a glass of water. The tall man appeared. 'You're Greg,' he said. 'Katherine's friend. I'm Roger Wells.' They shook hands. 'I'm Julia's ex-husband,' he explained. 'I just dropped by to say happy Christmas and hand over the cheque. Sometimes I wish I was a woman. You married?'

'Not so far,' Greg told him.

'Don't do it,' advised Roger. 'Look at me – business going through hard times and still paying Julia to live in the manner she's accustomed to.' He gobbled down some canapés, which sat on a tray on the table. 'I might as well eat all I can, eh? After all, I've paid for it.'

Julia came through the kitchen door and, catching the last words, cried, 'Do shut up, Roger. After all, it's Christmas.'

'I was just going anyway,' he said. 'Do you want to pop over to the pub with me for half an hour?' he asked Greg.

Greg shook his head reluctantly.

'Just half an hour,' Roger said. 'I'm very depressed. I'm due to spend Christmas with my mother and sister. They're here, backing up Julia about what a swine I am. I've sold my flat to support the business so when I get back to London I'm camping with friends. Come on, you'll be doing me a favour, stopping me from adding to the Christmas suicide statistics.'

'OK,' said Greg. They left the rectory and walked across the village green to the pub.

'Look at that party,' said Roger, sitting down with his pint. 'Alimony, inheritances, golden handshakes, early retirements – there wasn't a bugger in that room except Jim Maclaren doing a fair day's work for a fair day's pay.'

In Charlie's absence, the pub had taken on a noisier air, perhaps because it was Christmas Eve. Voices were louder; the juke-box was playing country and western music. 'This place must seem weird to you,' said Roger.

'I was in Britain a few years ago, on a scholarship to Cambridge,' Greg told him.

Roger ignored this remark. 'There's something awful about this village, I always think,' he continued. 'You're staying with Simon, I suppose.'

'Yes,' Greg said, his mind going back to the drawings by Eugene Hamilton on Simon's bedroom walls.

'He's a weird bugger, too. Not surprising, I suppose, with his legs gone. Still . . .'

He had sunk his beer and Greg got up to buy two more, though he was only half-way through his own. When he sat down again he asked, 'What's your business?'

'Ships' engines, mostly. It's tricky at the moment, but the orders are coming in. I think we'll weather it. What about you?'

Greg told him briefly about the biography.

'My dad was in that lot,' Roger said. 'Killed in the Normandy landings before I was born. My mother married again, rich bloke, nice man. He's dead now, too. She and Sis are living on his cash. That's what I say. Oh, to be born a woman next time around.' He looked at Greg enquiringly. 'Or something.'

Greg responded, foolishly, 'I guess you have to be one or the other.'

'Not necessarily,' Roger told him, in a significant tone. 'Take old Simon. He got that house and its appurtenances from this queer bloke everybody thought he was having an affair with – when he died, of course. House, pictures, furniture, land, the lot. Now, if I'd been a bloke like that, well . . .'

The barmaid came over with two more pints
paid. 'I hope I haven't put my foot in it,' he said.
it you're Katherine's boyfriend.'

'Yes. We met when we were students. I've just com
back and we got together again.'

'Right, didn't want to be offensive,' said Roger. 'Each
to his own and all that. No, this guy, Simon's benefactor,
so to speak, was, gossip hath it' – he stumbled over the
words – 'involved with this other guy, the traitor they're
bringing back from Moscow.'

Greg stared at him. 'You don't mean Adrian Pym?' he
asked. 'Is he coming back to Britain?'

'So it seems. I caught it on the car radio coming up. I
suppose they announced it today because it's Christmas
Eve – they always do when they don't want a fuss.'

'It's definitely Pym?'

'Yes. The guy they wrote the books about. You must
know the story. He and another bloke spied for the
Russians, then fled. They lived in Moscow for years, then
one of them died. They're saying this bloke, the one who's
still alive, is an old man now, sick, wants to come home
and so on and so forth. Immunity from prosecution – said
that all right, didn't I?' he congratulated himself. 'The old
pals' act, if the truth were known, I bet,' he added, lifting
his pint.

A girl lurched against Greg's chair, ''Scuse me, I'm
drunk,' she said. The juke-box started up 'Heartbreak
Hotel'. A group at the bar were singing 'The Wild
Rover'.

Greg was surprised. 'That was quick,' he said, more to

He added, 'I saw him in Moscow of what I'm researching. The war

, Le Carré stuff, letter-drops on ..., Roger said vaguely.

...ow does Simon Ledbetter come into the story?' Greg asked.

'Common knowledge. Didn't they tell you? The guy who originally owned the house and left it to Simon bought it for his retirement from some top Whitehall job. He was a relation of Simon's, so it's said, but really his boyfriend. Bloke died, left it to Simon. But, way back, he'd been involved with all these spies – the dead bloke, that is, the owner of the house. He was cleared, of course, but what does that mean? Mum read me out the obits over the phone when he popped off. It was big news round here at the time. I'd tell you his name but I can't remember it. Anyone round here could tell you, though.'

Greg was silent and thoughtful. Who was this man who'd left Simon his house? Hadn't the woman, Julia, called him Allie? Was that when Simon Ledbetter had made an excuse to go home? And he had Eugene Hamilton's drawings on his wall, but he hadn't mentioned it. Allie. Alexander Briggs. Greg's heart sank. The man who'd owned Simon's house had been Briggs. It had to have been him! Christ! Oh, Christ, he thought desperately. He caught Roger's eye.

'Thinking?' Roger asked.

'Yeah,' Greg said. 'In a big way. And getting nowhere. But life goes on. Should we be getting back?'

'Yes. I've got to drive Mum and Sis home,' Roger said.

'You can't do that,' Greg said. 'I'll take you. You insured for me to drive? Is it far?'

'Only two miles. And I wouldn't mind if you did, thanks very much. I've a few black marks on my licence already,' Roger told him. 'OK, let's go.'

As they walked back across the quiet village green Greg began to feel depressed. Anger might have been easier, but he couldn't manage it. Only depression.

'Where have you been?' Katherine asked him, as they came in.

'In the pub,' Greg said neutrally. He had realised Katherine must know about the house, about Briggs. But she hadn't told him.

'Listen,' he said, 'I'm sorry, Roger was planning to drive his family home, but he's had too much to drink, so I've volunteered. Should I go back for the car first and drive you and Simon home?'

But Katherine said she and Simon would be able to get back to Chapel Manor Farm together when they wanted to leave. 'Don't settle down with Roger,' she warned. 'He'll have you drinking till dawn.'

The road to the Wellses' led straight from the village. In the car Greg enquired, 'Mrs Wells, Roger was telling me Simon inherited the house from a friend. I don't suppose you remember his name?'

'Briggs,' she said. 'He was called Alexander Briggs.'

As Greg drove on into the darkness, she added, 'I met him a couple of times, with Simon, at Christmas, like now. He'd bought the place to retire to so he wasn't here much. Then he died just before he was due to move in

275

permanently. Rather sad. Of course, he left the house to Simon.'

'What did he retire from?' Greg asked.

'He was something very high up in the Civil Service,' explained Mrs Wells. 'He was knighted. He worked very closely with the prime minister, whoever it was at the time.'

'What was Briggs like?' asked Greg.

'I didn't know him well. He was tall and thin and very dignified, a sort of touch-me-not attitude.'

'I'm asking,' said Greg, 'because his name has cropped up in the research for the book I'm writing. I didn't realise he had anything to do with Simon Ledbetter.'

And Roger's voice came from the back of the car. 'Whoops.'

'What, Roger?' asked his mother.

'I just said, "whoops," – awkward territory.'

'Yeah,' said Greg. 'That's the impression I'm getting.'

They had arrived at Roger's mother's house. Roger opened the gate. Greg parked the car. He said he wouldn't come in, and refused Roger's offer to drive himself back to the village. 'I think I feel like some exercise,' he said.

Roger got him a walking-stick from the hall, 'You never know,' and they parted. 'Good luck, old man,' said Roger, looking at him with friendly concern. Drunk as he was, he had evidently noted that Greg was upset by the revelation that Briggs had once owned Chapel Manor Farm. He added, 'Thanks for the lift.'

'Don't mention it,' said Greg, and set off down the cold, quiet road. There were hedges and fields on either side. An owl hooted.

That explained the pictures, he thought. They'd probably been acquired by Briggs during the time Eugene was seeing Sally.

But nothing else was explained, he thought, striding through the darkness. The least of it was why his host hadn't told him about the Briggs connection when he had first heard what Greg was doing. What was more important was why Katherine hadn't told him. How long ago had she realised that her uncle was living in a house left to him by a man who had shared Sally's war years? From the outset – when he had first written to her saying he was coming to Britain and why? Or had it been later, after he arrived and started talking to Bruno Lowenthal? However long it had taken her to put two and two together, she must have known when he went to Russia to see Pym, must have known when they came down here. But she had said nothing.

Greg took a swing at a bush with Roger's stick. Well, shit, Phillips, he said to himself, face it. You've been conned. And the big question is, why? And when you and Katherine started sleeping together again, was it because she liked you or because she was just trying to find out what you were doing?

He needed to have it out with her immediately. It wasn't a very attractive idea, on Christmas Eve with the prospect of Christmas Day stretching ahead. But he was not prepared to wait. He wanted the whole thing out in the open, however much it hurt – and he was getting the idea it might hurt a lot.

Back at Chapel Manor Farm he found Simon and Katherine in the drawing room, by the fire. Katherine looked up. 'Did you get them back in one piece?' she asked.

'Yes, they're nice people,' he returned.

'You took quite a liking to Roger, didn't you?'

'Yes, though he's a little bitter about things. Perhaps he has reasons.'

'Maybe,' Simon agreed. 'Though Julia often describes him as an animal.'

'That's hard to imagine.'

'I can see him getting drunk and falling over the furniture,' Katherine said. 'Perhaps the animal she meant was a big clumsy dog. Do sit down, Greg. You look uneasy standing there.' Greg opened his mouth to speak when Katherine added, 'By the way, there've been phone calls – on Christmas Eve! All about your friend Pym.'

Greg poured himself a drink and sat opposite the fire. 'Roger told me in the pub there'd been an announcement he was being allowed back. Who phoned?' Greg asked.

Simon said, 'Well, as you'll know, this house was left to me by a former friend of Pym's, Alexander Briggs.'

Greg mentally congratulated the pair of them. Very good, very neat. They had guessed that by now he'd most likely have discovered that Simon had inherited the house from Briggs, and their strategy was to pretend they thought he'd known it all along. If he said he hadn't, they'd express amazement. They'd say, but surely – but they'd thought – but hadn't Katherine—? Suddenly, he began to wonder if he was being paranoid, if perhaps Katherine and Simon had genuinely thought he knew about Briggs. But what about Eugene's pictures? Meanwhile Simon was saying, 'I had to tell them there weren't any letters or papers. I sent everything like that to Briggs's sister when he died.'

'Who wanted the documents?' Greg asked.

'The Foreign Office.'

'On Christmas Eve?'

'That's always the way with civil servants. Forty years of inactivity and then a flurry on high days and holidays. I told them I'd sent everything on. There wasn't much here, a few personal letters, a set of notes for essays about some painters Briggs was thinking of writing after his retirement. There may have been some documents in the London flat, I don't know, but the flat and its contents went to his sister.'

Greg's eye went involuntarily to the grate, where the fire burned, as if he could see letters and documents going up in flames. Simon's eye followed his. 'What's it all about?' Greg said.

'God only knows,' Simon said. 'Pym's returning and the bureaucrats are getting their knickers in a twist, egged on by the spooks and watchers, who are short of work now.'

'I suppose Pym's arrival will delay your book, Greg,' said Katherine.

'I doubt it,' he said calmly. 'Why do you think that?'

'Won't you want to hear Pym's side of Sally's story?'

279

'Sure,' Greg said. 'But I'm not prepared to put everything on hold until he's prepared to speak with me, which could be never.'

There was a silence. 'You don't find that approach a little unsatisfactory, knowing there's further information to be got and going ahead anyway?' came Simon's voice.

'You're implying my attitude is unscholarly,' Greg replied. 'And I have to agree with you, in a way. But I've made the decision to deal with what material I have, not wait for Pym's revelations at some unforeseen time in the future. I'm assuming there's a strong possibility there will be no comment from Pym. From what he told me in Moscow he was trading his return here for his silence.'

There was an uncomfortable pause. Greg felt the room chilling and sensed than Katherine and her uncle wanted to continue to talk without him. Suddenly, he felt violent anger. Here was a lovely girl, beautiful and clever, his girlfriend, plainly wanting to spend the rest of the evening, Christmas Eve, talking to this elderly man about long-gone events that did not concern her, her life or her future. And he had started to think that perhaps he would be part of that future, she part of his. What a sucker. She'd been deceiving him all the time. He was sure of it. And why had she brought him here in the first place?

'Another drink, Greg?' she asked.

'No,' he said. 'I'll get along to bed.'

'I'll be up in five minutes,' she said.

Greg turned in and lay waiting for her. At least here, in bed, he'd have her to himself and be able to ask her about when she'd realised he was dealing with people who had known Briggs.

Katherine did not come up to bed five minutes later, as she had promised, or in ten, or in fifteen. Almost an hour later Greg drifted off to sleep, conscious of the little pile of brightly wrapped Christmas presents on a table by the door, winking at him as he lay alone in bed.

49

Late on Christmas Eve Bruno Lowenthal was alone in his pleasant flat at 11, Cornwall Street, though all too conscious of the others in the house. He could hear his tenants' damned record-player in the basement – even though he was two floors up – the damned *Threepenny Opera* blaring out, all harsh chords and coarse German voices. What a choice for midnight on Christmas Eve. 'Ach,' he heard himself say in fury. If he weren't so busy he'd go downstairs and complain. But he must get on, time was running out. He had rewound the tape he had been making for Greg and now pressed the button, pleased to find that he had operated the recorder correctly and that his own voice was coming out.

'Greg, I hope you're enjoying your Christmas now, though I've just had a phone call which makes me wonder if you are. Surprises, eh? Pym coming back after all these years. And you staying with Simon Ledbetter! *What* a coincidence, eh?

'Well, Greg, I'm beginning to think a biographer can be like a scientist – you know the theory, I expect, that the scientist himself, in doing the experiment, changes the result.

'Before you arrived Pym was safely away in Moscow where he'd been for forty years and where everyone thought he'd die and never trouble anyone again. And an old man would not have expected to have been rung up on Christmas Eve by one of Sir Peveril's minions, warning him not to say anything to the press and not to try to get in touch with Pym, which is what has just occurred. I have to tell you, Greg, that before you came here, as far as I know, Sir Peveril didn't even know where to find me, which made us – made me – very happy.

'I bought this piece of equipment when I heard the news that Pym was returning. You'll have noticed I'm speeding up. All right. I'll tell you the truth. When we first met my plan was to give you just enough to satisfy you, not enough to reveal too many secrets. Not now. Now is the time for the truth. I think it's important to get the story over with before the trouble starts. I think there will be a bit of trouble, Greg. There always is when Pym's about. He comes into the next part of the story in a horrible, grotesque way. But I mustn't interrupt myself. I must keep going from start to finish. And you owe me fifty pounds for this recording device, by the way. I bought it for your sake and I think you'll find it's worth the money. I'll get Fiona to drop the tapes over to you when I've finished. She won't mind – she has no life, poor girl.

'I must tell the whole story because when he returns

Pym may start talking – and he lies. He will lie or tell the truth according to what will bring him the most advantage.

'Perhaps the real truth has some value, even if it is an old truth told about a world that exists no longer, to a world that no longer cares. Truth is much like peace and motherhood, when you think of it – we all support them until it gets a little inconvenient. Then there are a thousand reasons why they don't matter so much. Just as there are a thousand reasons for telling a lie. People seldom have to explain why they told the truth.

'Well, I'm growing tedious in my old age but you, Greg, will never have heard a "Communist truth", in other words, a lie, nor did you ever live in Hitler's Germany. Now that was a place for lies . . .'

He trailed off, then began to speak again.

'It's odd, isn't it, that you came here as an ambitious young man with a project you saw as only half serious – it was a career move, you'll admit that, I'm sure. And how your very presence seems to have stirred up all those old things that were lying quietly at the bottom of the pond.

'But – you'll be impatient and I'm worrying about how long the tape will last, so let's return to the past, to Sally's marriage which is not a long story, God knows.

'Well, Theo began to take Sally out again. Pontifex Street thought little of it. We had seen Theo's returns and courtships before. Then one evening, early, we were sitting quietly, listening to some music, when in came Sally and Theo, and Sally opened her eyes and arms wide and said, "Darlings, you'll never guess. We're engaged!"

'This astonished everyone, but we all congratulated her and Briggs was kind enough to open a bottle of champagne he had been saving. Theo phoned his wicked old father, who was sitting in his crumbling castle in Ireland, drunk, I suppose. Sally put off making the call to her family. Then the happy pair went off to La Vie to tell Cora.

'After they'd gone Briggs said, "I don't believe this. Why?"

'"It must be the baby, Gisela," Julia said.

'"Ha, ha," said Pym, and he turned on the gramophone again.

'Cora came in not long after, in a beaded dress, and sat down comfortably. It was a surprise because Cora was not one to drop in. And she said, cheerfully, "I expect you've heard the news. Isn't it lovely?"

'"Incredibly lovely," said Pym.

'"So nice for Sally – everything she ever wanted, a dream come true," she said. "I shouldn't be surprised, though, if her fortune doesn't come into it somewhere."

'Briggs said, "Ah," and Pym opened his eyes wide.

'"Yes?" he said, getting ready to enjoy himself.

'"Well," Cora told us, "this is the story. I had it from a general. Geneviève Jackson-Bowles, you see, was one of three daughters. Her sister Madeleine married a doctor or a surgeon called du Tour, whom nobody had ever heard of, and then the second sister, Clothilde, married an industrialist, a self-made man of no family. Socially, all three girls' marriages were a disaster, of course – but Jerome Vincent, Clothilde's husband, was very successful and also very wise. In nineteen thirty-nine he put the bulk of his money in a bank in Switzerland. He was a patriot, but he understood Hitler and wasn't confident that the French would be able to withstand him. And a year later he died. About a week or so ago, so did his wife, Sally's aunt. They were childless," she said. By now Pym was laughing loudly. Cora ignored this. She went on, "I shouldn't be at all surprised if Clothilde hasn't left her nieces and nephews a lot of money. Perhaps Sally doesn't know yet, but I wonder if Theo has got wind of it?" And then she, too, started to smile for Briggs was grinning and Pym laughing his head off. Julia was looking rather annoyed at the thought of Sally's being an heiress. Briggs, though, said, "Poor old Sally. Theo is a vile deceiver. However, at least she'll be able to afford to replace the champagne."

Bruno continued, 'So Sally was rich. Her mother phoned next day to give her the news. Geneviève was angry because she and her sister Madeleine might have expected to get Clothilde's money. Even worse, Sally's sister Betty had been left nothing. It seemed Clothilde had changed her will after Sally's mission to France and had left her money only to Sally and her two cousins, Benoît and Charles. All were, as she put it in the document, fighting for France. However, the money was in Switzerland and the will in occupied France, so for a long time there was nothing. Sally said that she'd split the money with Betty, or give it all to her mother if Geneviève felt so strongly about it.

'In the meantime, though, Sally's father advanced her enough funds to buy a house immediately. Sally bought a fairly run-down place in the unfashionable area people then called "south of the park", the park being Hyde Park, of course. Theo was displeased. He would have preferred getting a short lease on a smart flat in a smart area. But Sally told him she had Gisela to think of and that a flat wasn't suitable. He sulked, but I think he decided that this was no time to start a fight with an heiress and must have thought that he could eventually persuade Sally to get something better.

'In the end Gisela didn't come to London. Sally's mother had a change of heart and decided the marriage would get off to a better start unencumbered by a child Sally barely knew and Theo had not seen at all. Of course, Geneviève was quite pleased by the marriage. By that stage almost any marriage of Sally's would have soothed her mother and the marriage to Theo was better than she could have hoped for. Theo, though he had no money, had a career on *The Times* and was of quite good family.

'The wedding took place at a register office on a cold January day in nineteen forty-four. It was supposed to be quiet, but by the time Pontifex Street turned out and Sally's anarchist friends from Kennington, her workmates from the Post Office, Vi and her brothers and quite a lot of the clientele from La Vie, including Cora, of course, it became rather noisy.

'Sally's sister was quite cross, actually, and she and her husband made unpleasant faces in the wedding pictures. They were still annoyed about the money. The pictures were a little odd because they were taken by an aircraftsman more accustomed to taking reconnaissance pictures from a plane. But I still have a photogragh

somewhere of Sally, looking very happy and excited, in a
silly hat with a veil, arm in arm with Theo and flanked by
Adrian Pym and Geoffrey Forbes. An historic photograph,
for ten years later Pym and Forbes were running like hell
for Moscow with the British authorities behind them.

'Briggs, Pym, Charles Denham and Forbes organised a
sweepstake on how long the marriage would last. I joined
in and drew three months.'

50

'Is there nothing at all to eat?' Theo Fitzpatrick was demanding of his wife on a gloomy winter's afternoon a month after the wedding. They were standing in the depressing sitting room of the house Sally had bought. The original lino was still on the floor. A small fire, made mostly of coal dust, smouldered in the grate. The view of the houses on the other side of the street was masked by grimy net curtains and the Edwardian wallpaper was coming off in patches.

Sally was lying on the sofa. Her friends Ricardo and Antonia were crouched in a wool rug near the fire. Antonia held a guitar but had stopped playing when Theo came in. Beyond the sofa stood a big table, with a typewriter and many papers and books. In a corner some shirts were drying on a wooden airer.

The Fitzpatricks were living on only two floors of the house. Downstairs, the basement was cold and damp; aloft, the roof leaked into the upper rooms.

'There's a saucepan of beetroot soup on the stove,' Sally said. 'The butcher gave me some bones. Wasn't that nice of him?'

'Is there anything else?' he asked.

'We've eaten all our rations.'

'God, Sally. Other people make them last. Or couldn't you have got something under the counter?'

'Vi's brother's promised me a tin of ham,' she said. 'I can't do any more, Theo. You know I don't like getting things other people can't have.'

'How very high-minded. Especially as Simcox's donations are knocked off at the docks. Well, I'm going out for a meal. You coming?'

She shook her head and he went out. He had not taken off his overcoat. This caused an awkward silence. Sally said to Ricardo, 'Marriage is rather amazing. I never realised it involved so much housekeeping. It's like some contract you sign thinking it's one thing and it turns out to be another.'

'With a person who turns out to be another,' Antonia remarked. 'But perhaps, as you would say, Theo only needs some re-education?'

'Only!' exclaimed Sally. 'I've spoken to him again and again. I think he believes there's an invisible servant living here and doing everything. My responsibility is to make sure this servant does her work. He feels better living in his imaginary world, with the imaginary servant, because that way he doesn't have to admit there's no one here but me to wash his clothes or cook. I'm fed up with it. It isn't fair. He's only been sitting in Baker Street, turning over a few secret documents, and I've been at work since seven thirty.'

Sally had given up her Post Office job when she moved away from Pontifex Street and had found employment in a small factory half a mile away. This produced cartridge cases, as it had since 1915.

The doorbell rang and Sally ran to answer it. She found Vi on the step in a headscarf, trousers and a mac holding the hand of her young brother. 'Ted turned up with a tin of ham and four cans of fruit for you,' she said. 'I rushed straight round with it.'

'Goodie – let's eat,' said Sally. The war-time bread was grey, and Vi said she'd kill for a tomato, but they all enjoyed the soup and ham, except Jack, who said it tasted horrible and he'd rather have Spam.

'Fancy – he's forgotten what ham tastes like!' Vi exclaimed. 'And he's never seen a banana – well, it's only food,' she added bravely. Nevertheless, she looked thin and pale. They all did.

'What a pity Theo went off like that,' Sally reflected, as she made tea. 'But I suppose you can't blame him. I can't manage properly. The meals, the laundry, the dust – there's always something to do. I'm beginning to see why my mother was always so agitated. And she had maids and a cook.'

'You should tell him he's lucky not to be dead,' Vi announced. Archie, her pre-war fiancé, was now presumed dead. Poor Mrs Hedges's husband had been killed the year before at El Alamein. It seemed likely, though, that Ted would marry her, but she had yet to get over the guilt of having fallen in love with Ted before her husband's death.

'I don't think Theo really understands about queues and things,' Sally said mournfully.

'He must see them,' Vi remarked bluntly. 'He's got eyes in his head. His mind's on higher things, I suppose. Mind you, Sally, if I had any choice I'd never have moved into this old-fashioned dirt-trap. I think I'm going to marry this Yank I'm going around with. His parents have got an Italian delicatessen in New York. It's like a grocer's. They've got fridges and proper kitchens and modern bathrooms – I wake up at night thinking about it.'

'Be careful of an Italian son and his mother,' Antonia warned. 'No woman is good enough for an Italian son.'

But Vi, who had stolen a glance at Sally's face, dropped the subject of her American boyfriend. She suspected that Sally had suddenly thought of Eugene. Small wonder, thought Vi, now that Theo Fitzpatrick had turned out to be just as bad a husband as she, Vi, had always suspected he would.

She changed the subject and said pleadingly, 'Sally, Vic's got a forty-eight-hour pass and we want to get down to Brighton. Ted and Lou Hedges can look after Jack, but I need someone to do my turn at La Vie tonight. Will you? Cora said she'd love to see you again.'

'Oh, I wouldn't mind,' said Sally. 'But I don't think Theo would like it.'

'He doesn't seem to mind you doing nine-hour shifts at the ammunition works,' retorted Vi.

'That's for the war effort,' Sally said diffidently.

Vi could feel the approval of Sally's Spanish friends, who might have been bomb-throwing anarchists with no decent standards and not even married, but seemed quite nice anyway and were certainly loyal friends. 'Part of the effort is cheering people up,' she said. 'Come on, Sally. Please. You'd be doing me a big favour. You can have the pay, for what it's worth.'

'Oh, all right,' Sally said. 'It's only once. I'll dig out my dress. Are you coming?' she asked the other two, but they said they would stay behind to finish an urgent pamphlet. So Sally ran upstairs, changed, and they left together. Sally, Vi and Jack got a bus into the centre of London.

'You still haven't sent for Gisela, then?' Vi asked.

'No, it's the bombing. And I don't really want her here.'

Vi took a deep breath. 'I don't want to be rude, Sally, but you don't act like Gisela's your child at all.'

'She's not,' Sally told her. They were going down Bayswater Road, past the park.

'She's not?' Vi repeated, hardly able to believe what she was hearing.

'Gisela's Jewish,' Sally said flatly. 'Half Jewish, actually. I had to bring her here from Germany, but at first I didn't dare say who she was in case the Germans invaded. I was afraid of what would happen to her if they did and they found out her father was Jewish. I let everybody assume she was mine. That way, if we were beaten she'd stand the same chance of survival as anybody else. Of course, with me being a Communist, Gisela was better off away from me with my parents. Not that I wanted to take care of her, anyway. It was bad enough getting her here.'

'Well, I'm damned,' said Vi. 'I've got to hand it to you, Sally. You're full of surprises. Poor little thing. Where are her parents?'

'Still in Germany. I wish I knew where. Listen,' she said, 'I'm only telling you this because there won't be an invasion now. But I don't want it to go any further. I don't suppose you could ask Vic to get me some nylons, could you? I haven't got any stockings left.'

'Course I will,' Vi told her. 'But I can't guarantee anything. Whoops! Come on, Jack, it's our stop.' She and her brother got up. 'Cheerio. Don't do anything I wouldn't do.'

'Just ask about the stockings.'

When Sally got to the Bessemer she was surprised by the warmth of Cora's welcome. 'Sing us some of those German songs – people won't mind so much now we're winning. And we need a bit of class, foreign languages and so forth. Vi's all right but she hasn't got your touch.'

A second surprise, less pleasant, came when she ran down the stairs of La Vie and found Theo sitting at a table with Charles Denham and Geoffrey Forbes.

'I'm just helping Vi out, darling,' she said, swooping past him to the rostrum, where the musicians were tiredly playing 'The St Louis Blues'. Yet another new saxophonist didn't help much, but Vincent Tubman was accustomed to Sally's repertoire and she managed a Kurt Weill song, a couple of cabaret numbers and the finale, 'Lilli Marlene', in which everybody joined. Sally felt energetic again, admired in her red dress, interesting once more. Bowing to the applause, she reflected that another surprising aspect of her marriage was that it made her feel unlovable and unattractive. No one warned you that could happen. Or was it just her?

She had noticed Theo rising half-way through her turn but, concentrating on her performance, assumed he'd gone off to the lavatory. When she came off the stage, Cora was in Theo's seat, talking to Charles, Geoffrey and a naval officer.

'Where's Theo?' Sally asked Charles. 'Has he gone?'

Charles nodded but said nothing else and Sally, despondent, asked no further questions.

'That was very nice, Sally. Have a gin,' said Cora.

'I won't say no.'

She got back to the house at one, driven by the sailor. Outside, he put his arm round her. 'I'm married,' she said.

'Oh, I see,' he replied, and took away his arm.

Sally went in, but Theo wasn't at home. She went miserably to bed and next morning, when she got up early to go to work, felt even worse for Theo had still not returned.

He came in next evening at eight. Sally jumped up from her chair and said, 'Guess what, Theo? We can have a ham omelette. Ted gave me some ham and the boss's daughter came up from Kent with some eggs and he gave me two.'

But Theo just put down a paper bag on the cluttered sideboard, took out a bottle of whisky and poured himself a drink – not the first he had had that evening, Sally thought.

'Do you want it now?'

'I can't think of anything I want less,' he replied.

'Why are you always in such a bad mood?'

'Look round you at this place and ask yourself if you need an answer to that question.'

'If you wanted a housekeeper you should have married one.'

'God, Sally, that's a bit banal, isn't it? When all I ask is the minimum of comfort, a little order, the odd meal. Look here, we can't go on like this. If you can't make the place comfortable why can't we get someone in?'

'Who?'

'Well, can't you find a woman? It's not impossible.'

'Where were you last night?'

'I don't think I have to account for my movements when I see you turning up out of the blue at La Vie.'

'I told you, I was just standing in for Vi. Anyway, why shouldn't I? I enjoyed it – Cora paid me. I think I'll go back if she'll have me. The money would be handy.'

'That's the other thing, Sally, this money. Can't you ask your father how long it'll be before he can get it transferred?'

'He's put some in the bank,' she said.

'What? It's here? What bank? Why didn't you tell me? Let's get hold of some of it, for God's sake. We could get out of this place for a start.'

'It's in his bank,' she told him.

'What the hell's it doing there? It should be in yours.'

'I've given it to him,' Sally said.

'You've *what*? You've given your money to your father? *Why*, for Christ's sake?'

'I said I'd give it away and he persuaded me not to. He made such a fuss that I said, "You keep it, then."'

'Oh, *God*,' Theo said. 'Well, look, darling. Get in touch with him, tell him you've changed your mind and ask him to hand it over. Ring him up. Do it now.' They had a telephone as Theo was on government work.

'I don't want to. I don't believe in inherited wealth. It perpetuates inequality. And I think I've heard you say that quite a lot over the years.'

'I certainly believe that in principle, in a proper society, inherited wealth should be abolished,' Theo told her. 'But that society has not yet come about. So in the meantime we're stuck with the old one. That being the case, I can't see any argument against your accepting your legacy.'

'Oh,' said Sally, thinking. Then she said, 'But how can we get to a perfect state of society if people go on acting in the same old way?'

'By the democratic will of the people,' Theo said, 'which they haven't yet expressed, not having had the chance to do so. You know perfectly well that individual actions are pointless and only collective action is of any use.'

'All right,' said Sally. 'If individual acts are pointless I won't do anything at all.'

'What do you mean by that?' he asked sharply.

'I won't ring up my father.'

'You will, Sally,' he said, with assurance. 'You will.'

'You said—'

'Look, you little nitwit, when I said individual actions were unimportant, that was a general statement. Theoretical.' He began to lose his temper. 'Theory, Sally. You know what that is, don't you? Abstract ideas, impersonal thoughts, guidelines, philosophy – products of the human intellect, nothing to do with ourselves. Theories,' he crossed the room, took her by the shoulders and shook her slightly, 'theories. Now do you know what I mean by *theories*?'

Sally looked him in the eye. 'I know you want Aunt Clothilde's money.'

He raised his arm as if to strike her, then pushed her away with his other arm and smote himself on the brow instead. He groaned. 'I'm sorry, Sally. Do what you like. Shall we have that omelette?'

51

Bruno said, 'Things were better between Theo and Sally for a few weeks. Perhaps Theo hoped to bring her round about the money. And Sally came back, a couple of nights a week, to La Vie. But Cora said, and Cora was always right, that Sally wouldn't ask her father for her share of Aunt Clothilde's money.

'So gradually it came about that on the nights Sally was at the club Theo wasn't, and on the nights she wasn't there, Theo frequently was, with other women, and later with just one, a girl called Penelope Forrester. She was in the ATS and working as a driver to some general. She came from a rich old family. Her father was a peer. Sally didn't know about Theo and Penelope, of course. No one told her. But you could see she was unhappy sometimes.

'The Allies had invaded Italy early in nineteen forty-four and Germany was being bombed heavily.

'Sally struggled on with her housekeeping. Sometimes she'd arrive at La Vie with a string bag containing some pathetic little items she'd managed to get – cabbages and a few potatoes, a little bit of fish and a tin of Vim for the bath, but the truth is, Theo didn't like the house and he didn't like Sally enough to try to make things work. And he was still angry about the money, too.

'Cora said to me one night, which was a surprise, "She might have been better off with the Yank. I don't like these black men going out with white girls, but Eugene was intelligent and respectable and he made her happy." Then she said a very surprising thing. "He wrote to me recently, you know. Said he had the idea he was going into action soon and asked me as a favour to tell him how Sally was, if she was well and happy. He asked me not to let her know he'd been in touch. He'd heard she was married to Theo."

'She told me she'd written back to tell Eugene Sally was alive and well and still in London. But she added, "I didn't say anything about her marriage. I couldn't bring myself to say she was happy, when anyone can see she isn't. I don't know what he'll have made of that. There was another thing, too. He said he'd asked his commanding officer to let me know if he was killed. He'd enclosed a letter to Sally, to be given to her in the event of his death."

'I asked was it sealed, and she said of course it was, and then I asked, "So, Cora, what did it say?"

'She told me, "He said he loved her, he regretted the quarrel, would she forgive him? Rather touching," said Cora. She'd resealed the envelope after she'd steamed it open and read it.

'Then she said, "I was tempted to tell him she wasn't

getting on with Theo, and invite him to come back and try again, but it's not my business to interfere. Theo and Sally might be perfectly all right when the war's over. It puts a strain on everyone. In my opinion she ought to get her money from her father so that the marriage would stand a chance. A man like Theo needs money the way a plant needs water. You can't blame the plant, can you?"

'It was inevitable that one night the accident would occur. Sally had taken over from Vi one evening and Theo didn't know. He came in with Penny Forrester. If Cora had been in charge she would have prevented this, but that night she wasn't.

'Sally saw the couple, I think before they even got to the foot of the stairs, and her voice faltered. Then she stopped. She took in the situation at a glance, went white and just walked out, past them. She sent all Theo's clothes and personal things round to the Bessemer in suitcases two hours later in a taxi. Theo was astute enough to stay at the hotel that night. He knew it was over.

'He was posted back to Washington soon afterwards and took Penny with him. He married her after the war. After that, of course, Theo Fitzpatrick never had a worry again – she bore him sons, her father provided money, all was well.

'Sally told us. She was sad, but she added, 'I suppose, in a way, I'm glad he's gone. What a washout. What a fool I've been. I don't think I ever understood Theo at all.'

'And Briggs said, we were at Pontifex Street, "The rest of us did, dear."

'"That's because you're all the same as he is," Sally told him.

'And Briggs told her very firmly, "No, Sally. Not quite the same."

'We all dreaded her moving back into Pontifex Street, now that she was alone, but she didn't. No one told Sally's parents that the marriage was effectively over so Gisela stayed where she was and Sally remained in that leaky house. She went on working at the factory, and doing her act at La Vie in the evenings. And the war went on and we were waiting for the invasion of France.

'But before it came Hitler launched the V-1s – the flying bombs – on Britain like the last bite of a mad dog. They came in flights, making a noise like a train, then cutting out, without warning, coming straight down and exploding.

'Our nerves went – even Sally's – and a million people left London.

'After the V-1s came the improved version, the V-2 – rockets – which made no noise at all. Imagine a rocket coming overhead, silently, through the cloudless blue, and you didn't know where it was going to land. The fact that these rockets were unmanned made it worse. It seemed so unfair. There, a man at any hour of day or night pushed a button. Here, half an hour later a house exploded, a family was killed. You felt helpless. They started shooting them down, of course, but still they came. And all the while we were bombing Germany savagely. The punishment on both sides was dreadful. And the rockets kept on coming.

'Then Sally's mother became ill and this time she had to go home. Her father could not manage alone – and there was Gisela, who was four now.'

52

Sally found herself back in the big house in the country in which she had spent so little time since she left home, and not much before that: she had been away at boarding school from the age of eight.

Geneviève Jackson-Bowles had been diagnosed as having leukaemia, for which there was no cure. Harry still went to his Birmingham factory, though as his wife gradually weakened he cut down the number of days he spent there. Geneviève fought, but there was no hope for her.

When Sally arrived in July she found her sister Betty in charge, but itching to get back to her own home. Her suitcases were ready in the hall when Sally entered the house one afternoon and went into the kitchen, where Betty was making tea. Gisela, in a red jumper and short kilt, stood by.

'God knows how you'll manage, Sally,' Betty told her, pouring water into the teapot. 'This place needs a staff of five. You know what there is now? A daily and an old man who turns up to do the garden when he feels like it. I've applied everywhere but I can't get any more help. If you ask me, Maman's exhausted herself trying to take care of everything.' And she shot a look at Gisela.

'That's why I came,' Sally said. 'I suppose we can close up some of the rooms and move downstairs.'

'You're accustomed to primitive conditions,' said Betty, who had visited Sally in London. 'Maman isn't.' She picked up the tray and started to leave the room.

Gisela looked at Sally and said in a clear voice, 'Are you my mummy?'

Sally paused, then replied smoothly, 'I'm not really, darling.' She took the tray from her sister. 'Your mummy and daddy are abroad and they can't get here because of the war. I'll explain it to you later.'

'They might have died in all the fighting,' said Gisela.

'I know, sweetheart,' Sally said. 'We'll try and find them when the war's over. I'll tell you all about it soon. We'd better take this tray to Granny, now.'

'Not so fast,' said Betty. 'What are you telling the child?'

'The truth,' said Sally. 'She's old enough now.'

Geneviève was in the drawing room. She held her cup in a thin hand. 'I'm afraid this illness of mine is being a great bother to you all.'

'Nonsense, Maman,' Betty said briskly. 'We're only too glad to do all we can for you.' She turned to Sally and said, 'Look here, Sally. About Gisela. I don't know what you're saying, but I think it's time you told us who her father is.'

Sally glanced at Gisela, who was looking out of the window at the birds on the ragged lawn. 'I think I ought to tell her first.'

'Never mind that. She's only four years old.'

'Nevertheless—' Sally began.

'I wonder if someone would have the goodness to tell me what you're discussing,' Geneviève said. Gisela was suddenly at her side. Geneviève sighed. 'I see whatever it is will happen with the minimum of decorum.'

And so Sally explained who Gisela was, concluding, 'You see, Gisela, your mummy and daddy will come back if they can, and if they can't – we don't know yet – you will stay here with us. You do understand, don't you?'

'Will Nanny come back, too?' the child enquired.

'I don't know,' Sally said.

It was a bleak moment for the adults. 'Oh dear,' said Geneviève. 'This war.'

Betty rallied, saying briskly, 'Well, I suppose some organisation could take responsibility for Gisela.'

Sally laughed.

Betty was stung. 'I suppose you think that now you've got the money it'll be easy to keep her.' The business of Aunt Clothilde's will still rankled. She added, 'Just as well you've got the money, since your husband's left.'

Geneviève observed, 'I confess, I always thought I might have a vulgar daughter but I suspected her to be Sally. Can I have been mistaken? Or perhaps it's both of you, in which case I've been very unfortunate.'

Betty got up. 'Well, at least I can ring Daddy.'

'Why?' Sally asked.

'To tell him the good news about Gisela. Gideon will be mightily relieved, too, I can tell you.'

As she left the room Gisela ran towards Sally, stumbled over an invisible obstacle, fell down and began to cry.

'Oh, Christ,' said Sally, picking her up. She sat down with the child on her knee and lit a cigarette. 'I'm sorry, maman. I think we need to get some chickens – for the eggs.'

'I don't really think so,' Geneviève said faintly.

Gisela had brightened up, 'Can we have chickens? Can I have a kitten as well?'

'We'll see,' Sally said. She was saying to her mother, 'Perhaps chickens aren't a good idea,' when Betty came back into the room.

'How did Daddy take the news?' Sally asked.

'He said he wasn't altogether surprised,' Betty reported. 'Gideon's thrilled to bits.'

'Why on earth?' Sally asked.

'Because he's very likely to stand for Parliament as a Conservative at the next election and, well, you know what I mean – no one wants a blot on the escutcheon.'

'He'll be a blot on mine!' Sally cried.

'Really!' Geneviève said, and then added, weakly, 'I must go and rest now.'

Sally jumped up. 'Let me just put a hot-water bottle in your bed. It's still frightfully cold up there.'

After she had helped Geneviève to bed, Sally made a phone call, then went into the kitchen to prepare dinner. She told Gisela to lay the table and ruthlessly fended off questions about her parents and kittens.

When Harry Jackson-Bowles returned from Birmingham Betty and her husband had left and Sally was making soup. Gisela, who had put a blanket in a cardboard box, as a bed for the hoped-for kitten, had crawled into it herself and fallen asleep.

Harry peered into the box and said, in a low voice, 'Poor little thing. I wonder if she'll ever see her parents again.'

'There's one bit of good news,' Sally said. 'I've phoned up Nanny Trotter and told her about maman. She says she'll come back. I've offered her a big pay increase. I'd better have some of Aunt Clothilde's money, Daddy. I know it's privilege but it's what Aunt Clothilde would have wanted. The trouble with Maman is that she's not good at releasing the purse strings. Have a gin. I brought some down with me.'

'Thank you, darling,' he said. His face was strained, for he knew how very ill his wife was.

Sally had returned – Gisela had parents. War threw up some strange situations, he thought. Indeed, War had made his own marriage. He remembered himself as a young soldier being greeted by the stuffy French family who had offered him hospitality, remembered the sudden intoxication of his first sight of Geneviève

Février de Roche, the steady charming gaze of her brown eyes.

And God alone knew what Sally was cooking up now on that stove.

Each summer evening at nine Sally, her father and Miss Trotter would gather in Geneviève's bedroom to listen to the BBC news. Already Rome had fallen; the Russian army was routing the last of the Germans. Britain had become an armed camp in preparation for the coming invasion of France.

Geneviève slept early and after the news the others normally went downstairs for cocoa or a drink.

It was Miss Trotter who said, one evening, 'I think Mrs Jackson-Bowles is staying with us by will-power. I believe she's waiting for the liberation of France.'

In the country, despite the absence of the men and the presence of the called-up land-girls in their brown breeches, much was still the same. Fields, hedgerows, the small roads, the swelling hills were as they always had been. In London, though, the rocket attacks continued. At Glebe House they waited.

Sally, whose grip on her purse in contrast to her mother's was excessively loose, threw ration books and principles to the winds and soon became part of a rural network of illicit food-providers. After dark parcels were delivered to the back door. Sally pedalled the lanes on her bicycle with eggs and bacon in the basket under her mac.

There was game, too, in more than one way, for Sally

had begun a flirtation with George Pomfret, the game-keeper of the local estate. Everybody in the neighbour-hood, including his employer and the local policeman, knew that George had deserted the Army after Dunkirk but no one was prepared to turn in Jenny Pomfret's only boy.

The plan to rear hens was abandoned but a kitten came back from a farm in Sally's bicycle basket. Gisela was overjoyed. Better still, from Sally's point of view, was the return of Miss Trotter, who, with money available for local bribery and corruption, soon managed to secure more help about the house.

And Geneviève's strength ebbed.

One May morning she said to Sally, 'I should like to see France free again.'

'Have you regretted your life in England, Maman?' Sally asked her.

'Of course not,' she replied. 'Your father is English. It is enough to have led my life with him. I'm sorry, Sally, you have never found that kind of happiness.'

'There's still time,' Sally said. Though Geneviève did not reply, her expression indicated that eternity would not be long enough to see her awkward daughter happily settled.

One evening in June, late, the still-light sky was darkened by thousands of planes, drumming overhead, thick as clouds. 'It's happening at last,' said Geneviève. She lived just long enough to see Paris liberated in late August.

It might have been true that, during those final months, Geneviève softened towards her difficult elder daughter but this sentiment was not reflected in her will. She had evened the score between Sally and her sister by dividing the bulk of a fairly large fortune between her husband and Betty. To Sally she left nothing but a picture of her own mother and her love.

Harry Jackson-Bowles was inconsolable, yet allowed no one to see his feelings.

It was after Geneviève's funeral that he told Sally, 'I've been putting some money aside for Gisela and now I can do a little more for her.'

Sally was touched. 'That's good of you, Daddy, especially now that you know she's not your granddaughter.'

'She'll need it more, perhaps. Jewish, isn't she?'

'Half Jewish.'

'Well, she doesn't look it so far,' he said. 'That's lucky. And, after all, there are many cultivated Jews.' These were the code-words for wealthy European Jewry, used by people such as Harry Jackson-Bowles, whose own culture went little further than Gilbert and Sullivan and one or two plays by Shakespeare.

Once the mourners had gone Harry, Sally, Betty and Gideon Cunningham and Miss Trotter were left alone in a house which, lacking Geneviève's presence, seemed lifeless.

Christmas 1944 came and went, and with the spring it had become obvious that the end of the war was now only weeks away. A general election loomed in the summer and Betty and Gideon had begun a campaign to move permanently into Glebe House with Harry. The house was bigger and more impressive than their own and would be useful for the launch of Gideon's political career. Betty had already mentioned this possibility to her father. But Harry was unready, so soon after his wife's funeral, to consider such an upheaval. Moreover, Gisela's name had not been mentioned and it seemed the new ménage Betty was planning did not include the little girl.

One evening, as the family sat together, Miss Trotter quietly knitting, while Gisela, on the floor, looked through a book, Betty reopened the subject.

Miss Trotter burst out, 'What about Gisela?'

Harry, profoundly tired, opened his mouth to speak. Betty got in ahead of him and was saying, 'That's Sally's responsibility, surely,' when the telephone rang in the hall.

Harry got up to answer it, returning shortly after to tell Sally, 'It's Adrian Pym for you.'

'Oh, Lord,' Sally said, and went to the phone. Less than five minutes later she was back in the room, chalk white. She said, 'I'm terribly sorry – I have to go back to London very quickly. I'm so sorry, Daddy.'

'I hope it's not bad news,' he said.

'I'm not sure,' she told him. She ran upstairs to pack.

'Rather a funny moment to leave,' Betty said into the silence.

'Perhaps there's an emergency at the Post Office,' Gideon suggested.

Not long after, Sally had made her farewells and was bumping towards London in George Pomfret's van, illegally fuelled with blackmarket petrol. Before she left she'd whispered to Miss Trotter, 'It's about Gisela's mother. Don't tell the others.'

'Is she alive?' the other woman murmured.

'I don't know,' Sally replied.

53

Into the silence of the early hours of Christmas Day Bruno Lowenthal said, 'So that was why Sally went to Dachau to find Gisela's mother, Claudia Stein.

'This was not easy. Dachau was still full of what came to be called displaced persons. Even though the camp had been liberated in April 1945, they had not opened the gates to allow the sick and starving to flood out. Typhoid fever had broken out. The US Army was guarding the camp.

'What Pym had told Sally as she stood, almost fainting, in the hall at Glebe House, was that Frenchmen on a mission to the camp had found in its prohibited area, where the hopeless cases, the dying, were penned, a skeletal figure who had spoken to one of them by name. They had barely recognised the figure of Claudia Stein. They had wrapped her in a sheet, as people wrap a dead body, and smuggled her from this area of the dying to the survivors' part of the camp, where they had covertly laid her down

314

by a hut to give her some minimal chance of life. They could do no more, had only been able to do this, they said, because there were no guards around. The soldiers were all in the guardhouse, hiding, afraid of typhus.

'In London Pym told Sally, "I've got you a plane and I've made some telephone calls. If you want to get her back you have to go there. You'll have to get past the guards somehow."

'Sally got in touch with Benoît and Charles du Tour in Paris and they called on a contact who had been in the Resistance. Through him they obtained French Army officers' uniforms and false papers. Sally was provided in London with a British nursing officer's uniform and had papers to match.

'They drove all day from Paris and by the next morning were at the gates, beyond which lay the acres of mud, the huts, the chimneys of Dachau.

'As they walked up to the guard-house, they saw an officer in the uniform of a US captain put down the telephone he had been speaking into, then quickly put on his gas mask.

'Benoît and Charles presented their papers and a sergeant, in helmet and gas mask, ordered the gates to be swung back. 'See Hamilton – he's over there in that block,' he told them, pointing.

'Sally, shocked by the mention of Eugene's name, dared say nothing.

'They marched forward over the mud, passing hundreds of ragged figures, hollow-eyed, skeletal and silent. The air was rank.

'In a small hut Eugene Hamilton sat at a desk, a man and a woman beside him, both evidently former prisoners. Others sat on chairs in front of the desk, waiting. He looked at Benoît, Charles and Sally as they came in and something like a smile crossed his weary face. Sally stepped up to him. "Eugene, I've come to take a prisoner out. Please let me – it's Gisela's mother."

'He said something to one of his helpers, who stood up. "We'll take you," Eugene said. "Sally?"

'"Cora told me about the letter. Will you come and see me – afterwards?"

'He nodded. Then she and Eugene, with Benoît and Charles, followed the tall, thin man, conducting them back into the smell of death.

'"What are you doing here?" she asked.

'"My regiment's been put to guard the camp," he said. "The captain won't come in and a lot of the other guys can't take it."

'A truck meandered towards them over the mud, followed by a crowd of prisoners, some barely able to walk.

'A gas-masked soldier looked out of the truck's window. "Hey, buddy, where do you want the load dumped?"

'"Over there," said Eugene, pointing to a heavily guarded shed.

'"What is this place?" the soldier asked.

'"You have come to Dachau," he said.

'"I've come to hell," said the driver, and he started up the truck again.

'"How can we find her?" Sally said, looking about. A

crowd of skeletal people were approaching them, languidly, and she felt as if her senses were leaving her.

'"She's lying down, in a sheet, we know that," Benoît said. His voice caught in his throat.

'And they found her, alone, for no one wanted to go near. She was almost unrecognisable to Sally, but as she looked from face to dying face, one skin-covered skull opened its eyes and whispered, "Sally."

'Charles carried Claudia in her sheet across the compound to the gates. Half-way across, Sally, tears running silently down her face, said to Eugene, "I loved you. Really, Eugene, I did." Then they parted.

'At the gates, Sally said, "We have papers for this woman. She is an important scientist required by the British Government. The papers are signed by General de Gaulle himself. These officers are the escort he has provided."

'And they were allowed to pass.

'They stretched Claudia out on the back seat of the car. She was unconscious now. The twins and Sally squeezed together in the front seat. Sally took the wheel.

'Claudia became conscious again and asked, "Gisela?"

'"Gisela's alive and well."

'"And Simon?"

'"I don't know. We can only hope."

'They had to stop every half-hour, because of the dysentery. The car was full of that smell and with it the smell of the camp. They stopped by a river, washed Claudia a little, for that thin, fevered body was too frail to endure much. They dressed her in a cotton frock. She became unconscious again. They carried her back to the car and continued the dreadful journey.

'"Where are we going?"

'"Paris."

'"I won't get there."

'"You will," Sally asserted, but she did not believe it. She thought of Gisela, running about in the big house in England.

'"We must – must – find Simon," Claudia said, as if the miracle of her own discovery could be achieved again.

'"The news is coming through, slowly, in Paris. Trains are coming back. There are lists of those returning every day in the papers," Benoît said. "There's a bureau – crowds go there every day for news. We'll investigate. There is hope."

'The faint voice came from the back of the car. "I think I'm beyond hope." There was a pause. Claudia said, "Not the Germans. Not people. Governments. The governments create all this."'

54

When they reached Paris, exhausted, they carried Claudia upstairs to the handsome flat and laid her on a bed in an empty room. Benoît fetched boiled water and as Sally moistened Claudia's cracked lips she heard the sounds of argument outside the room. The voices began to repeat again and again. 'What has she got? Typhus! And what else? She must go to the hospital.'

'Hospital – typhus – this is unbearable! She must go! Hospital – typhus. We must have the flat fumigated. Intolerable. Unbearable.'

Then orders were shouted, feet thundered to and fro, there were thuds and bangs.

Five minutes later there was silence. Benoît came in with a carafe of water and a glass half full of milk. They propped Claudia up. She drank the milk greedily and said, 'More.'

'The doctor's coming,' he said. 'No more till then.' Claudia closed her eyes and moaned. Then she seemed to sleep again.

Benoît muttered to Sally, 'Mother and Father didn't like it. When we refused to move Claudia they took the line of least resistance and left for the farm with Célestine.'

'That's all right, then,' Sally said.

The doctor paused in the doorway, looking at the form on the bed. He didn't understand. Then he realised that Claudia was not yet dead.

Her temperature was 105 degrees. The doctor shook his head. Shortly after he left the phone rang.

'It was Adrian Pym,' Charles said, putting his head round the door. 'How did he get the number?'

'He can do anything,' Sally said.

'What does he want with—?' Charles asked, looking at the woman they all thought would die.

In the panic of finding Claudia, Sally had not considered Pym's motives in wanting her saved. Now she paused briefly, to ask herself the question. For a long time Pym had been feeding her with stories of the German treatment of European Jewry, from sources public and secret. Now this. She looked down at the skeletal figure, lips blackened with fever.

'What?' Charles asked again.

'I don't know.' Then she looked at Claudia, thought she was dead, put her hand on her brow. She was hot, so hot.

'Shall I get the doctor back?' he asked.

'Yes – yes.'

The doctor came once, twice, sometimes three times a day, for a week, during which it seemed impossible that Claudia could survive.

And then the fever broke. She began to recover.

Sally thought of Eugene, who must still be in Dachau. She wrote to him.

She began to visit the Gare d'Orsay, the station at which the deportees arrived back in France. They were mostly prisoners-of-war, and men who had been taken off to forced labour. Among them were some concentration-camp survivors, although so far only a fifth had been released. With the others she joined in the chorus of names of the missing, 'Simon! Simon Stein!' as the long lines of returning men came through the station, walking, supporting each other. The name was never recognised.

'There's still hope, Claudia.'

But Claudia said nothing, as if she did not wish to hope, or was certain that her husband was dead.

Eventually Claudia was fit enough to travel in a plane. Adrian Pym arranged the flight and met them in a car at the airfield in Kent. As they drove to London it became plain that he had assumed they would take Claudia to Pontifex Street. But Sally, now suspicious, refused to do so. There was a row as they neared London, in which Claudia took no part. She still weighed less than five stone and was confused much of the time. She was dazed, often afraid, always hungry. Sometimes she thought of her daughter, or of Simon, and wept silently, tears rolling down her wasted, papery cheeks. For long periods of the day she was motionless, inert, yet at night she could sleep only after taking heavy sleeping pills.

As the argument in the car went on Sally began bitterly to regret having taken up Pym's offer of a flight back to Britain. It was true that they could not have stayed on much longer in the du Tours' Paris apartment for the parents were still angry about what had happened and always on the telephone asking how soon Sally and Claudia would be leaving. Nevertheless they could have gone somewhere in the countryside, where Claudia would have gained strength before any further journey. And now Sally asked herself again about Pym's motives in organising the rescue. She had believed he had done it to help her which, she now thought, had been pretty naïve of her, considering what Pym was like.

'Claudia's coming to my house,' Sally shouted. 'And then, when she wants to, up to my parents' to see her daughter. I don't know why you're doing this, Loomie, why you pushed so hard for us to come back. What do you want? She can't even climb the stairs at Pontifex Street. Everything's ready at my house. She'll be by the door – she can come and go when she wants, when she's strong enough.'

'Your house is dilapidated,' Pym said. 'It's not fit for someone in Claudia's condition.'

'I don't understand this,' said Sally.

'There are people who want to see Claudia.'

'Who? What's going on?'

Something alerted Claudia now. 'I'll go to Sally's,' she said.

'Good,' said Sally.

'It's unsuitable. I'm not taking her there,' Pym said.

Sally said nothing. They were going through Croydon.

When they reached the centre of London, she said, 'Stop the car.'

'Don't be absurd,' he said, driving on.

'Stop by this cab rank,' said Sally, who had spotted the war-time miracle, a stationary cab, at a rank. 'I'll get a policeman,' she threatened. 'I'll accuse you of kidnap.'

Pym, sulking, complied.

Sally helped Claudia out. No one was in the cab so, with Claudia leaning on her, Sally went into a nearby café and shouted, 'Is the cab driver here?'

'I'm eating my dinner,' said a man at one of the tables. Doubtful eyes were now taking in the sight of Sally, in a rage, and Claudia's death's-head face.

'Please,' said Sally, 'can you drive us? This woman's just come out of a German camp.'

The man stood up and walked over to them. 'Is she all right?' he asked Sally.

'I'm all right,' Claudia said. 'Please take us.'

55

Bruno Lowenthal stopped the tape recorder. He had scarcely rested since he had opened his shop yesterday. It was now two thirty on Christmas morning. The streets were silent. The noise downstairs had ceased around midnight.

Tomorrow he would face the annual ordeal of Christmas dinner with that madwoman in the basement and her family.

But he had, he considered, almost finished his story. He would complete it the next morning and get the tapes to Greg Phillips. Now he must sleep.

Rising tiredly from his chair he went to his warm bedroom, undressed and got into bed. He felt a long way from the world he had been describing. Wars, armies, cities in flames, death – fifty years was a long time. It was strange that the arrival of that young man, Greg, which had at first seemed such a nuisance – indeed, potentially so threatening – had turned out to be ... what did one call it? A blessing in disguise.

He drifted into sleep with muddled images of himself and Briggs, young and loving, in Berlin, before his eyes. He saw Sally at the cabaret, faces in torchlight, swastikas flying. He heard the sound of breaking glass. He slept.

56

At Chapel Manor Farm Greg, alone upstairs, heard, in his sleep, what he thought were phones ringing. Each time when he half awoke at the sound he found the house silent – but Katherine was still not in bed.

Next morning dawned clear, bright and cold. The bed was still empty.

Mad thoughts went through his brain. Katherine had left the house that night – both she and Simon had packed up and left as he slept – she was in bed with her old crippled uncle – they had locked him in his room.

His blood racing, he showered, dressed and went downstairs. At the breakfast table sat Simon, composed and clad in a blue cashmere sweater and well-pressed jeans. Katherine was beautiful, but pale and withdrawn, wearing a soft red woollen dress, her hair piled up and secured with a gold comb.

'Happy Christmas, Greg,' she greeted him.

'Happy Christmas to you – and to you, too, Simon,' he responded, and sat down.

Katherine got up quickly. 'What would you like, Greg?' she asked. 'Sausage, bacon and eggs? Boiled egg? Mushrooms?'

'Just coffee and toast, thank you,' he said.

He looked at Simon, whose face was taut and eyes a little worried, and thought, Greg, you've spent the night in an empty bed, you've come downstairs and found your girlfriend and another man eating breakfast. They both look a little embarrassed. They're bright and friendly but they can't meet your eye. Haven't you been here before, sucker? OK, it's not very likely Katherine's sleeping with a crippled man twice her age who also happens to be her uncle, but that's not the point. Something's going on. This is a relationship – Katherine and Simon. Forget Katherine and Greg.

Simon said encouragingly, 'Have a proper breakfast, Greg. It's Christmas Day, after all.'

He himself had abandoned a boiled egg half eaten. Katherine's plate contained only toast crumbs.

Katherine sat down again. Greg had the idea she would have felt more comfortable if she could have run into the kitchen to produce a large British breakfast, but he didn't feel inclined to let her off the hook, Christmas or no Christmas. He said, 'I kept having the idea, all night, that the phone was ringing.'

'It must have been jingle bells,' Katherine said. 'Which reminds me, we thought we'd open our presents before lunch. We've got a last-minute invitation to pre-lunch

327

drinks with some friends of Simon's near Dorchester. It's a bit of a drive – we'd have to leave about eleven thirty. Will that be all right?'

'Excellent,' said Greg. He drank his coffee and stood up. 'I'll take a walk,' he said, and left the room, sensing the relief behind him. He put on his jacket and took the path by the tor down to the river.

It was quiet. The sun shone and he heard church bells ringing in the distance. A little edgy after a night spent in and out of sleep, he looked across the small, slow-moving river and thought, They say you can never step in the same river twice, but he had tried, with Katherine. And it hadn't worked. That pretty, clever, loving young woman of six years before had toughened up. Perhaps she'd had to. Times had been hard in Britain. There wasn't a lot to go round and to get what little there was, he imagined, it probably paid to be in with the right people, the great and the good. Those people had connections in the Oxbridge world to which she belonged, that world which still had its roots deep in the heart of the Establishment, whatever they said. Perhaps Katherine wasn't just venal; perhaps that was where her loyalties really lay. With her uncle and her uncle's old lover, Briggs; with Sir Peveril and his kind.

So whatever they said, Katherine had, in his parents' terminology, sold out. Sold him out. Because he might start a scandal for them. Now they were really scared because here was Pym coming back with secret files. More scandal.

Well, Greg thought, this certainly was a beautiful spot and he certainly felt lonely in it.

He walked along, then turned towards Merricombe. When he came to the village pub, he stopped outside it, as he had planned. From the call-box there, he telephoned Bruno Lowenthal.

When the old man answered, Greg said, 'I hope I'm not too early for you. Merry Christmas anyway.'

'Greg?' came the harsh voice. 'So good to hear from you. Merry Christmas – at least, I hope it's being a merry one.'

'It isn't,' Greg told him.

'I'm not surprised. Listen – I'm finishing the story on tape! What a surprise for you, eh? Will that be your best Christmas present? I think so.'

'God, Bruno, that's good of you.'

'We've no time to waste so I have purchased this little machine, just like yours, and you will be surprised to learn it obeys me completely.'

Greg said, 'I would always believe you could do anything you wanted to do, Bruno. But I have a problem. I've discovered I'm staying in the house Briggs gave to his lover Simon Ledbetter, who happens to be my girlfriend's uncle.'

'It's a nice house, eh?'

'Very nice. And he has some nice paintings – and several drawings by Eugene Hamilton he didn't mention to me.'

'I heard of the house, dear boy, many years ago. And I have to tell you, Greg, I got a call from someone in Sir

Peveril Jones's employ. They told me where you were. They want to meet me – to shut me up, I suppose.'

Greg was shocked. 'Bruno, I'm sorry. Do you think I'm responsible for all this – stirring things up?'

'Don't worry. I've suspected for many years that one day there'd be a problem. The bomb and the fuse have been in place for many years. All you did was strike the match.'

'They've been up all night here on the phone.'

'Romantic for you.'

'You can say that again.'

'It doesn't go well?'

'It goes horribly. They're worried about the book, I think. And Pym's return.'

'And your girlfriend has turned against you?'

'I'm beginning to wonder if she was ever for me. She must have known for some time about her uncle's connection with all this but she never said a word.'

'Do you think Ledbetter was working for Briggs – also for the Soviets?'

'Oh, Christ!' said Greg. 'I don't know. I don't think so. He said his career had been in medical research at Cambridge.'

'It depends what kind of medical research it was,' Bruno said. 'But in a world of secrets one suspects everything. Never mind. Tell me, when are you coming back?'

'Tomorrow. The atmosphere's terrible here. I'd leave now but to walk out on Christmas Day would be too much. There's no transport and I've got the car. I'd be stranding Katherine.'

'Come back as soon as you can,' said Bruno. 'You'll like what I have for you. I'm sure of it. Merry Christmas again.'

'Merry Christmas to you too,' Greg said glumly.

He put down the phone and walked resolutely back to the house. At least he had Bruno's new material to look forward to – if he nourished that thought he could get through Christmas Day without disgrace. Mercifully, by the time he got back to the house it would be time to set out for the drinks party with Simon's friends. Then there'd be Christmas dinner with other people and all that socialising would cut down the amount of time the three of them would be obliged to spend together. With luck, Greg thought, he could keep Christmas Day civilised and get away early next morning.

It was in this more philosophical mood that he entered the house and ran upstairs to change into his suit. As he did so he thought that they were supposed now to open their presents. Well, if no one else mentioned it, he certainly wasn't going to.

Their hosts, the Hope-Rudstons, lived in a long Jacobean house, set in an old garden. Behind it were water meadows and a lake. Greg suppressed impatience as they entered the house and met their hostess, a smiling, needle-thin woman in pale cashmere. He was becoming tired of these nice houses in nice settings in the country, tired of feeling like a stranger in what was beginning to feel like a strange land, tired of watching Simon's back as he whizzed off into the centre of a crowd of friends.

Katherine hailed him from the middle of the room, and

331

when he joined her she introduced him to a beautiful girl with long blonde hair, Amelia. 'Thank goodness,' she told Amelia. 'I don't know a soul here.'

'Here's Rupert – Rupert Hennessy,' Amelia said. A tall young man in black joined them. 'Jon Hope-Rudston,' said Amelia. As Greg turned his head to say hello his glance struck a large mirror hanging over the fireplace. Reflected in it was a group of five men near the opposite wall talking. One of them, full face to the room, was Sir Peveril Jones and he thought he saw Sir Peveril's eyes flick towards him, then away.

Interrupting Jon Hope-Rudston, who was saying something about a party, Greg said, directly to Katherine, 'Why, there's Sir Peveril Jones over there by the wall. Who'd have thought it?' A promising chess player at high school until he'd got tired of being called a nerd and started concentrating on football, Greg decided that the situation merited a random opening gambit and, turning abruptly, marched straight over to Sir Peveril. They said that if you went up to a hundred people and hissed in the ear of each, 'I know everything,' ninety-eight would go pale.

Apologising, as he pushed past the men with Sir Peveril, he went up close to him and said, in a low voice, 'I know everything.' Then he turned and walked out.

And that, he thought, starts and finishes the game.

He would not go back to the party. He would not have what he believed was an arranged interview – set up by Simon and Katherine – with Sir Peveril Jones.

On the other hand, he couldn't bring himself to drive off, leaving Katherine and her crippled uncle stranded.

He went to where the cars were parked, opened the door of his own, got in and sat down to wait until the party ended.

Half an hour later a face appeared at the car window, that of the lean black-clad young man to whom Greg had been introduced.

'Jon Hope-Rudston – we met,' he said, apologetically. 'They sent me off to find out where you were.'

'Well, I guess you know now,' Greg said.

'Had enough of the party? I don't blame you,' he said. 'Mind if I join you?' He opened the door on the other side of the car and climbed in. Then he produced a packet of cigarettes and took one out. 'Do you object?' he asked.

'No.'

Jon lit up, and from the smell Greg deduced that this was no ordinary cigarette. Jon took a drag then offered it to Greg. 'Do you inhale at all?' he asked.

'Thanks,' Greg said, taking the joint and breathing in deeply. He handed it back.

'Sorry about the intrusion,' Jon said. 'Any particular reason why you're sitting in the car?'

'I found out I don't like my host, Mr Ledbetter, he doesn't like me and neither does my girlfriend. It's Christmas Day, I'm six thousand miles from home and I think I'm being conned,' Greg replied.

'I see,' Jon said. He smoked the joint pensively for a few moments, then passed it back to Greg. 'I hope you don't mind me sitting here,' he said. 'You know what Christmas is like, a bit of a strain.'

'Do you live here all the time?'

'No, in London. I'm a solicitor, very junior.'

He lit another joint, took a drag and handed it over. 'I don't want to use up all your supply,' said Greg.

'It's all right. I've got loads. Anyway, if I run out I can get some more from the gardener.'

'He grows it?'

'No, he buys it in Dorchester.' He stretched. 'I'd better go in and say I found you, I suppose.'

'Tell them I'm asleep.'

'OK. Nice meeting you.'

'Thanks for the smoke.'

'A pleasure,' said Jon, and went off. Greg shut his eyes, relaxed.

Not long afterwards, Katherine came to the car. Greg got out. 'Jon said you were asleep,' Katherine said.

'I did drop off,' Greg told her. 'Sorry.'

'We're about to leave. Do come back inside and say goodbye.'

'Sure,' said Greg amiably. He realised there was no way out of the interview with Sir Peveril, but the difference was that now he didn't care much.

'Sir Peveril was a bit put out by something you said to him before you went out,' Katherine said lightly, as they walked towards the front steps. 'Apparently you went up to him and said, "I know everything."'

'It was a joke,' Greg told her. 'I never called him an asshole – or a traitor – and I guess he's both.'

She stood still in front of the house. 'Greg, you're being very peculiar.'

'Jon Hope-Rudston offered me a strange-tasting cigarette,' Greg said.

'He didn't – Oh, God, you haven't?' Katherine said disgustedly. 'Can you drive?'

'I can drive. I just can't connive,' said Greg, and smiling widely, he bounded into the house.

Sir Peveril dropped any pretence that this was a casual meeting. He was waiting in the hall when Greg walked in and came up to him immediately. Grasping Greg's arm he said, 'I wonder if we could have a word in private.'

'Sure,' Greg agreed, moving to regain possession of his arm.

'This way, then,' Sir Peveril said, and led the way to a study off the hall. They sat down in an atmosphere of furniture polish and unread books.

Greg leaned back in his chair, still a little irritated that the determination of the Ledbetters and Sir Peveril had forced him into a conversation he did not want. He said, 'I don't really want to be here. Is this about Adrian Pym?'

Sir Peveril, evidently deciding it would not serve him well to take offence, replied, 'It concerns Pym indirectly, more particularly perhaps it concerns your book. You've been talking to Bruno Lowenthal, of course, about Sally Bowles.'

Greg said the first thing that came to him: 'Is she dead?'

Annoyed at being deflected, Sir Peveril replied brusquely, 'Dead? No, she's not.'

Greg was very startled by this answer, which he had not really expected. 'She's not? So where is she?' he demanded eagerly.

'You'd better ask your friend Mr Lowenthal. I'm surprised he hasn't told you,' Sir Peveril replied. 'Now, concerning Pym, obviously he has the capacity to do immense damage to this country's reputation . . .'

But Greg was hardly listening. He knew more or less what Sir Peveril was about to say. What shook him was that Sir Peveril had no doubt Sally was alive or that Bruno – Bruno! – knew where she was. The old bastard. The evil old bastard. Sir Peveril leaned forward and tapped Greg's knee as if to attract his attention. Greg hated that tap. He was caught by another mention of Bruno's name.

'No doubt Lowenthal's inaccurate anecdotes involve Pym during the war. If you publish these damaging statements, Pym may be tempted to retaliate. The developments could be dangerous.'

'It was a long time ago, sir,' Greg told him. 'Fifty years. Most of the people in the world weren't born then.'

'That's not relevant to what I'm saying. The times we're talking about are on the borderline between present time and history, close enough to have a bearing on the future. In particular, on our relationships with other countries, including your own.'

'Once upon a time,' said Greg, still thinking about the extant Sally Bowles, 'there was heavy Communist infiltration of the British secret service. The traitors worked undetected for many years, were exposed and fled in the nineteen fifties. The damage they did is accounted for. From what I understand there's nothing dangerous in what I have to say.'

'Let's say I might know a little more about that than you,' Sir Peveril told him.

The room was suddenly too hot and too small. Greg wanted to get out. He forced himself to reply. 'I'd be grateful for any comments you might like to make when my book is complete.'

'There is a likelihood that publication of the book will be stopped,' Sir Peveril said.

Greg had half expected this. 'I'll be sorry if that happens in the UK.'

He knew Sir Peveril must understand that an embargo in Britain would make little difference to him. His contract was with an American publisher. News of British censorship might even help sales.

'I think the State Department might easily come to the same view as the British Government,' Sir Peveril replied.

Greg, half stoned, child of freedom marchers, stood up and said, 'I don't, I have to tell you. Any British cover-up would be more to protect the reputations of a small group here than to serve any public interest. I think my government would feel the same. There's nothing you can say that will stop me from writing the book, Sir Peveril.'

Sir Peveril sighed and looked at him coldly. 'If that's the case, I have to tell you your presence is no longer welcome in this country. Mr Phillips, you are under a deportation order, effective as of eight o'clock tomorrow morning, the twenty-sixth. A BA flight to New York is leaving at ten a.m. tomorrow and your name has been placed on the passenger list. If you do not avail yourself of your seat, you render your status that of an illegal immigrant. You may be arrested by the police and imprisoned until deportation.'

Greg laughed. 'If you want to attract the attention of the world to Pym's return, you're certainly going the right way about it.' He left the room.

Katherine was in the hall, waiting for him.

'It looks like I have to leave the country,' he said to her.

'My God,' said Katherine. 'Why?'

As if on cue, Simon came up in his wheelchair. 'We must go,' Katherine told him. They all said goodbye to their hostess and silently got into the car, Simon in front as usual, Katherine in the back. Driving along, Greg said, 'I'm getting deported, but I guess you knew, so it'd be nice if nobody started saying, "What a shock, Greg. I'm so sorry." I'll leave right away.'

'Oh,' said Katherine. 'You must stay to lunch.'

'Yeah – we can pull crackers and put on paper hats,' he said. 'Tell me this, Katherine, if I hadn't got in touch with you, once you heard what I was doing, would you have got in touch with me?'

'It was just a coincidence,' she said.

'Fuck you,' he said.

The rest of the journey passed in silence.

Back at Chapel Manor Farm he parked. They all got

out of the car and Greg went upstairs to fetch his bag. As he closed the front door he heard the phone ring. Katherine and Simon, together in the drawing room, did not come out to say goodbye.

57

After Greg's call from Dorset Bruno sat down again and continued to speak into his tape-recorder.

'Claudia began to live in Sally's house. Antonia and Ricardo spent a lot of time there, helping. I would go when I could, for it was only by chance that I had avoided the fate of Claudia and Simon Stein. Of Simon there was still no news.

'It was terrible,' Bruno said. 'It was quite terrible. Claudia's state of mind was not good. When you think what had happened to her, what she had seen, what she had endured, that was not surprising. She was like a zombie, clear about only one or two things, one being that her daughter must not see her until she looked more like a mother – anyone – should. The other, that her husband was dead.

'So I would go there and help, cleaning, that sort of thing. Sally was hopeless at it. In any case, the house was unmanageable. Sometimes I'd cook some German food and Claudia and I would talk. It was easier for her to use German, though difficult for her to speak at all sometimes. Sometimes she would pause, look ahead of her into space and tears would begin to run down her face. This was difficult for me,' Bruno said. 'I'm not good at such things. She was so broken, so weak. There would be these long silences, where you could almost feel the nightmares building in her head. And at other times she would speak fluently, but of times and people I did not know – of her childhood, of films she had seen before the war, but never about Dachau. It chilled me. It frightened me. Many times I did not want to be there. Sometimes I would arrange to go and visit her then cancel at the last moment. I am ashamed of this, but I am a selfish man. I can only take so much.

'But you must have the whole story. Well, then,' said Bruno. At this point he got up and poured himself a brandy. He sipped a little and went on speaking. 'The Steins met at the Berlin Institute of Technology before the war. They were both top of their classes, sometimes Simon in position one and Claudia second, sometimes the other way about. But, of course, Simon was a Jew. Claudia was not. They married in nineteen thirty-six, the year Hitler made it illegal for Jews to marry Gentiles, but Claudia and Simon did it anyway. They had to keep the marriage a secret.

'By this time Simon could not get the work he was qualified to do, because of his race. But Claudia was taken on by Walter Dornburger at the experimental rocket station at Kummersdorf-West, not too far from

Berlin. I don't know if you appreciate fully what this is all about, Greg. I think you will know the name of Claudia's superior, though. He was Werner von Braun. So there was Claudia in the Army Weapons Department, involved in developing rocket technology, while Simon worked as a hospital orderly, which was all he could get. The country was becoming a hell for Jews. And they were living apart, at two different addresses, pretending not to be married.

'Of course, they should have left but they couldn't see into the future, could they? Clever as they were, they couldn't know . . .

'Later, around nineteen thirty-eight, Sally returned to Germany and tried to take up again with Christian von Torgau, to discover that this once enlightened and civilised man, free-thinking and cultured, had become a fanatic. How such a thing can happen I don't know. It's possible to understand the poor and deprived adopting a philosophy that promises them power and wealth and tells them they have a natural superiority over another group of people, so they can treat others as they themselves have been treated – but a von Torgau? A man with almost everything? What did he want? A faith? More power when Hitler had conquered the world? I don't know – some things you can never know.

'His wife Julia was not with him in this. Julia's family was even older than von Torgau's. She was more aristocratic, even, than he. She was a cold woman, haughty, and I don't know what their marriage was like. It was suitable, though, and two sons were born, which, I suppose, was the point of it. Julia disliked Sally, but not because she was von Torgau's mistress – I expect the marriage was by that time beyond love, jealousy, all the rest. No, I think she disliked Sally because Sally was Sally, disorderly and English, and she didn't know the rules. I suppose a woman like Julia would expect to be respected by her husband's mistress, as she might have been respected by anyone who was, in some way, in the family service. Which Sally didn't understand and didn't care about. However, when it came to the point, Julia couldn't believe in Hitler. She believed in her country, but not in Hitler. So there it was.

'Now the von Torgaus and the Steins were friends, which you might think strange, but no, Simon Stein's father had been the von Torgaus' banker. The Steins were greatly cultured, something, perhaps, of more importance in Germany than in Britain. And Christian and Julia had a passion for music, as had Simon and Claudia. Julia was a good pianist. She had a natural talent. Simon was a fair violinist and Claudia played the cello. They would meet often, sometimes just for a meal or to talk, sometimes to play music, purely for the fun, because they loved it, a feeling which transcends class and race and politics. Musicians are musicians. You will remember I told you I was there one evening, before the Nazis put an end to everything good, including their music. Von Torgau's conversion ended their friendship also, but Julia maintained her loyalty to her friends and continued to see them.

'By now Claudia was working on rocket fuels. This was crucial work, of course, for without light fuel the necessary impetus could not be achieved for successful launching. The scientists weren't keen on the weapons side of the affair. It was the rockets themselves they were interested in. There was a lot of politics – for the first three years of the war Hitler, for example, was not convinced about the use of rockets in warfare. Just as well – if he'd become keen earlier he might have won the war. Never mind, it didn't happen.

'Claudia got pregnant about the time Britain declared war, and went back to her parents to have a child few knew about. Fewer still knew the paternity of the child, not even Claudia's parents, who had to accept that their daughter had come home to bear an illegitimate child in secret.

'The child was born. Claudia returned to Berlin with her and gave her to a woman in the house where she lived to bring up. She went back to her work.

'Remember, the child was half Jewish, the marriage had been illegal. All three, Claudia, Simon and the baby, were in grave danger. Each year the punishment of the Jews grew worse. In the week of Claudia's return Simon was arrested. He had been picked up at the hospital where he worked and accused of theft. This was probably the action of a malicious fellow worker. It's certain he was innocent. But he was a Jew. He was condemned, he disappeared. It was Julia who made the enquiries – Claudia could not afford to be so involved. But even Julia got nowhere. As for finding Simon, he had disappeared, no one knew where. Claudia's position was impossible – her husband was missing, perhaps dead, her child, in Nazi Germany, half Jewish, and then there was her work – poor woman, poor woman.

'And so to Sally. I think she was what they called a stay-behind. There was a secret service organisation, called Department D, as it had been since the days of the Fenians at the end of the last century. Even before the war began they started persuading people to stay behind in Europe – most important, of course, were those prepared to remain in Germany. I think Pym, who was well placed in intelligence at the time and who had known Sally in Berlin, was responsible for persuading her to stay in Germany. And report back. I think Theo Fitzpatrick, who was also up to his neck in the secret world, was in it too. I think Pym was "running" Sally, as they put it. Imagine how furious he must have felt when she turned up in London with Claudia and Simon's baby instead of staying where she was sending information. The fact that remaining in Germany put her in a position of extreme danger wasn't likely to worry Pym. That's what I guess. It's not what I know.

'Anyway, Julia von Torgau knocked on Sally's door one day and offered her money and the right papers to leave with the baby. Julia and Claudia knew that this was the last possible moment to get to safety. If Sally could go to France, which was still fighting, then she would be all right on her British passport, Julia thought. No one anticipated then how quickly the French Army would collapse.

'And Sally agreed. She told me that in Germany she'd been getting more and more frightened. Julia's offer came at the right moment for her. Claudia, poor

woman, brought the baby one night and Sally left with
Gisela.

'As I say, Pym must have been furious when she turned
up. He was a man who played chess using people as the
pieces on the board. Sally's arrival must have seemed as
if a rook had got up and strolled off.

'Sally claimed that Gisela was hers and Pym at first
believed her but then he found out who Gisela's parents
were. He had another contact, a man in the same building
in Berlin where Sally had lived. This man had seen a
woman arrive with a baby the night Sally left. That led
Pym to guess the baby wasn't Sally's but he would never
have found out who the mother was if Claudia hadn't
broken down and prevailed on Pym's contact to get a
message to Sally to discover if she and the baby had arrived
safely. Of course, the message fell into Pym's hands.

'He was delighted. Now he had a woman at the
Kummersdorf research institute, right at the heart of the
experimental work on rockets. And he had the woman's
child in Britain. So he could threaten Claudia with taking
her baby from Sally if she did not send information
through his contact. And he had Sally where he wanted
her by telling her that if she put a foot wrong he would
turn Claudia in. Whether he would or would not have
done so, that is not the kind of bluff you call.

'Blackmail – double blackmail – of two women and a
helpless child. Pym must have thought his lucky day had
come. And all the time he could feed a percentage of his
information to the British Government and quite a lot to
the Soviets, securing his position in both places.

'He must have been happier still when he heard of von Torgau's appointment to the German general staff in Paris. Here was the chance for more blackmail. Sally had to go to von Torgau because Pym threatened that if she didn't he'd betray Claudia to the Germans. Von Torgau, Pym thought, would have to co-operate with Sally, to some extent, because if even a portion of the story between them came out he would have been ruined as a serving officer. All this was a triumph for Pym, there behind the scenes, pulling all the strings. What he didn't know was that it had been Julia von Torgau who'd organised the removal of the baby. He was furious when he found out.

'Meanwhile, poor Claudia was providing information on all the work at Kummersdorf and of the internal politics behind it, the decisions, the funding and so forth, and also the location of the rocket launching station they had built on the Baltic coast. All this she did for three years. I don't know how she bore it. Then the entire project fell under the control of the SS and something went wrong. I don't know what it was, but Claudia was caught, tortured and thrown into Dachau.'

Bruno sighed and was silent for several minutes. Then he poured himself another brandy, sat down and spoke on.

'You are amazed, aren't you? But there's more. Pym wanted Claudia to go to Russia – that was the point of the rescue from the camp. She was going to be a sort of present from Pym to the Soviet Union. She'd been working under von Braun for several years (and the Americans already had *him*, for their rocket programme).

'The race was on between the Soviets and the Americans. Pym had to help the Soviets – yes? They needed the rocket launchers to launch atomic weapons, just like the Americans. They wanted to get into space too. This was a race to control the world. And Claudia had been in Dachau for only a year. She could still be useful. She knew the direction of the research, the problems, some of the solutions – oh, yes. She could still be useful in Russia. Pym was playing for high stakes, eh, Greg? Now you see what kind of a man you spoke to in Moscow. Who Pym is. Why, old as he is, people are still frightened of him.'

'But before Pym made his next move Claudia and Sally went to see Gisela. Sally said the visit started badly.

58

'Sally and Claudia arrived, very tired from the journey, and walked up the drive to the front of Glebe House to find a large furniture van parked in front. The Cunninghams were moving in.

'Betty was addressing one of the removal men in harsh tones as he brought a box from the van. "For God's sake, be careful what you're doing, man." Gideon Cunningham was outside with Harry Jackson-Bowles, while the Cunninghams' two boys, Neville and Christopher, were chasing Gisela's cat across the lawn. It climbed an ornamental peach-tree, which they shook to and fro to dislodge the animal.

'At that point Gisela was holding Miss Trotter's hand at the front door near Gideon and Harry, with an expression of intense confusion on her face.

'Then up the drive came the two tired and shabby women – Sally and Claudia. By agreement Miss Trotter had told Gisela only that Sally was coming with another lady and the child had enquired no further, like the well brought-up child she was. But she had plainly suspected all along that the other woman might be her mother. After all, Sally had said they were looking for her. Therefore, the moment she spotted the pair she broke free of Miss Trotter and rushed to Sally and Claudia. Claudia looked pitifully down at her daughter's bright little face and tears ran down her cheeks as she knelt, painfully, to be closer to the child. Gisela looked into that tear-stained, wasted face, shocked and half fearful. Claudia was not the happy, pretty mother a young child might have imagined. Yet, I suppose, when she looked into those eyes she saw a kind of love she hadn't known before, for she smiled at the woman, kneeling there, and said, 'Are you my mother? Did Sally find you?' And Claudia just nodded and they embraced each other.

'Betty came straight up. She just said, "If you're staying, I hope you've brought your ration books." Can you imagine it? She must have been keen to get rid of Gisela, who would have spoiled the image she was trying to present. She didn't offer them a cup of tea, even. They only stayed an hour or so, and when they left, Miss Trotter went with them, saying that now Gisela had her mother back she would no longer be necessary. This didn't please Betty.

'Anyway, Sally, Claudia and Gisela, with the cat in a sack, got back to the railway station in the furniture van, by now in good spirits. Incidentally the arrangement at Glebe House didn't last long,' Bruno said. 'Harry Jackson-Bowles couldn't stand his home being taken over and full of Gideon's political friends, and Betty was cultivating the county people, who rather looked down on him. He sold Glebe House and bought a small place in the village. Miss Trotter returned as housekeeper and they spent the rest of his life together. They went abroad a lot.' Bruno observed, 'He was a nice man. When he died he left Miss Trotter all his money. Betty wanted to challenge the will, but Sally wouldn't. In the end Gideon Cunningham was not even elected. There was an enormous Labour Party victory that year and the Cunninghams, in disgust, emigrated to South Africa. Betty and Sally never met again.

'Anyway, for the time being Gisela, Claudia and Sally all lived together in Sally's house. There was still no news of Simon. I don't think there ever was.

'Then one day – and here comes Pym again, like a stage villain – Sally came back unexpectedly to her house. The war against Japan was not over so she was still at the munitions works. But that day the power had failed. She found Claudia in tears in her room, trying to pack. It was just as well that Sally turned up when she did – a fluke – for in another half-hour Claudia and Gisela would have left the house.

'Of course, Sally wanted to know what was going on. Then, to her enormous surprise, Pym emerged, saying, "Claudia and the child are going to the Soviet Union. All the papers are ready."

'There was, of course, a problem with Claudia. All countries were reluctant to take in sudden influxes of displaced persons. The war in Europe had just ended and millions were in transit, trying to get back to places that no longer existed, trying to find somewhere to live. There were procedures, health checks, investigations. Claudia had been through none of these. She had been abducted from under the nose of the American Army and smuggled into Britain.

'They were starting to sort it out – it would all have worked in the end, but Claudia's nerves were out of order. She had Gisela to worry about and was terrified that once again they would be separated. Imagine what she'd been through. So when Pym came along, with all the right papers, a job fixed for Claudia in Leningrad and many threats about how she would become a stateless person if she stayed in Britain, that she and her child would be flung back into the European tide of refugees, she believed him. Pym had fixed it with the Soviets. Claudia was going east.

'What a row there was! Sally knew that what he was doing was wrong. All right, politically she sided with the Soviets, but instinctively she knew it was wrong for Pym to use Claudia, in the state she was in – and Gisela, of course – as pawns in his game.

'Sally got a message to Ricardo and Antonia and they arrived. As anarchists they had no love for the Soviets, who had betrayed them in the Spanish Civil War. The row raged round the house, Claudia in tears, saying first one thing, then another, Pym threatening her, Gisela bewildered and frightened.

'Sally phoned me at the hospital. Thinking the easiest thing to do was remove Claudia and Gisela from the house, at least until the plane left, she asked me to get hold of Briggs's car. It was an emergency, she said. Well,

I couldn't get the car because Briggs had taken it to work. I didn't know what was happening so I rang Briggs and said there was a crisis at Sally's and he went round quickly. He didn't know what Pym was up to and was surprised – horrified, I think, though he tried to hide it – when he found out what was happening

'I arrived a bit later. Claudia was saying that no, she would not go to the Soviet Union, Pym was yelling at her that if she didn't she'd be a stateless person, back in a camp with Gisela, did she want that? Gisela was huddled in the corner with her precious cat wrapped in a blanket and struggling to escape.

'Now, theoretically Briggs ought to have been in favour of sending Claudia to the Soviet Union. He argued, weakly though, that she should go. The situation was shaping up for a scandal – Sally was ringing Winston Churchill, her old war-time supporter, out of office now but still powerful. And I think, to do him justice, Briggs disliked the whole thing – a woman in a nervous breakdown, a little child and Pym.

'The doorbell rang and Sally ran for it, shouting to Pym, "That's someone from Winston Churchill's office—" But it wasn't. She came back into the room, radiant, arm in arm with Eugene, in uniform and still carrying his kit-bag.

'Explanations were made – shouted – and Eugene went over to Claudia. He said, "Wait. Don't do anything now. It's too soon." That seemed to calm her.

'Pym yelled into her face, "So you want to be a displaced person, without a nationality, a passport? You want your child to grow up in a camp?" He turned to Briggs, "You tell her."

'Eugene said to Briggs, "Are you going to let Pym bully this woman into going to Russia where we don't know what will happen to her?"

'"She shouldn't go to America to assist their war effort," he managed to bring out.

'"Hell, Briggs, she doesn't have to go anywhere," Eugene told him.

'"I'm surprised you're backing a country where there's no justice for your race," argued Pym.

'"I'm surprised to see you putting pressure on this woman to make decisions she's in no state to make. I know where she was a couple of months ago," Eugene retorted.

'Pym, of course, guessed that after Sally's phone call to Churchill back-up would arrive so he quickly put his hand into Briggs's pocket, where he knew he always kept his car keys, and pulled them out.

'Then he picked up Claudia's suitcase, put it under his arm, went over to Gisela and grabbed her round the waist. Gisela screamed at being held and because Pym's sudden move had startled her into dropping the blanket containing the struggling cat. Her scream was overwhelmed by Claudia's. Claudia howled and leaped forward. She could not endure the sight of anyone about to lead her child away.

'I was outraged. Eugene looked at me and our eyes found Ricardo's. We all three moved forward in a group. Eugene grabbed Pym, who struggled a bit then gave up. Gisela ran back to her mother, who clutched her, sobbing. We bundled Pym along the passageway and out of the house.

'And that was how Claudia missed the plane to Moscow. They went to Israel, eventually.' Bruno sighed. 'So that was Pym. What a devil that man was – is.'

He continued, 'Sally and Eugene married, you know. That was why you could find no records of her. She had changed her name again. I'm sorry, dear boy. There were reasons why I couldn't tell you. But now you know everything and my story's over.

'I'm tired now,' he said. 'I'm going to get Fiona to take these tapes to your flat.'

59

Greg drove fast back to London. Around him were silent, peaceful fields, farms, small villages with smoking chimneys, all places, he guessed where people – other people – were enjoying Christmas. While he himself was on the near-empty motorway, furious and humiliated. An innocent academic, with nothing more on his record than a few speeding tickets and a drunk-driving charge from his student days, under a deportation order. The might of the law of this strange little worn-out country had descended on his head. It didn't seem credible. It was a joke – if he hadn't been so angry he'd have laughed. Suppose he didn't comply and just stuck around until he'd finished his work. Would they really arrest and deport him? Would they risk the international scandal, boosted by the return of Pym, that such an action would create?

What wasn't so funny was Katherine's part in all this. How could she have sided with her uncle, with Sir Peveril Jones, with the whole, stinking rotten lot of them, against him? Just for a bit of promotion, if it came, and to keep their dirty names clean. And he'd believed in her. What a fool.

In this mood he entered Everton Gardens and took the narrow stairs up to his flat.

There was a package in a Jiffy-bag on the doormat outside. Bruno had been as good as his word. Thanks, Bruno, he thought, and here's hoping the contents will be good enough to make up for all this.

And he remembered, as he threw his travel bag into the clammy bedroom, that Sir Peveril had told him Sally was alive and that Bruno knew where she was.

Shivering, he lit the gas fire, and turned on the recorder. For the next hour and a half Bruno's voice filled the small room. When the tape ended Greg stood up, went to the window and stared out, sightlessly, over the bare trees of the square opposite. Then he hit his head, walked round the room, poured a whisky, sat down, stood up and shook his head. So that was it then, the whole story. What a book it would make, he thought. What a book! He was suddenly exhilarated. So what if he was under a deportation order? So what if he'd been betrayed by his girlfriend? For all he knew the SAS, under the instructions of one of Sir Peveril's minions, was about to raid the building, grab him, drive him to the Essex marshes and execute him. And he didn't care now. He felt weak. Then he felt strong – he felt hungry. It was almost five and all he'd had since morning was a slice of toast and a glass of whisky. He needed to eat and he needed to see Bruno. There was no food in the flat.

He'd go out, try to get something at a 7–Eleven, then go straight to Bruno's. He called and left a message on his answering machine.

Then he went to the bedroom to change out of the suit he'd put on for the drinks party that morning and noticed a page hanging from his fax machine. He read it. The Atlanta lawyers representing Mr Courtney Hamilton, the nephew of Mr Eugene Hamilton, about whom Mr Phillips had enquired, had been instructed to inform Mr Phillips that Mr Eugene Hamilton had died in London three years earlier. Mr Hamilton, wrote the lawyers, had preferred to live in Britain with his family and in 1950 in order to secure the privacy he desired he had handed over responsibility for dealings connected with his artistic work to his brother in the United States. Mr Hamilton's brother had now died, so this responsibility had been assumed by his son, Mr Courtney Hamilton.

The letter went on. On receipt of Mr Phillips's enquiry Mr Courtney Hamilton had, as a matter of courtesy, contacted his uncle's widow and to his surprise this lady, who had up to that time chosen to maintain a distance from anything connected with her late husband's work, had stated that she would be prepared to meet Mr Phillips. Mrs Sarah Hamilton's address in London was given below. A copy of this letter would follow by post.

Greg looked at the address of Mrs Sarah Hamilton on the fax. A broad grin spread across his face. He remembered his first visit to Bruno. 'Mrs Bulstrode. Mrs Bulstrode,' he said aloud. 'Oh, yes. Mrs Bulstrode. Yes, yes, yes.'

He did not stop to change but raced from the flat and drove like a maniac through empty streets to 11, Cornwall Street. Somebody who had once owned that house 'on the wrong side of the park' had fallen on hard times and sold it to Bruno Lowenthal. That somebody had been involved in wartime espionage, had probably told the authorities what she knew about Adrian Pym in the 1950s when he had fled. Then she had gone to ground, hiding out to enjoy a happy private life.

That somebody was still there, still living in the same house . . .

Greg parked, went down the basement steps and banged heavily on the door.

A tall, brown-skinned young woman of about his own age opened the door. She looked at him and smiled. 'Bruno said you'd come.' She nodded him in.

There was an internal lobby, then a long room where a lighted Christmas tree stood. At a table, at which Christmas dinner had evidently been eaten and on which still stood cheese, fruit and the remains of a Christmas pudding, sat eight people, two couples in their fifties, and a young man who, by his appearance, seemed to be the brother of the woman who had let Greg in. Near the end of the table was an untouched place, with a full complement of knives, forks and glasses. At the head of the table was an old woman, bright-eyed, heavily made up and smiling. Beside her was Bruno, who stood up.

'Welcome, Greg, we saved a place for you,' he said.

The old woman now also got up. She was wearing a

black beaded dress. She held a gold-tipped black cigarette holder. Bright-eyed, wreathed in smoke, Sally Bowles cried, 'Darling! I've heard so much about you! Come and sit down. Will someone open a bottle of champagne?'

AS TIME GOES BY

Michael Walsh

Here's looking at you, kid ...

What happens to Ilsa Lund and Victor Laszlo? Did they make it to America? Do Rick Blaine and Louis join the Free French garrison in Brazzaville? How did Louis end up in Casablanca? What secrets prevent Rick from returning to the States? And most of all, will Rick and Ilsa ever see each other again?

From sun-baked Casablanca to the smoke-filled speakeasies of prohibition New York, *As Time Goes By* continues the story of Rick, Ilsa, Victor, Louis, Sam and even Sacha and Carl – the men and women who made Casablanca so unforgettable. Here they are once more: Rick sounding so much like Bogey, you'd swear Bogart wrote the dialogue; Louis, dapper and ironic; Ilsa as incandescently brave and beautiful as ever.

HALF HIDDEN

Emma Blair

The news of her fiancé's death at Dunkirk was a cruel blow for Holly Morgan to suffer. But for Holly – forced to nurse enemy soldiers back to health while her beloved Jersey ails beneath an epidemic of crime, rationing and the worst excesses of Nazi occupation – the brutality of war has only just begun.

From the grim conditions of the hospital operating theatre, unexpected bonds of resilience and tenderness are forged. When friendship turns to love between Holly and a young German doctor, their forbidden passion finds a sanctuary at Half Hidden, a deserted house deep within the island countryside. It is this refuge which becomes the focus for the war Holly and Peter must fight together – a war where every friend may be an enemy …

A PECULIAR CHEMISTRY

Kitty Ray

A tale of extraordinary passion, courage and sadness, coloured by the effects of war …

Fiercely independent, single and pregnant, university lecturer Ellis Jones has fled her career and found refuge in the small primitive Suffolk cottage she inherited from her Great Aunt Nell. Here she intends to spend the rest of her pregnancy on her own, sparing her young lover Joe from being saddled with fatherhood before he is ready. In the dusty fireplace of the cottage, she finds a diary hidden in a package addressed to herself.

Savouring the spidery entries night by night, she slowly pieces together the extraordinary story of Nell's own life, her love for the untouchable Lawrence, the baby she too, bore alone and the abandoned garden which becomes her solace in the face of overwhelming tragedy.

Other bestselling Warner titles available by mail: